THE ANNALS OF THE MIND LEGION

VOLUME 1: THE RESURGENCE

BY

CRAIG WOLL

Manufactured in the United States of America

Summary: In this first volume of the Annals of the Mind Legion,
fourteen year old Darius Shannon discovers the secret of the
Mind Legion and becomes its newest member.

ISBN-10: 0985171405

ISBN-13: 978-0-9851714-0-7

For

Emily

CHAPTER 1

I am Darius Shannon. These annals contain a year's worth of history regarding my life and the proceedings of the Mind Legion on the planet Earth. The Mind Legion is a secret organization that pursues the advancement of humanity by silently influencing the lives of individuals and organizations. This record was commissioned shortly after my fifteenth birthday by order of the Great Council of the Mind Legion, which governs the affairs of each planet belonging to their dominion.

Each day last summer I awoke with a strange feeling that there was something more to be gained in this life. I was a dreamer, but I never believed my dreams could become reality. I believe now that most people felt as I did. They live each day as if it is of no consequence because of the dissonance between hope and reality. Only a few snap this pattern and reach for hope in the absence of empirical evidence. In my case, reality collided with my dreams and made them come true.

It was my fourteenth birthday and I asked for only one thing, in hopes that the lack of an alternative would increase the likelihood of obtaining my desire. I attempted to keep my expectations in check, but I was impetuous. My gifts had always been practical and predictable in the past, yet somehow I felt that this year would be different. I knew that money was not reticently available. I had been privy to more than one heated conversation between my mother and father where money was the central theme. My mother liked to say that she was frugal, but I knew that just meant we couldn't afford to buy certain things.

I sat at the kitchen table on my big day and stared through the bay window onto a perfect scene of small town life. The sun was high but moving down in the summer sky as the afternoon waned. The Tetons loomed before me as I glanced over the fence line of the yard behind our house. The mountains were dark with evergreens and speckled with dark cliffs of black stone. Rivers and trails interlaced the canyons near our home.

My dad was crossing back and forth before me, pushing our old lawn mower. It, in some ways, reminded me of him. The paint was worn off in patches and the engine sputtered every few minutes. Dad was in his mid forties, what was left of his hairline was creeping back, and a small belly was starting to show under his worn t-shirt. He had a perpetual smirk on his face as he was doing things. It was always like he was thinking back on some funny experience he had recently witnessed. He lifted his gaze on one of the passes across the window and caught the eye of my mother and flashed one of his classic smiles. Mom smiled back before turning back to her flowers edging the periphery of the small backyard. She had a pretty but aging face. She was plump and pleasant. She worked harder than anybody I knew and never seemed to complain. Her clothes were a few fads behind but she kept them tidy.

The stress of waiting for the birthday cake and presents was killing me. After a rousing song and blowing out candles I opened my first gift. There was no surprise— underwear. Plain old tighty whiteys. Not the brand name ones, but the generic brand. When I looked at the size, I was crushed. My mother had bought them one size too big in the hopes that they would last a little longer. I knew I was being set up for utter humiliation. The elastic would wear out before I was upgraded to new underwear, and the only thing between me and complete embarrassment would be the hope that somehow I would never be forced to reveal them to anyone. My mother obviously had no experience with high school.

The only other gift that year was a small box. I shook it prior to opening and heard the hollow rattle of a single object inside the box. The object turned out to be a key.

"Well, you better go into the garage to see what that belongs to," my dad said with another smirk. Then he winked at my mother

This was a running joke in the family. Every year or two, someone wrapped up a key or the garage door opener. We'd all go around to the front of the house, open the garage, and sure enough some unexciting present would be sitting in there. And yet, we fell for it every year. One year for Christmas my dad had the audacity to wrap up a refrigerator box in Christmas paper and a giant bow. We all ran up to it and began rocking and shaking it. There was obviously something heavy in it. Our excitement rose as we tore off the wrapping paper. The box was sealed with duct tape. We finally had to get a utility blade to open it. When we peered inside we all audibly sighed in disappointment. The box was weighted down with various heavy objects from the garage. At the top of these objects was our last hope—a tiny box. In it was a box of microwave popcorn and a movie. My dad laughed for days about that one. In fact, it was fun for the whole family. The hope of something great was enough for us.

With key in hand I walked through the kitchen to the door that led to the garage. I guessed no-name socks would be sitting out there. They would be one size too big, trailing around my ankles. As I opened the door, to my surprise a semi-new bike was standing proudly in the middle of the garage. I stared in awe. I had secretly wished for a bike, but had mentally prepared for the worse. The white bike was not the latest model—it was used, but it had been carefully cleaned and repaired. My father had probably worked on it, though I wasn't sure how he found the time. A lock was attached to the frame, and I realized that the key in my hand really did open something spectacular. With the bottom of my dirty t-shirt, I wiped a tear from my eye. I walked into the garage to inspect the best gift I had ever received. I never bothered to thank my parents at that time, but they were rewarded in their own way.

I rode that bike every day that summer. This was the year that I took my first breath of life. One afternoon was embedded in my memory with vivid clarity. I rode with an unquenchable desire to achieve something: To push my body harder and further than ever before. It was the first time that I was able to conquer the body through the concentration of the mind. The ground beneath me turned to a veritable blur as if it was going out of focus. Undeterred by the speed, I downshifted and pedaled in quick spurts to increase the velocity. My only connection to the earth was an occasional bump against the worn and ruddy tires as I descended the mountain trail. I could smell my own perspiration and crinkled my nose in disapproval. I lifted one hand from the handle bars to brush my disheveled hair out of my eyes. I was living my new dream. It was mid-August in Driggs, Idaho, and there was not a cloud in the sky. The heat was noticeable, but not oppressive. It always seemed to be that way once I left the concrete confines of the city and entered the mountain trails. Another small bead of sweat trickled down the side of my tan, dust-ridden face as I rounded the last corner of my favorite downhill stretch. This was my favorite bend because it hugged the incline on one side and was bounded by a cool mountain stream on the other. It marked the transition from the natural canopy of trees and vegetation that covered the trail, opening up into the brilliant sunshine.

I was blinded for a moment by the sunshine as I emerged from the trees. This heightened the exhilaration of the curve because I had to begin making the turn on faith that I was still on the trail. Today was shaping up to be like dozens of others. I smiled, unaware of the significance of the event that would occur momentarily. It would be the single most important event of my life—the event that defined my future and possibly that of all mankind.

I began to decelerate in preparation for the turn, and just as I started to lean into it, there was a jolting shock against the front tire, and I felt myself lift into the air over my handlebars. I recall looking down at the ground and seeing a brown blur below me turn a murky blue as I sailed out over the river.

Time seemed to stand still as I took in the scene. A smile was pasted on my face, as if I were in denial of my circumstances. I heard the bike crashing and coming to a rest near the bank of the river. I looked up, or down—depending on how you looked at it— over the trail at the foliage that lined the soft, reddish-brown dirt. I thought I saw two heads peering from between the bushes. That seemed strange since I had hardly seen a soul for the last few months that I had been riding the trail.

I glanced down and realized I was directly over the water. A sense of momentary relief enveloped me as I realized that the landing would be a soft one. Then my mind recalled the drowning from the previous summer of a boy a few years younger than I. All of these thoughts seemed to pass idly by in my mind but the reality was that only a few seconds had transpired.

I entered the water head first and felt the cool stream slow my momentum. When my head popped out of the water, I was already a good fifteen yards downstream. Fortunately I knew how to swim, but I was merely an average swimmer. I focused all of my efforts on reaching the shore. After a few minutes of exertion, I lifted my exhausted body from the stream bed and lay face down on the turf that lined the water.

When I rolled over and sat up I realized my mistake. I had reached the far side of the river. A glance upstream was all it took to identify the spot where I entered the water. It was 100 or more yards further up, marked by a bike hanging from some roots that belonged to the lone tree near the bend in the trail. The rear wheel was spinning in the current as the water just touched the surface of the tire. I sat up in amazement at how far the current had dragged me in what seemed like so short of time.

"Ah crap!" I groaned in agony as my eyes swept over my front tire. Even at that distance I could see that the rim was no longer serviceable. Whatever I had hit had left an impression on the bike. It was a miracle that I was not injured, but none of this mattered. I was too busy cursing my bad luck.

The stream was moving swiftly due to recent rainfall, and it was not crossable for at least a half mile further downstream where a hiker's bridge crossed over, leading back to the main road entering the canyon.

I was practical like other boys my age. I spent several minutes cursing and muttering to myself about what I was going to do to the person that messed up my perfectly good trail and forced me to ruin my bike. I even wandered a few yards up stream on my side of the bank to get a better look at the damage. At some point, I finally relented and picked my way through the foliage toward the bridge. It took twenty minutes to get to the bridge, and it was only a matter of a few moments to cross and begin ascending the trail. By the time I reached my bike, the sun was just preparing to fall behind The Big Hole Mountains across the valley.

The trail had been covered by a collapse of the uphill bank scattering several small boulders into the path. I edged my way to where my bike had settled. I put one arm around the trunk of the tree and leaned out and took hold of the front tire. Five minutes later, I laid the bike on the bank of the river and scrambled back to the trail.

I let the bike know what I thought of its damages, using every obscenity I had learned from school and TV. I then dragged the bike across the path and leaned it on the uphill slope. With the light waning, it was difficult to see if the bike would be sufficiently serviceable to get me home.

I lowered my head until it was only a few inches above the surface of the trail in order to examine the bent rim. My eyes trailed off a few degrees and fixed on something that I had originally mistaken for one of the small boulders littering the trail. From this new angle I could vaguely make out a star-shaped design on the underside.

"What's this?" I exclaimed as my frustrations with the wrecked bike vanished in the exuberance of youthful curiosity.

I lifted the stone and dusted it off, revealing an intricate star pattern on a black surface. I ran my hand across the pattern on the surface of the smooth stone. It was maybe eight or nine inches in diameter at the widest point. While handling the stone, I noticed there were indentations on the opposite side of the patterned surface and it was surprisingly light for its size. The final rays of the sun had disappeared some time ago and darkness made it impossible to decipher more. After a few moments deliberation, I shoved the stone in my wet-soaked backpack, disregarding the half-eaten peanut butter and jelly sandwich that got mutilated in the process, which left a sticky residue of strawberry jam at the bottom of my bag.

I jumped on the bike and tried pedaling down the trail toward home. After a half rotation of the front rim I'd realized that it wasn't a good idea. For the second time that day I flew over the handlebars. This time the water did not soften my fall. I worked my way through the previous list of profanities to be sure that I had not missed any the first time around. I dusted myself off and soaked my scratched palms in the river to get a better look at the damage.

"Why me?" I muttered in all the anguish of a fourteen-year-old soul.

I picked up the bike and slung it over my shoulder, then started down the trail. By the time I had crossed the bridge, a welling pain shot through the shoulder where I was resting the bike and a similar pain in the other from the second fall.

Suddenly, two headlights shone on me from the trailhead parking lot as I exited the brush, dragging my bike behind me.

"Is that you, Darius?" chuckled a voice from behind the beams. "You look like you've been through hell."

"Maybe I have."

"Do you want a ride home?" asked the voice with more concern.

I inched closer. Mr. West, the freshman English teacher, slid out of the car. He was tall and slender with an athletic build. Even though he appeared to be roughly the same age as my father, he had aged more gracefully. The first thing most people noticed was the shock of dark hair that covered his head. It seemed like more than one head could handle. He had a winning smile that made up for the narrow eyes that were slightly more recessed than normal. My mother never stopped complimenting his good looks when my father wasn't around.

"Yeah, that'd be great," I muttered. Mr. West loaded the bike in the trunk and secured it with a bungee cord so that the trunk wouldn't bounce up and down as we drove.

As I stumbled from behind the car toward the passenger's door, I noticed somebody sitting in the front seat, so I opened the rear door and sat down.

"Darius, this is my boy Tommy," said Mr. West, nodding his head toward the young man that looked about my age. "He'll be a freshman this year as well."

I peered at the back of Tommy's head and then glanced from him to Mr. West and back again. Their heads looked identical. Tommy was a little shorter and less refined than Mr. West, but was obviously his offspring.

Mr. West was one of those teachers that just understood kids. He won Teacher of the Year almost every year, and none of the other teachers ever questioned the results. They knew he was the best. He had great success academically and socially with the kids. This, however, didn't stop most of the teachers from resenting him to some degree.

"So, what happened?" asked Mr. West, concern in his voice as he headed away from the canyon and toward my house.

"I hit some boulders coming down the trail and bent my rim."

"You're lucky you didn't kill yourself," Tommy said dryly.

"Maybe, but I'm as good as dead when my mom sees me," I responded dejectedly.

"Is this your place Darius?" Mr. West asked as he pulled into the driveway.

"Yep."

"Do you need any help getting your bike into the garage?" Mr. West asked as he removed the bike from the trunk.

"No thanks, Mr. West," I said as I grabbed the bike. "I should be okay from here."

"Okay then. I'll see you in a few weeks at school. Will you be taking Freshman English from me or Mrs. Williams?"

"Mrs. Williams," I responded unenthusiastically.

"I'm sorry we won't be working together."

"Me too," I said, wincing in pain at the thought of Freshman English with Mrs. Williams. English had never been my best subject, and Mrs. Williams was not the school's most desirable teacher. There was nothing appealing to a young boy about Mrs. Williams.

According to my older brother Jim, she taught with a vengeance.

Mr. West misinterpreted the wince and assumed I was in physical pain. He relieved my burden and carried the bike closer to the garage and leaned it against the house.

"Thanks, Mr. West," I yelled as I opened the garage.

Mr. West gave me one of his patented smiles as he drove off into the night. "It's no wonder he's always voted Teacher of the Year," I thought wistfully as I stared down the street at his taillights.

I dragged the mangled bike into the garage and leaned it against the wall. I kicked open the door and yelled, "Mooooom!"

A sinking feeling welled up in the pit of my stomach as the scene in the kitchen reached my eyes. My family was sitting around the table with their heads bowed, and my father was mouthing the words of the blessing on the dinner. I waited restlessly by the door for what seemed like forever. "This prayer will never finish," I said silently as I stood there clutching my damp pack. I wondered if my father could sense my agitation and was therefore prolonging the experience. *Why did adults always do that?*

The scene was peaceful. Mother was seated to the left at one end of the table, and Father was on the other end. Jim had his back to me, and I could see his ball cap hanging on the edge of his chair near his right shoulder. Rachael, the youngest of us, had her head bowed slightly and her arms folded. One eye was open, trained on me, and a smile was creeping on to her lips as the prayer continued.

The light reflected off the shiny spot near the widow's peaks on my father's head. He was getting older. Mom's timeless face and bright eyes almost hid the wrinkles that came with age. She was often quoted saying that she needed to drop a few pounds. Somehow, she never did and it never mattered. As usual, her hair was pulled back, and she had a grin on her face. One of her eyes was also cracked open, and she was beaming at my father. They were always sneaking peaks at each other, and up until the last few years I enjoyed this game they played. But at fourteen, it became one of the many things that my parents did that made me nauseous.

Jim was about six feet tall and every inch of him was athletic. He, like my dad, always carried a smirk on his face. The sandy colored hair on his head fought against itself on which direction it was going. Might be why Jim always wore a cap. He and I could have been twins, but he was a few years older, better looking, and more athletic. Besides that we were like two peas in a pod. He was the best of the best at everything he did, and girls were always calling him. Sports and school were his priority so he blew them off most of the time.

Rachael didn't seem to fit the family mold. She had inherited my mom's big eyes and it was clear that she was going to be quite a looker when she grew up. Her hair was dark, straight, and long. This was a mystery to us because mom and dad both had sandy colored hair like Jim's. At 12 she was generally just a nuisance to me. She lurked about the house looking for opportunities to tell my mother about whatever I was doing.

"Amen," my family recited in unison at the conclusion of the prayer. Jim immediately dug into his meal, but Rachael and my parents looked over to the door where I was standing.

"Mom, Dad, you will never guess what happened to me," I belted out.

"Son, before you go a step further into your mother's clean kitchen, you need to take off those filthy shoes and put them in the garage."

Mother looked over at Dad and smiled in a way that was also on the list of things that my parents did that made me nauseous. She continued beaming at Dad, and when she caught his eye, she gave him a little wink.

"But, Dad, you won't believe..." I said trailing off as I perceived the dissatisfaction in my father's eyes as he glanced from Mom back to me.

"There will be plenty of time for your stories once you take off your shoes and go downstairs and get cleaned up," my father said, smile emerging as he turned to look at Mom. He must have noticed my ruffled hair and clothing. He turned again and winked at Mom before digging into his meal.

"All right, all right, I get the picture," I said, controlling the dry heaves and returning to the garage to remove my shoes.

As I walked through the kitchen toward the stairs to the basement I noticed that they were eating tuna casserole again. Mom saw the disgusted look on my face and stated warily, "You will eat what is prepared and you will like it."

"I'll just have a PB&J," I responded as I dropped down the stairs taking them three at a time so she wouldn't have time to respond.

My room was in the furthest corner of the basement. Even though it was the smallest room in the house, I shared it with Jim. The door had been removed for some reason many years prior and was still missing. This didn't bother us much. I threw my pack to the side of the bed and yanked off the dirty trail clothes, throwing them on the floor. I streaked into the bathroom across the hall for a quick shower.

A few minutes later I crept quietly up the stairs to eavesdrop on the table conversation. The conversation was light and casual. My mother commented on the wonderful recipe for a new tuna casserole that the neighbor down the street had recommended she try. I peeked my head around the corner to see my father trying to sound interested as he eyed the clock.

"Well, its game time," Dad stated enthusiastically when the minute hand reached the top of the hour.

This was my cue. I crept around the corner and said, "I'll get the popcorn and meet you on the couch."

"Not until you have scraped this plate clean, young man," my mother sternly admonished with a head nod toward my end of the table.

A plate was piled high with tuna casserole and accented with cauliflower. An audible, "rats" escaped my lips as I slipped into my chair at the table.

My only hope was to take the pain quickly. The casserole disappeared at an astonishing rate as I realized just how hungry I was. I slipped the cauliflower to the family dog, Patsy, who turned up her nose in disgust. Throwing the plate into the sink with the others, I headed to the couch to enjoy the game.

CHAPTER 2

After two overtimes and a dramatic loss to a bitter rival, I realized I was emotionally and physically drained. Within minutes of diving into bed, my breathing was in a measured sequence as my body relaxed and fell into a fitful sleep.

I was startled into consciousness by a lack of oxygen. I could feel a hand clasped across my mouth and nostrils, cutting off all breath. A short struggle ensued, followed by a gasp of inhaling air as I cried out, "Jim! Leave me alone. I'm trying to sleep."

Jim smiled and laughed. "I'm just trying to keep you on your toes. Someday you'll thank me for keeping you alert of your surroundings."

Jim was two years older and derived great pleasure from trying various pranks on me. A few weeks ago, Jim and his friends had actually carried me out to the back lawn during the night. I had pulled the covers over my head to protect me from the open air, but water from the sprinklers began to seep through my comforter. It was 6:00 a.m. when I threw off my covers and discovered the prank.

Jim knew how to exploit my weaknesses better than anyone. Whenever he pulled a nighttime prank I would just give in since I was too tired to offer up any more resistance. Tonight was no different. Once I could breathe again, I rolled over and was sleeping before Jim had time to slip off his shoes and jump into his own bed.

That night I dreamt as I had never dreamt before. It was as if I was viewing my own life as a silent observer. My dream self reached down next to my bed and opened my backpack. Inside the backpack lay a carefully polished stone. It appeared to be the same stone that had led to my unfortunate accident and subsequent soaking in the river. It was smooth like glass on the outside, but light as a feather, as if it were hollow. The stone was slightly larger than my hand and rounded on one side. It had the shape of a star protruding from the flat end. The star came out about a half of an inch, and the edges reached the circumference of the stone.

The dream Darius turned over the stone in his hands and noticed a design on the rounded surface that was shaped like a hand but had intricate designs lacing in and out of each finger and the thumb. I watched myself put my hand on the surface as indicated by the design. For a moment nothing happened. Then I heard a subtle exclamation slip from my own lips and felt a mild tingling sensation rush through my entire being.

The sensation startled me into consciousness and I realized that it was only a dream. I rolled over and saw the dimly lit outlines of 1:00 a.m. on the clock beside the bed.

"What's up, bro?" Jim asked.

"Nothing, I just had a weird dream."

"Okay," Jim responded as he settled into his bed.

I realized I'd only been asleep for a few minutes. It was one of those phenomena that accompanied sleep. Sometimes you could sleep for hours and it felt like seconds. At other times you could sleep for minutes and it felt like hours. This experience fell into the second category. Slightly aggravated, I turned over and struggled to go back to sleep.

As I fell in and out of sleep, I noticed that I was having a second out-of-body experience as I began to dream again. It was as if my previous dream had rewound or started on an infinite loop. It proceeded exactly as the first, but this time I paid attention to every detail and waited anxiously for the moment that I would once again grasp the handprint on the strange new stone. The drama of the moment captured my absolute attention. As my skin made contact with the stone, another thrill filled my body and snapped me back into reality.

I jerked to a sitting position. A quick glance at the clock confirmed that what had felt like only a minute was indeed several hours. I looked down at my hand and involuntarily flexed my fingers into a fist. I tried to rationalize what was happening. Finally, it dawned on me. I was feeling the aftershocks of the crash from the previous afternoon. Clearly the accident had been a little more serious than I had anticipated. This settled my mind somewhat, and I laid back down, content with my explanation for the events in my dreams. As I pondered the situation, I slipped back to sleep, and a few moments later I repeated the sequence for a third time. This time I was determined to avoid the shock and attempted to warn myself in the dream. It was like yelling underwater. I was making noise, but my dream self could not hear or deviate from the scripted path. For the final time, I reached out and grasped the stone with my hand. As I reached for the stone, I dropped out of bed onto the floor.

"What time is it?" mumbled Jim.

I rolled over on the floor and looked up at the clock. "It's five," I said and glanced over. Jim was already asleep.

"This is crazy," I mumbled as I crawled back into bed and passed out for the fourth time.

When I woke, light poured in my window and a firm hand was shaking me.

"Get up. Church starts in thirty minutes," my father said with some urgency.

"I'm not going. I'm too tired."

"I wasn't giving you a choice. I was just informing you. I'll see you in the car in twenty minutes."

When my father used that tone you knew the discussion was over. I moaned as I rolled out of bed and headed in the direction of the bathroom. Two steps from the door, Rachael squeezed past me.

"Sorry, Dari. I'll make it quick," she yelled as the door slammed shut in my face.

"Quick? When are you ever quick?" I conceded without much effort. I was still too groggy.

I went toward the kitchen for a bowl of cereal. I arrived in time to see the last bit of the good cereal poured into an enormous bowl by Jim.

"Sorry, bud. You'll have to eat that stuff Mom likes," he said with a sly grin as he poured the milk, spilling cereal out over the bulging edges. "They say the fiber will help keep you regular."

By the time I had eaten and made my way back downstairs, I had less than five minutes to spare. I splashed some water on my face and pulled a wet comb through my ratty hair, missing a large patch near the crown of my head.

I rambled into my room where I threw on my slacks and a button-up shirt along with an old pair of sneakers. I reached the foot of the stairs just as my father's booming voice yelled, "Darius! You have ten seconds to be in this van. Ten, nine, eight..."

I waited by the garage door until my father reached three and started to open the driver's door to come into the house.

"Three...It's about time. Get in."

After church, I threw myself down on the couch in the basement for a Sunday afternoon nap. I kicked my shoes into the middle of the room and began to relax. Just as I started to doze I remembered the stone in my backpack. I jumped up and ran to my room. "Now let's take a look at what's inside," I said as I lifted the bag.

As I pulled the stone out, it appeared to be a much less brilliant version of what I had seen in my dreams. It was covered with dirt, peanut butter, jam, and a little piece of bread was hanging off the base. I pulled it closer for examination. A tiny piece of sandwich was ignored as it fell to the floor near the foot of the bed.

"Darius? Where are you?"

"Right here, Mom," I responded as I dropped the stone back into the bag.

"How do you live in this place?"

"Most of it is Jim's stuff."

"What about those dirty shorts and that half-eaten sandwich?" she said as she scanned the room. "I want this place immaculate before dinner. We have company coming."

"Oh no, not again." I threw the sandwich across the room, barely missing the garbage can. Fortunately, there was enough jam on the bread and it stuck to the side of the can. Both of us stared at the bread as it slowly slid down the side until it touched the floor.

"Ugh," sighed my mother. "These are important friends of your father's and mine from college," she said. "They have twins that are about your age. They'll be going to your school in a few weeks when they finish building their home near the mouth of the canyon."

"Okay, Mom. I'll clean up," I said, trying not to stare at the mess I had just created.

"Well, this is unexpected. Since when are you willing to clean your room the first time I ask you?"

"Maybe I finally learned something in church," was my sarcastic response as I began to throw dirty clothes in the hamper.

"Let me take this backpack out to the garage for you," my mother offered as she bent over to pick it up. "I have to go upstairs anyway to prepare dinner."

I snatched the backpack from my mother and said, "Thanks Mom, but I got it."

"Okay," she responded with furrowed brows. "I know when my help is not wanted."

"It's not that...I just had a little problem with my sandwich that I wanted to clean up before I take it outside."

"We are eating at six o' clock sharp," my mother warned with a knowing eye.

"You bet, Mom. I'll be there."

Her footsteps faded down the hall, and could be heard ascending the stairs as she made her way to the kitchen. Not wanting to risk exposure, I grabbed the pack and locked myself in the bathroom. I slowly reached into the pack and removed the stone in order to examine it more closely.

"Now let's see what you look like without this dirt."

I grabbed Rachael's towel from the holder near the shower and wetted it in the sink. I slowly worked the towel over the entire surface of the stone, rinsing it until the dirt was cleared. I ignored the mess I'd made on Rachael's towel and returned it to the holder where I found it.

I stared in awe at the stone's shimmering surface. It reminded me of a stone I had seen when my father and I visited some Indian ruins. He had called it "obsidian." He had said that the Indians used to shape the stone into various tools and weapons. But this stone was huge and didn't seem to have any flaws. I couldn't find a crack or discoloration anywhere.

I stared at the stone, noticing the tiny engravings on the surface. The shape of a hand was inscribed with intricate designs tattooed on the fingers and thumb. As I looked closer, I noticed a slight smooth indentation at the base of the thumb and the pinky where they joined the palm of the hand.

"What are these for?" I thought as I stared at the grooves.

The indentations were rectangle and slightly deeper than any of the other grooves found on the surface. I stared for a long time before I realized, "Rings! These must be there to match rings worn on those two fingers."

I hovered my hand over the indentation, preparing for it to shock me like I felt in the dream. As my hand nearly touched the surface, I heard my mother yell, "Darius!"

I jumped up, nearly dropping the stone and scrambled to find a good hiding place. I unlocked the bathroom door and looked both ways before dashing into my room and opening my dresser drawer. I placed the stone in the drawer, hiding it behind my birthday underwear, and carefully shut it before walking out of the room.

"There you are," my mother said as she stepped aside to reveal a perfectly clad family of four. It was like the families you see in the empty frames at the store. Pressed slacks and polo shirts were worn by the boys and skirts and blouses by the girls. All of them decked out in the latest style. "These are the Smiths. They are friends of your father and mine from college. This is John and Susan, and the twins are Richard and Valerie."

"Nice to meet you," I muttered, glancing away shyly from the penetrating glare of the entire family.

I couldn't help but notice Valerie in the exchange. She was slightly taller than me and had rich brown hair and dark brown eyes. Her eyes were deep and knowing and seemed to see right into my thoughts. On top of that, she was gorgeous. I self-consciously put my hand to the crown of my head in an attempt to flatten the rooster that I knew was there. Why didn't I shower this morning? I tugged at my top lip insecurely. There was a scar there from a collision with Jim while playing football in the living room four or five years earlier. Since I didn't trust myself to look at her quite yet, I looked down and noticed that I was covered with dirt and dust from cleaning the stone. Apparently my mother had noticed as well. She pulled me aside as my father casually asked the twins questions.

She whispered, "Run downstairs and get cleaned up for dinner. You don't want to make a bad impression."

It was a little late to make a good first impression, so I descended the stairs listening to the conversation in the background.

"So how old are you two?" my father asked the twins.

"We are both fourteen," said Richard dryly.

"But we have different birthdays," said Valerie in a voice that was as smooth and classy as was her appearance. "I was born at 11:58 pm, and Richard was born at 12:04 am."

"That's the same age as Darius," responded my father as the conversation faded behind me.

I entered my room and threw on a pair of jeans from the floor and a t-shirt hanging on a bedpost. They looked clean enough, so I slipped on my shoes and headed back upstairs.

The rest of the family was seated around the table with the Smiths, leaving one vacant spot next to Jim and across from Valerie. I slipped into the chair, and my father offered a prayer on the food. My mother opened the lid of the dish and said, "I hope everyone likes tuna casserole."

A groan escaped me and my eyes met Valerie's as she responded to my mother with enthusiasm, "Tuna casserole is my favorite, Mrs. Shannon."

That comment took a load off my mind. How could I be intimidated by someone that liked tuna casserole? I dished up a plate of food and began to eat, glancing occasionally at the twins as they responded to questions from my parents.

"Valerie, what do you and Richard like to do for fun?" my mother asked during the next lull in the conversation.

"We both like to ride mountain bikes whenever we have some free time," Valerie responded.

"She is just being modest," Richard said. "Val is the top girl rider in the region for her age."

"Oh Richard, you can't be sure of that. There are a lot of very good riders out there," Val responded as her cheeks reddened. She sneaked a glance in my direction.

"She doesn't like to say it, but she even beats most of the guys in the races we enter."

"What about you Richard? How do you do in the competitions?" my dad asked. It was just like him to take the pressure off of someone when they were embarrassed. My parents had this rare ability to make everyone feel comfortable except me. They found great pleasure in embarrassing me at every opportunity. Sometimes I thought it was a game of theirs to see how awkward they could make me feel. One time they went so far as to pull out some pictures of me naked in the tub when I was a baby to break the ice with some neighbor kids they wanted me to befriend. It didn't work.

"I was the best in the state until I took a bad spill this last spring. I'm still trying to get back into form."

"Darius likes to ride as well," my mother stated, turning her attention toward me. I was pretty sure she felt that further humiliation would somehow help me become friends with the twins.

"Not anymore," said Rachael.

"What does that mean?" my father asked. .

"I saw his bike in the garage," Rachael responded. "He broke his tire."

"You didn't mention anything last night. What happened?" My mother asked with a concerned look on her face. She had never liked it when I rode alone all day in the canyon.

"It was nothing; I just hit a few stones in the path and bent my rim and forks," I responded, trying not to glance at Val and Richard. Rachael's timing was impeccable as usual. She had an uncanny ability to bring up these juicy bits of information at precisely the wrong moment.

"Well, from now on you don't ride alone in that canyon," my mother said sternly.

"But Mom, there's nowhere else worth riding around here," I protested. I stared into her concerned eyes. I was still desperately avoiding eye contact with the twins. This was a critical situation made worse by the presence of a pretty girl and her twin brother. From the corner of my eye I could see a smirk on Richard's face as if he was trying not to smile at my predicament.

"Well, maybe Richard and Val will ride with you once they unpack their bikes," my mother responded in an attempt to smooth things over without conceding her ground. How did she always do that? It was impossible to remain angry with her because of this characteristic.

"Sure, that would be fun," responded Val. "You can show us the best trails in the canyon."

She said it with such conviction as if she actually meant it. In retrospect, she probably did but at the moment I was in no mood to give up my freedom and give away my secret trails.

"Thanks anyway, but I like to ride alone," I quipped without hesitation.

The room fell silent as everyone stared at Val and me. It was an awkward moment before I mustered the strength to glance into Val's eyes. Her eyes were shiny as the impact of my words seeped in. She was obviously hurt but didn't want others to notice. I attempted to retract my brusque comment by saying, "Maybe I could show you the trails and then let you ride on your own."

It was too late. The damage was done. Val was quiet for the rest of the evening and avoided looking my direction. Richard seemed oblivious of things as he actively listened to the conversation as the Smiths inquired about Jim and Rachael. They showed sincere interest in what they were doing. Mr. Smith was especially interested in Jim's exploits on the football field, and I could tell that Richard was envious as my parents recounted all the athletic awards that Jim had received over the years. For the most part, Jim just ignored the accolades. He was used to it and didn't seem to let it go to his head. At the end of the evening we walked the Smiths out to their car and wished them goodbye.

I went back inside and headed downstairs after watching some TV. I reached the bottom of the stairs in time to hear Rachael scream in disgust from the bathroom, "Darius! What did you do to my towel?"

I smiled and continued to my room, deriving some mild satisfaction that maybe this evened things up after she spilled the beans on my bike situation to the parents in front of the Smiths. I doubted she felt that way as she spewed self-indulged commentary about how disgusting boys were. She was probably right, but that was the least of my worries.

That night a fading image of Val's face flickered into my mind and I began to replay the conversation. I fell into a fitful slumber as I berated my stupidity. Had I not been so exhausted I may have given myself an emotional and possibly a physical beating in self flagellation to atone for my bad behavior. But, as usual, in a few moments I was asleep before I could resolve my internal conflict.

Another dream plagued my sleep. I knew it was a dream, yet it still somehow felt strikingly real. My senses were fully functioning as if I were truly touching, smelling, and hearing the things that I'd encountered. I reached down and slipped the black stone into my backpack and stealthily crept from the room so as not to wake Jim. I opened the garage door and light flooded in as if it were early in the day. My bike was where I had left it, but the repairs had been completed. I lifted the bike and felt the cold steel. I mounted and pedaled out of the driveway.

I rode toward the hills and followed my regular trail in the canyon. The sweat trickled down my face as my body responded to the warmth of the sun combined with the physical exertion. As I descended the slope toward the cutback near my previous accident, I turned off the trail into the foliage. I emerged from the undergrowth onto an ancient trail that had been hidden for some time.

The trail took me about a hundred yards into the interior of the hill before it turned parallel to the main trail and rose steeply toward a cliff face. When I reached the cliff I stopped and dismounted from my bike, leaning against the rock wall. I looked up as the sun just slid behind the mountain above me. It was a sheer rock face for about two hundred feet straight up.

Back in my room, a shadow crossed my face as I slept but did not wake me. I was deep in slumber as I felt a hand grasp my exposed shoulder. It shook me into consciousness.

"What do ya want?" I asked groggily.

"You were tossing and turning all over the place again," Jim responded. "Try to keep it down. I have football practice at 6:30 and need some rest."

"Okay, what time is it?" I asked as I wiped the sweat from my brow with the blanket.

"1:00 a.m."

The dream repeated itself in its vividness and entirety two more times that night just like the previous night. By morning I was completely exhausted when Mom called for me at 9:00 a.m. "I'm going to the store. Do you need anything?" she asked.

"No," I responded and then recounted, "Wait! I'm coming with you."

I jumped out of bed and threw on the same clothes I had worn the previous evening. I ran upstairs and grabbed a granola bar before running out the door and telling Mom to open the back doors of the van so I could throw my bike in.

"So that is why you were interested in coming," she said as she smiled at me. "And I thought you just wanted to spend some quality time with your mother."

"Yeah right," I said. "That was my real reason for coming, but since I'm going out, I figured I would bring the bike along to get fixed as well."

We dropped the bike off at the local shop in the mall before running to various department stores. I tried not to look at the lingerie as my mother took me through the women's portion of the department store. It always felt like every woman in the place was staring at me as we passed through this section.

After a lunch in the food court, we went by the store to pick up the bike. As the bike tech brought the bike to the front of the store, I noticed that the new forks matched those I had seen in the dream the night before. When my hand touched the metal, a sensation of déjà vu crept through me. I jumped on and tested the new forks and rim in the parking lot while Mom paid for the repairs.

"I can't believe how expensive these things are," she commented as I pulled up alongside the van. "It's a good thing your father got that raise last month or you would be hiking instead of biking."

"Thanks Mom!" I said with genuine appreciation. "It was fun today."

By the time we got home it was early afternoon. I turned to my mother and said, "I want to make sure everything is in working order. Is it okay if I take a short ride before dinner?"

"Yes, but be careful."

I rode up the canyon and found the spot where I had wrecked on Saturday. The trail was still partially covered by the small rockslide, so I jumped off my bike and cleared the trail. An inspection of the hillside above the trail revealed the cause of the small avalanche. A decayed wooden box was sticking out of the dirt entangled by the roots of an old elm. It appeared that over time the dirt eroded away around the box until there was no longer sufficient adhesion to maintain the shape of the hill. All around the box were scrapings that verified that someone or something had been attempting to free the box from the hold of the roots.

In order to get a closer look I scrambled up the hillside. There were shoe prints below the box. I put my foot next to the prints and saw that they were about half again the size of my shoes. The side of the box facing me had corroded away and inside there was nothing but a few straggling spider webs and a little dust from what appeared to be an extended entombment beneath the earth. The box tilted slightly down on the open side as a result of the shifting soil beneath.

Obviously the black stone had been inside the box at some point, and when the hill gave way and the box tilted down the hill, it slid out onto the trail with the other clods and boulders where I so cleverly found it with my front tire.

As I looked below, I remembered the two sets of eyes that I saw as I was descending into the river. Could it be that they were the ones trying to get the box? It was pretty obvious that someone was digging around the place. They must have heard me coming and hid in the bushes.

I glanced up the hill to where the canopy of foliage started. I walked around, looking for the spot that I had seen in my dream. It was difficult to locate the offshoot that was so vividly displayed the night before. Finally, I wandered a few feet into the shrubbery and began to walk parallel to the trail in hopes of spotting the path.

Where was that trail?

After several false starts I finally found the trail. There were scuff marks on a stone that was part of the old trail that cued me into its location. I wove my way back to the cliff where I had seen myself standing in the dream. It was eerie looking up at the rock face. I looked closely at the wall and saw that there was no way to ascend it without a rope. In fact, the face was slightly inverted. Even the most daring rock climber would sweat a little at the prospect of climbing the rock.

Looking back down the trail, I noted that it was impossible to see the rock face because of the trees and foliage that surrounded it.

This would make a perfect hideout. I stared back in the direction of the trail. I turned again to the face of the cliff and noticed the shadows from the western sun slowly climbing up the wall. I looked out over the valley below and thought I saw a car entering the canyon.

Not wishing to be seen by whoever might be coming up the trail, I jogged down to my bike and dragged it back to the trail from its hiding place behind two large trees. I jumped on and sped toward the recently cleared curve, exhilarating in the experience I'd been robbed of a few days before. From halfway up the hill I was unable to reach the speeds I was used to, but it was reassuring to come around the corner and continue down the trail without spending any more time in the river.

As I came to the trailhead I saw Mr. West and pulled on my brakes.

"Hi Mr. West."

Mr. West was peering at the trail with his nose inches from the ground. He jumped up, as if I'd surprised him. He focused his eyes on me and his stern countenance melted into a glowing smile of realization.

"Darius! You startled me. I was just getting ready to go for my evening jog. What brings you out here this late in the evening?"

"I was just clearing off the trail where I wrecked the other day," I said, not wanting to elaborate on the true reason for visiting the canyon.

"I'm glad to see you up and moving. I thought you might be a little too bruised to be back on the trail so soon," Mr. West stated as he stretched his legs.

"Nope, I'm okay," I responded. "It was my back that took the brunt of it."

"Well, you better get home before it gets dark. It's not safe to be out on the streets on a bike so late."

"Thanks Mr. West," I responded as I mounted my bike and pedaled down the trail.

The dreams continued for a third night. This time I saw myself standing at the rock face holding the stone in my hand. I held the stone by the rounded side and scanned the rock face as if looking for something. I woke and glanced at the clock. The dreams came like clockwork—1:00, 3:00, and 5:00 a.m.

I groaned. It was so early, and my eyes were burning from not enough sleep, but I felt restless. I snuck out of the room, being careful not to wake Jim. I took the bike out the side door to avoid waking my parents with noise of the garage door opener. It was my belief that my father purposely let the chain rust so that everyone in the house would be perfectly aware of his return home each day from work. The noise literally shook the entire house.

I rode to the spot, clutching the stone in my hand, and staring at the rock face. I could not fully understand what was happening, but something urged me on, as if there was a great importance attached to the events that were occurring. As the sun started dipping below the mountains, my stomach grumbled and I gave up and headed dejectedly toward my bike.

"What a waste," I muttered as I stood at the trailhead. I stared up the trail at the location of the rock wall in hopes that I might think of something I missed earlier.

A rock ground on dirt and I turned and noticed that Val had ridden up behind me as I was lost in my thoughts. Sweat was trickling down the side of her face from beneath her helmet. The exertion brought color to her face and enhanced her natural beauty. Her skin had taken on a nice tone from all the riding in the sun. Her jersey was zipped down to just below the nape of her neck revealing a tiny mole. It was probably her only imperfection. Sunglasses covered her eyes. She was smiling.

"What did you say?" she asked.

"Oh nothing. I was just talking to myself."

"Come on. The way you were looking up the hill I thought you had seen something."

"Nope, I was just wishing I'd had a better ride today," I said.

"I just had a great ride! In fact, you should come with me sometime," she said smiling again.

"That sounds like fun," I said with genuine interest.

"I thought you only rode alone," she teased with just a little hurt in her voice.

I winced as I recalled my harsh words of the other night. "Yeah, sorry about that," I said lamely. "When did you want to go?"

"How about we go tomorrow?" Val asked.

"Uhhh, okay. What time?" I said unenthusiastically.

CRAIG WOLL

Val's countenance fell and the smile disappeared. "It's okay if you don't want to go. I'll understand."

"No, it's not that," I stuttered in embarrassment, "I just wasn't sure if I could make it or not." The reality was that I wasn't sure what was going to happen that night and didn't want to commit to something I couldn't do.

"Okay, I was thinking of leaving after lunch. I have piano lessons in the morning, so I can't do it before then."

Relieved, I answered, "I'll meet you at your place at about one o'clock."

If we left at one, that would give me all morning to figure out the next piece of the puzzle. It never occurred to me that there may not be a next clue. I just assumed that this craziness would continue until I figured things out.

I turned to begin riding down the hill and realized I didn't know where Val lived. "So, I guess if I'm going to pick you up I better find out where you live first," I said as we mounted and prepared to go.

"Oh yeah, we live in the new houses just outside of the canyon. Ours is the first one on the left as you come in on Aspen Street. We just moved in on Saturday. If you want I could show you on the ride home."

Val and I rode back down the hill together. At Aspen Street she turned into her driveway and came to a stop. I pulled up beside her and said, "Well, I guess this is it. I'll see you tomorrow at one."

With that, I turned my bike around, and with a wave I continued on as she pulled her bike into the garage. Once she was out of sight, my mind wandered back to my previous failure. I could not understand why nothing happened. The previous dream led me right to the rock face. Why would I stand all day looking at the wall and then nothing happened? There should have been some sign or something. It didn't make sense to just stare at the rock.

Again, my sleep was troubled with a dream. This time I saw myself standing in front of the rock wall holding the black stone in my hand. After a few minutes, I placed the stone into the rock wall. It appeared that one of the crevices matched the star pattern found on the stone.

I awoke abruptly to the dream on the same schedule as the previous nights. I must have looked exhausted because the next morning something caught my mother's attention at breakfast.

"Darius Shannon! Where you up all night watching television?" she snapped.

"Nope," I responded half-heartedly.

"Well, why do you look like you haven't slept in days?" she asked as she put a hand to my forehead to feel for any signs of a fever. "You don't seem sick, but you look horrible."

"Thanks, I appreciate the morning pep talk," I responded. I shoved my spoon into the bowl, and cereal spilled over the sides. This was pretty much a daily ritual. I wasn't sure why I never got a bigger bowl or why I didn't just pour two bowls each morning for breakfast. It was a sort of challenge to eat the cereal with as little spilling as possible.

"I see that whatever it is, it hasn't affected your appetite any," my mother said dryly as she eyed me from across the kitchen.

I looked up with a smile as milk dripped from my chin. I made no attempt to respond to the allegation. It was true. I was starving.

By nine that morning I was in front of the rock wall scouring its surface for a crevice that mirrored the star design on the black stone.

"Where is it?" I said as I ran my hands across the surface.

I started to try and fit it into various crevices that looked like they might be a match. After what seemed like hours, I stepped back from the wall to examine it again from a distance. I closed my eyes and drew up the image from the dream. I could see the location in my mind. I focused on the spot where the stone was inserted and noticed it was slightly to the left of a root that stuck out from the wall. There were three tiny crevices between the root and the location.

When I opened my eyes I walked back to the rock wall and located a root that seemed to be the right one. I counted over three tiny crevices and noticed a slight circular indentation about the size of the stone. It was filled with moss and dirt that must have collected there over time.

I looked around for something to clean out the indentation. With a small stick I had broken off of a nearby tree, I carefully scraped away the moss and other debris and blew in the indentation to clean out any dirt.

"Aha! There you are," I exclaimed as a star-shaped indentation emerged.

I placed the stone into the indentation and stepped back again to relish in my accomplishment.

"Now what am I supposed to do?" I mumbled to myself once the elation of the discovery wore off.

The shadows were climbing up the rock wall, and I had an eerie feeling that someone was watching me. Despite turning around several times and looking into the surrounding foliage, I never saw anyone. I grabbed the stone from the wall and reluctantly put it in my bag for the ride home. At that moment I looked down at my watch. "Ah crap! Val is going to kill me."

I ran down the path toward the trail and sped off on my bike. As I reached the bottom I saw Val approaching.

"Looks like you found a better offer," she said icily as I skidded to a stop in front of her.

"I'm so sorry. I totally forgot."

"Well, I'm glad that I left such a strong impression," she said sarcastically. "I hope you enjoyed your ride."

At that she mounted her bike and rode off toward her house.

I stared after her as she rode away and berated myself for my own stupidity. I hadn't even started dating and I was already standing up pretty girls.

"You got yourself in deep this time, Darius," I said out loud as I rode down the hill toward the mouth of the canyon. As I came up on Val's neighborhood I turned on instinct and leaned my bike against a tree in her front yard and approached her door. I knocked and Richard answered the door.

"You've got a lot of gumption showing up here," he said with a mischievous smile. "Val is out back if you are hoping to apologize. But you are better off letting the dust settle."

I ignored Richard's advice and headed around the side of the house and through the gate. Val was sitting on one of the swings of the swing set, facing the mountains. She was staring off with a look of dejection and sadness. She was still in her bike shorts and jersey but had on some sandals instead of her biking shoes.

Val turned as I approached. "What do you want?" she asked coldly.

"I just came to apologize and ask if there is anything I can do to make it up to you."

"Well, for starters you could tell me what was so important that you forgot about our ride."

I paused, trying to think of a viable story, but nothing came to mind. "I really don't have a good excuse. I just forgot."

"I guess all boys are the same. All they can remember is whatever is important to them."

"I'm sorry. Do you want to go for a ride tomorrow?"

"Maybe some other time, Darius."

At that moment, Val's mom called her in for dinner. I walked out front and rode home in silence.

Again the dreams returned. This was the fifth dream and more vivid than the previous dreams. It seemed like each night the dreams became more and more real. It was almost to the point that I didn't even consider them dreams. They were almost like little video clips of my future being played to me in the present.

I saw myself turn the stone in the wall. It seemed so effortless. I just placed the star-shaped design into the indentation on the wall, and with my right palm flat on the smooth, black surface, I turned the stone clockwise about a quarter turn.

I awoke even more exhausted than the previous day. I was so tired that I laid back down for a nap after breakfast. It was a quarter past two when I woke with a start. I ran out the door with my pack in hand and headed for the canyon.

I reached the spot in front of the rock face and counted over three crevices from the root to find the indentation. I placed the stone in the hole and remembered the first dream. I prepared myself for an electrifying shock as I slowly put my hand palm down over the hand impression on the stone. I drew my hand away rapidly, then realized that nothing had happened. I tried again with the same result.

Nothing.

Since there was no shock, I tried to turn the stone clockwise in the star indentation like I had seen in my dream. It didn't move. I tried again and again over the course of the next hour until the palm of my hand was rubbed raw.

"Why won't you turn?" I asked myself over and over again, first in legitimate concern and later with a tinge of anger in my voice.

I couldn't believe it. It appeared so simple in my dream. Up until this point every dream had played out almost exactly as I had seen it. Sure, there was some unforeseen difficulty that I had to overcome prior to accessing the secret, but up until now it had been a somewhat simple solution.

The sun dropped in the west over the mountains on the other side of the valley just as I emerged dejectedly onto the trail. I mounted my bike and rode home through the deepening darkness.

Surprisingly, I had run into Mr. West almost every day on my way home. I usually talked with him for a minute or two, and then I would ride home and Mr. West would go for his run. I was a little sad that I wasn't in Mr. West's class this upcoming year. I was really starting to like him.

I opened the door in time to see my mother place the last dirty plate from the table into the sink. "You're late. You know I don't like you riding after dark," she stated. "And even worse, you stink like you haven't showered in days."

"Now that you mention it, I haven't," I responded, smelling my armpit.

"Get downstairs now and shower before you eat your dinner," she demanded.

"But I'm sooo hungry I could eat tuna casserole," I whined.

That comment got her attention. "Well, we have some leftovers in the fridge if you prefer that over the spaghetti we had tonight."

"I'll be right back," I replied as I bounded down the stairs with my shirt already off.

The dream that night began with me inserting the stone into the rock wall and turning it slowly clockwise. I wanted to yell out, "But it doesn't turn!" Instead, I waited for some time, then heard a loud crack. The rock wall split in half before me and slowly opened like two giant rock doors swinging inward.

SMACK!

I jumped out of bed to see what had happened.

Jim was smiling broadly and holding his belt in his hands. He had used it as a whip against my bedpost.

"You were tossing and turning like you were having a nightmare," he said as he hung his belt in the closet.

I was drenched in sweat.

I walked to the bathroom and washed my face. I looked in the mirror and saw why Jim was smiling. My hair was standing straight up. Ignoring it, I went back to bed. The clock said 1:05 a.m.

By morning I was anxious to get on the road. As I went to the fridge, I saw the chores list posted. I had bathroom duty this week. I hated it when I had bathrooms. Both Jim and I had inherited our aim from our father, so all three bathrooms were a little unpleasant to clean.

Having tried and failed throughout the summer to get out of my chores, I was determined to finish as quickly as possible. My mother watched me as I worked up a sweat cleaning her bathroom. An hour later, I saw my mother getting in her van to go grocery shopping. She signaled for me to hold up and struggled to roll down the window before realizing the van was not turned on so the automatic windows were not working. She opened the door instead.

"Don't you dare leave without finishing your chores young man," she demanded.

"Already done, Mom," I replied with a smile and a wink.

For the first time in my life my mother was speechless. She just sat in the van and watched me ride down the street toward the canyon entrance.

At the rock wall I placed the stone in the same spot and spent the rest of the day attempting various ways of turning it. As the sun sank in the west, I slipped the stone in my pack and rode home even more depressed than I was the previous afternoon.

What was I doing wrong?

Did I miss something?

I continued questioning myself until I pulled up in my driveway.

The clarity of the sixth dream surpassed the others in poignancy. I saw myself reach the rock wall after deviating from the trail. I turned and faced a large aspen tree about twenty yards from the wall. I took three steps toward the tree and turned right until I was facing a short pine tree. I took five steps in that direction and began to dig. After a few moments I hit something solid and pulled a box from the earth.

The dream ended before I opened the box, but returned two more times that night. When I woke up after the third dream it was 5:00 a.m. I grabbed my pack and snuck out of the house, grabbing a couple of apples and three granola bars. By sunrise I was breaking off the trail, heading toward the rock wall.

I leaned my bike against a tree near the clearing by the rock wall and set my pack next to the bike. I reached inside and pulled out my dad's fold-up army shovel and walked toward the rock face. When I reached the spot with the star-shaped indentation I turned and located the aspen tree from the dream. I took three steps toward the tree and turned to my right. I took five more steps toward the small pine. I unfolded the shovel and began to dig. The first hole reached twelve inches deep. I sat down to rest on a rock near the hole wondering if I would find the buried box.

As I stared out over the valley there was a reflection of the sun in the east off of an object on the west side of the valley. This wouldn't have registered with me if it hadn't repeatedly caught my eye. I tried to make out what it was reflecting off of but I couldn't decipher any details from this far away.

After a few minutes of rest I picked up the shovel and began to dig again. The shovel struck something solid. I cleared off some of the loose dirt, revealing the top of a wooden box. The shape of a box emerged slowly as I removed the layer of dirt from the top corners and edges. It was still too compacted in the hole for me to pull it out. I reached for the shovel and attempted to pry the box out using the leverage of the shovel. In my youthful exuberance I merely scratched the side of the box. Finally, I resigned to enlarging the hole. Within a few minutes I had the box in my hand. It was old. That much was clear by looking at it more closely. Dirt was caked on the surface, and the decorative wood elements of the box had rotted away, exposing a rusted metal beneath.

I searched for a way to open the box but couldn't find a latch of any sort. I pulled and pushed on the box for a while, and I even tried hitting it with my shovel and a rock. I got a water bottle from my pack and poured the contents over the surface to clean it off a bit. It seemed to be perfectly sealed. Frustrated and tired, I finally just yelled out, "OPEN!" followed by the few explicatives I had mastered in the past week.

The box instantly opened to reveal two shiny silver rings inside.

"Whoa," I muttered as I picked up the box for a closer look. There was some sort of writing on the inside, but it was in some other character set that I had never seen before. After examining the box, I took a closer look at the rings. One was slightly larger than the other and also slightly thicker. I turned it around in my fingers and noticed some writing on the inside. There were no jewels on the ring, just a silver band with writing on it.

I tried the ring on several of my fingers, but it didn't fit on any of them. I then placed it on my thumb.

"A perfect fit," I said. "What are the chances?"

I left the large ring on my thumb and picked up the smaller ring. It was engraved in an identical fashion as the other ring. I also tried it on all my fingers before it slipped onto my pinky.

The instant the ring was in place I felt a surge of energy burst into my body from my right hand where the rings were positioned. My mind raced through all the events of the past week in a few seconds. I saw the wreck and the meeting of the twins. I saw each of the dreams followed by the events they predicted up until the moment I placed the second ring on my pinky.

When I came back to reality I was lying on my back staring at the sky. The sun was now near its apex, so I realized I must have been laying there for more than two hours. Hunger pains hit me, and I stumbled over to my bag and ate an apple and two granola bars. I looked at the watch on my bike and saw that it was 11:45 a.m. I had been laying there for hours. I got up and filled in the hole, trying to erase any trace of my discovery. I wasn't sure why I did this, but it just seemed like the right thing to do.

I dusted off the box and placed it in my backpack, then slung it over my back. I walked to the rock face and placed the stone in the indentation. I placed my right hand on the stone over the intricate hand design and noticed that the rings fit into the grooves on the thumb and pinky as if they were designed to do so.

The moment my hand was in place, a power surged through me and my mind went perfectly clear. I could sense every tiny aspect of my surroundings. I looked around and saw a dragonfly a few feet off. I could see each wing beat, as if time was slowed down. I could hear the leaves rustling behind me and cars speeding down the highway a few miles away. My heart beat in a cool regular motion, and I willed myself to turn my hand in a clockwise direction. The stone slowly turned and...

CRACK.

The wall parted and dust flittered down the rock face, coating me in a blanket of dirt. I was pulled back into reality as the doors swung inward and my contact with the black stone was broken.

CHAPTER 3

I stood staring into the dark opening. After a moment's hesitation, I slowly walked from the bright sunshine into the dark room. All that was visible were some dust-covered designs on the floor near the entryway. One appeared like the tip of an inverted triangle. As I passed through the opening into the room, I cautiously put my hands out in front of me to avoid running into anything that might be in my path. I squinted to see into the darkness ahead but nothing was visible. The stillness was eerie and sent a chill down my spine. *What did I really know of this place?*

CRACK.

The door shut behind me, engulfing the room in utter darkness. I groped my way back to the door and began to frantically feel around for a handle or some way to open it again. My hands slid along the hard, smooth surface of the wall. There were no imperfections in the wall within the reach of my fingertips. A bead of sweat slid down my cheek despite the coolness of the room. Once I realized that there was not a door handle in the immediate space in front of me, I slid along the wall to my left, and after several minutes I reached one of the corners of the room. I continued and reached another corner a few moments later. The corners were not right angles and seemed to be more obtuse, making the room circular or octagonal.

As my courage mounted, I picked up speed, and after another few corners, I was in the open again. Spinning quickly in all directions with my arms extended, I feared that I might now be lost. My breath came a little more rapidly as I stopped and slowly retraced my steps back to the wall I came from. There was a right angle going into the wall. I placed my hand against the wall and lightly dragged it behind me, afraid that I would wander again into the open. My left hand groped the air before me. This wall seemed to be leading me deeper into the mountain. I took several steps and became confident that this was a long passageway and picked up my pace. Immediately I regretted my decision as I smashed into a wall directly in front of me and fell back on the ground.

I rotated slightly and leaned back against the wall. I rubbed my forehead and checked my nose for any blood. No blood, so I wiped the tears caused by the contact. The pain subsided as my curiosity aroused my senses. I carefully stood and felt my way to the corner and continued along the new wall.

THUD.

"Not again," I blurted out softly as I limped about in pain. I had jammed my thigh into a very hard object. That was going to leave a bruise. I felt around and realized I had slammed into some sort of platform or table.

CRASH.

This time I found myself sprawled on the floor rubbing my shins where they had smacked against another solid protrusion. I inched my way back to where I had tripped and found something shaped like a chair facing the wall. The low profiled, chair-like object confirmed that I had found some sort of desk. I sat down to think about what I should do next.

A few moments later I concluded that I must go on and find a way out. I stood and carefully made my way around the desk, only to find a second chair next to the first, then a third and a fourth. I inched along until I came to the wall again. This led to another wall at a right angle, which I followed until I found a right angle heading out of the room where the desk was located.

Progress was slow as I held my left arm forward and slowly inched along the wall to avoid any additional collisions. After what seemed like a long time, I came to another opening and found that it was identical to the first. This experience repeated a few more times before I realized I was going in circles and there was really only one room.

I finally sat back down at the desk, exhausted, hungry, and scared. I concluded there was no exit. I had no food or water since I had left my pack just outside the entrance. There was no way to call for help. Reality sunk in and fear overcame me.

"What now?" I moaned as I rested my head in my hands and cried.

"I could die and nobody would know what happened to me" I blubbered.

Then a new and greater fear arose in me as I realized that my mother was likely to send a search party into the canyon to find me when I didn't return home at my expected hour. An unreasonable surge of emotion welled up inside me. I feared that someone might find the black stone sticking out from the rock wall as part of the search. The reaction was unexplainable, but real. It was irrational and uncontrollable concern of being found out. Somehow, somewhere deep in my unconscious was an intimate understanding of the importance of what I had stumbled into during the last week.

"I must find a way out," I blurted out in determination. "If only there was a light switch."

I explored around on the wall directly in front of me and on the flat surface that was parallel to the floor just above my knees. I felt an imprint in the shape of my hand at just about an arm's reach. I placed my hand in the imprint and felt the contour of the imprint. After some time, I leaned forward, resting my head on the desk and mumbled to my maker, "Please, give me some light so I can find my way out of here."

Before the final words left my lips, the room illuminated. I immediately sat up and was blinded for several moments as my eyes adjusted to the brilliancy.

I shielded my eyes with my arm and slowly attempted to adjust my eyes by peeking out in front of me. Everything slowly came into focus as I absorbed my surroundings. A wall with four protrusions about three five feet up from the floor extended out directly in front of each chair. These protrusions were approximately three feet high and four feet wide and covered in a silvery reflective substance. Below each protrusion was some kind of writing. There seemed to be series of phrases in some ancient script. Each phrase was separated by a small space and a star directly in the middle. They looked like study cubicles that I'd seen in the library except there was no partitions separating the desks.

On the desk in front of each chair was an indent for a hand. There were also numerous compartments outlined in the table. They were locked, and my attempts to open them were unsuccessful. One of the compartments had an impression that looked like headset symbol seen on most electronic devices. It was horseshoe shaped and was etched into the space.

I stood and turned to explore the rest of the space. There were three other workstations—a small desk and chair—and they appeared to be identical to the one I had been exploring. The only difference was that the one on the far right had some sort of symbol above it. It looked like a star within a star.

The ceiling was probably more than twelve feet high and covered in polished black stone, similar to the stone that had gotten me into this whole mess. I thought it was odd that someone would go to all the trouble of polishing the ceiling. *What kind of person did that?*

Through the opening into the main room I could vaguely see the outline of what must have been the entrance. The light from the small room was filtering into the larger space and partially lighted a path. I walked out of the smaller room into the larger opening and looked around. The only thing I could see was my own shadow reaching out in front of me. It had even covered the outline to the door as I filled the entryway into the other room. The floors contained intricate designs of triangles, squares, circles, and other shapes, including one that matched the star found on the black stone. And like the small room, the floor was black except for the designs that appeared to be inlayed silver.

I looked around, and then addressed the Supreme Being, looking for another miracle. "Can you please light this room?"

Nothing...not even an echo.

I walked just a few steps into the darkness, and then turned to return to the small, illuminated room. My eye caught an indentation on the wall and something just clicked. I raised my hand almost involuntarily and placed it in the impression. This time I addressed the room, "Please turn on the lights."

Brilliance. Absolute brilliance. There it was. I could control the room. The technology was far beyond anything I'd ever seen or even dreamed.

The room was many times larger than the previous room. As I had so ingeniously discovered in my explorations in the dark, the room was polygonal. There was so much for my young mind to absorb. Facing one wall were a row of desks. The wall was covered with the same shiny material I saw in the smaller room. It was classroomesque. The rest of the large space was empty. I counted twelve walls that had shiny rectangles at about eye level. They were about the same size as those found in the smaller room. In addition, a hand impression was found to the right of each of them.

The ceiling in the larger room was many times higher than that of the smaller room. It appeared to also be polished black stone, but it was inlayed with similar silver designs like those found on the floor. One enormous star was the centerpiece of the design. It had twelve tiny stars forming a circle inlaid in the center. Two of the stars were larger than the others.

I wasn't usually a fan of artsy things, but I stared in awe at the floor and ceiling until my neck ached. As I rubbed my neck, I looked at the outline of a door in front of me. A hand imprint accompanied the opening similar to those found in other locations throughout the space. I walked forward and without further thought put my hand in the proper place and said, "Open."

CRACK.

The door opened and I was back outside, the sun blinding me. I stood in the clearing just before the wall and stared back into the room.

CRACK.

The door closed again before me, and the black stone spun to its original position. Fearing that I may not be able to open the door again, I placed my hand on the black stone and twisted it again a clockwise quarter turn.

CRACK.

The door opened again. I stood back and let it close before removing the black stone and putting it into my backpack. Apparently, my explorations had taken quite some time. It was getting late, and there was just enough sunlight to allow me to reach the trailhead before dusk turned to darkness. I did not enjoy riding down the trail in the dark, so I grabbed my pack and fished my bike out of the bushes before pedaling down the trail.

That night I slept soundly for the first time in a week. The only interruption that occurred was when Jim turned on the light just after midnight. I merely rolled over and fell into a deeper slumber.

Church was a blur for me that Sunday. I remember being asked a question to which I responded incorrectly. The teacher just looked at me in confusion and went on with the class.

Later that afternoon my mother confronted me. "Is everything okay?" she asked.

"What?" I answered absentmindedly as I looked up from a book I was holding.

"Is everything okay?" she repeated.

"Oh, yeah, everything is just fine," I responded, smiling faintly at her before returning to my semi-catatonic state.

"How's the book?"

"It's all right."

"Do you always read upside down?" she asked with a smirk.

"Oh, I guess I was thinking more than reading."

"Does this have anything to do with standing up Val the other day for a bike ride?" she asked without trying to sound too curious.

"What?" I asked, waking from my thoughts. "How did you hear about that?"

"I'm friends with her mother. She called me and filled me in. I guess Val was pretty upset about things. She also said that Val was feeling bad about how she treated you and wondered why you haven't stopped by again to apologize."

"Humph," I said, trying to disguise the ounce of hope that just entered my heart. My mother was a great, but she could not keep a secret, especially from one of her friends. There was no way I was going to appear interested.

"Maybe you can patch things up at school tomorrow," she remarked casually.

"I forgot that school started tomorrow," I said with a groan.

"I want you in the van at 7:30 a.m. sharp so I can drop you off."

"I think I may ride my bike to school this year," I responded deep in thought.

"Okay, but you need to be out the door by 7:15 or you'll be late for the first day," she replied with some doubt as to my capacity to be ready by that time.

My thoughts had already trailed beyond the conversation as I reflected on the experiences of the previous day. I descended the stairs and headed to my room. There was a package on my bed. It was wrapped in leftover birthday wrapping paper and had a white bow on it. I picked it up and saw my name written in marker on the paper. I tore it open and there was a brand new backpack inside. It was the one that I had been admiring in the bike store the previous Monday while I was getting my bike fixed. I couldn't believe it. It even had a built-in hydrations system so that I could drink water from a removable plastic pouch that zipped into the front pocket without removing the pack while I was riding.

I reached for my old pack so I could transfer the contents to the new bag. I looked around, but it was not beside my bed where I normally kept it. I crawled on the floor to see if it had been inadvertently shoved under the bed. Nothing was there.

I began to panic. "Where could it be?" I muttered as I rummaged through my room.

"Whatchya lookin for?" asked Rachael slyly from the doorway.

"Buzz off, it's none of your business," I retorted.

"Dad said I could have your old pack since he bought you a new one," she said coyly.

I glared at Rachael. "Where is my pack?" I demanded.

"I'm not telling," she responded, backing away from the doorway. "Dad said I could have it."

"It's my pack and I'll decide who gets to have it!" I yelled.

"Well, can I have it?" she asked.

Taken aback by her question, I pondered for a moment. "Yes, if you let me get all my stuff out of it first."

"Oh, I already dumped it all out into a bag in my room," she stated and smiled. "I'll go get it."

"I'll come with you," I said as I approached the doorway.

Rachael turned and headed down the hall to her room. She walked over to a pink bag in the corner that was once our grandmother's. She grabbed the bag and walked back toward me, taking one last glance at the contents. "What are you going to do with that shiny rock?" she asked.

I froze. "I don't know, I just thought it was cool," I responded, trying to sound disinterested.

"Can I have it?" she asked with pleading eyes.

"No!" I responded a little too quickly and a little too sharply.

"Fine, be that way." She handed me the bag. "Take your junk. I don't want it anyway," she chimed in, taking one final glance at the black stone.

I walked away and mumbled to myself, "That was a close one."

I redistributed the contents of the old pack from the pink bag into my new pack. One of the pockets seemed to have been made to hold the black stone, so I stuffed it in after carefully looking down the hallway to make sure nobody was watching.

CHAPTER 4

At 7:15 I saddled my bike and headed toward the high school. It was freshman year, and I had all the anxieties and high aspirations associated with the transition out of middle school. As I coasted on to the school property, I was jolted from my reverie on accolades yet received. Something nicked my handlebars and sent me careening into the vegetation in front of the main entrance. Before I came to a complete stop, I could hear the blaring of the horn as the driver stopped just long enough to drop off a passenger and speed in the opposite direction.

The other students were laughing and jeering at me as I pulled myself from the bushes. I was covered in dirt and discarded rubbish from years past. I glanced at the passenger and saw that he had joined the others in jeering my escapade. He even had the audacity to tell me to watch where I was going. I hoped this was not a bad omen.

Still jolted from the near fatal experience, I walked into Mrs. Williams's freshman English class. I sought a seat near the back of the room and sat down, setting my new pack next to my chair.

"Young man, you are going to have to put your bag in your locker," Mrs. Williams said, looking at me with a stern glance, giving me a disapproving stare as she inspected my disheveled hair and clothing.

"Okay," I muttered, realizing that this was a bad start to my first day of high school.

I pulled out a crumpled slip of paper from my pocket with my locker number and combination and began to search for the locker. As I scanned the row of lockers I saw that several were open with eager freshman standing in front of them. When I reached the locker with my number on it I was surprised to see it was already open and there was girl standing in front of it.

"I think you might have the wrong locker," I said as I approached the girl.

She turned and said, "Hi Darius."

"Oh, it's you," I said lamely.

"I'm glad to see you too," Val said without missing a beat, but I could see that she was disappointed with my reaction. As usual, I botched every conversation with my lack of exuberance and spontaneity. I had somehow been born with an inability to display the proper emotion at the proper time. Some might argue that I didn't show any emotion at all. I wasn't sure if this was a matter of nature or nurture. Either way it led to a social isolation throughout my short life.

"Sorry, I was just surprised to see you at my locker. Maybe the office made some sort of mistake," I said, ineffectively attempting to smooth things over.

"Actually, when we registered last week we found out that the freshmen have to share a locker with somebody else since there were not enough lockers for everyone to have their own." She paused, eying my reaction to the statement, and then continued, "I'm glad it's you and not some complete stranger."

My ears burned and I felt the blood rush to my cheeks as I looked into Val's eyes. I wanted to say something intelligent but responded with a dull, "Oh," confirming my hypothesis of being inept socially. The recent experience of standing her up for the bike ride was still fresh in my mind, yet it appeared that Val was no longer harboring any ill feelings.

"The locker is all yours I have to hurry or I'm going to be late," she said as she turned down the hall. I watched her walk away. She turned part way down the hall and waved. I waved and then turned back to the open locker, slightly embarrassed that she caught me staring.

I hung my pack next to hers in the locker and noticed it was identical to mine, except she had a pink trinket tied to her zipper. At least she had good taste in packs even if she did like tuna casserole.

When I returned to the classroom all of the desks were occupied except for one in the front row directly in front of Mrs. Williams's desk. As I continued surveying the room in the hopes of finding some other option, the bell rang. I scrambled to the open desk and slid into the chair.

"I presume, young man, that this will be the last time that you are tardy to my class. This time I'm just giving a warning, but in the future after your second tardy you will be given detention," Mrs. Williams said in a stern tone that made it evident that this was not negotiable.

Rumor had it that Mrs. Williams seemed to be really displeased with her life choices. She was unmarried. She had a dead-end teaching job at a second-rate high school. She was plump but not obese. But above all she was just plain mean. Her voice always had an edge to it, and sometimes she was one octave away from being shrill. It was just my luck to be in her class.

During lunch I sat alone at a table nibbling on my lunch, contemplating how much high school felt just like middle school except I was now the youngest and one of the smallest people. I was used to sitting alone at lunch. In middle school, I had become adept at being invisible. This was partially for my own protection and partially because I enjoyed my own company to that of the other kids.

"Do you mind if we sit with you?" I heard a familiar voice say as I gnawed on a soggy French fry.

"Sure," I said looking up at Richard and Val, trying not to act surprised.

"Did you make it to class before the bell?" asked Val as she sat down across from me.

"No, I missed it by a few seconds," I responded.

"So, when are you going to show us your secret trail?" asked Richard as he bit into his chicken sandwich.

"Anytime you guys want."

"How about this afternoon," Richard replied, looking up from his tray. "Val and I need to get a couple more training runs in before our race this Saturday."

"Okay," I replied, wondering how Val would respond to this line of inquiry after the last time I'd stiffed her. I also began to wonder if this was going to hurt my chances of returning to my secret room. I doubted that I should show Val and Richard what I had discovered. The less people that knew about the room the better it would be.

"Let's meet at our place after school," Val said, eyeing me cautiously.

"Sounds good. What time?" I asked, trying put some enthusiasm in my response but only succeeded in sounding less sincere.

"How about three-thirty. That should give us enough time to run the trail and get home before dark," Richard replied as he turned his attention to his lunch.

I looked over at Val. She was looking down at the table with an air of concentration. I thought she might be upset at the prospect of being stood up again. Instead she said, "Where did you get those cool rings?" She reached out and grabbed my hand to get a closer look.

"Uh, these?" I stammered. "I found 'em in the canyon."

"Can I see them?" she asked, still holding my hand in hers.

I was feeling *a little* uncomfortable. Never in my life had a girl held my hand, and to top it off we were in the middle of a busy lunchroom. I retracted my hand and attempted to remove the ring from my pinky for the first time since I'd put it on. I pulled, but the ring would not budge. Same result with the thumb ring. After a minute of tugging on my fingers, I muttered, "I can't seem to get em off."

"That's okay," Val said, grabbing my hand again. She examined the rings as she twisted my hand back and forth, looking at the inscribed letters.

A burning sensation filled my face and body. Richard was glancing over enviously at the rings or at the attention that Val was giving me. I wasn't sure which, but I didn't care too much at that moment.

Val finally released my hand and said, "I have never seen writing like that before. Where do you suppose they came from?"

"To be honest," I replied, "I'm not really sure."

"Well, I like them, and if you ever find another one I would buy it from you."

"If I find another one, I'll let you have it," I responded without thinking, then realized that I wasn't sure if I could keep my word, but it was too late to retract the statement.

Val smiled with the slightest tinge of embarrassment, "I'd like that."

With that the lunch bell rang, and the three of us returned our lunch trays before heading to our next class.

On the ride home from school, I wondered how I was ever going to get back to the secret room with Richard and Val tagging along for the ride. In the end I decided it would have to wait until tomorrow.

At 3:30 I rode into the Smith's driveway that led to their enormous two-story house. Richard and Val were standing in the garage looking over their bikes. They were both wearing their team outfits. They also had the top of the line bikes with full suspension, disc brakes, and all the latest technology.

I looked down, embarrassed by my worn-out shorts and dirty t-shirt and realized I might be out of my league. My bike was also only a fraction of the quality of theirs.

"Are you two just going to stare at your bikes all afternoon?" I asked, forcing a smile to disguise the feeling of inadequacy that washed over me.

They both looked up and grinned. Richard was immediately in his seat. "Let's see if you can keep up, Dari."

All three of us rode up the canyon at a brisk pace. We briefly stopped at the trailhead, and I explained how the trail was laid out and cautioned them about the turn near the river. I led off up the trail with Richard right behind me, and Val following behind him.

I loved a good ride and was really enjoying the trail. When I reached the top I stopped on the side of the trail near a fork between two trails to wait for Richard and Val. Richard reached me a few moments later and said, "If I keep going on the left will this take me back down to the trailhead?"

"Yep."

"See ya!" Richard yelled as he sped down the trail on his own.

I waited a minute or two for Val before turning my bike around and heading down the trail the same way Richard and I had just ascended. I found her a few hundred yards back walking her bike up the trail. She smiled as I rode up and said, "My tire is flat and my pump was packed up in the move, so I don't have it on my bike. Do you think you can help me out?"

"Sure," I said as I jumped off my bike. I pulled off my backpack and set it next to hers on the ground by her bike. "I owe you one since I dogged you on the last ride we were supposed to take."

I put some air in the tire and handed her my pump. "Why don't you keep this. You might need it again if we get separated."

"Thanks! But I'm pretty sure I can keep up with you, " Val said.

"You think so? Well, let's find out!" I slipped the pump into the pack and handed it to her. I slung my pack on and jumped on my bike.

We ascended to the fork in the road and began our descent. She was right about keeping up, but we did have to stop two more times to put air in her tire before reaching the trailhead where we found a note from Richard.

"I got tired of waiting so I headed home to get something to eat."

"Sounds like Richard," Val said with a shake of her head. "All he cares about is Richard."

The sound of an engine filled our ears as Mr. West's car pulled up. He climbed out with a questioning look on his face. "Who's your new friend Darius?"

"Uh, Mr. West, this is Val. Val this is Mr. West."

"Nice to meet you," they both said simultaneously and then laughed.

"How was your ride today?" Mr. West asked.

"It was okay. Val got a flat tire, so it took a little longer than usual."

"It's getting dark. You should probably get this young lady home before her parents start to worry."

"Okay, see you later," I responded as Mr. West turned up the trail and jogged off.

We filled up Val's tire with air one last time and rode back to her house. "Thanks again Darius," Val said, handing me my pump.

Our hands made contact as I grabbed the pump. She looked up and smiled before turning and running into the house. At the door she turned and waved saying, "Thanks again!" Then she stepped into the house, holding the door open to watch me drive off.

"No problem. I'll see you tomorrow," I yelled as I rode down the driveway.

The next morning as I grabbed my bag I noticed a pink trinket hooked to one of the zippers. "That was nice of Val to give me her trinket," I thought.

As I unzipped the backpack and looked inside I realized that it was Val's pack. It only took a moment for the reality of the situation to dawn on me. She had my black stone.

I rushed to school and found Val outside of our locker holding my bag with a big smile on her face.

"It looks like we switched up bags on accident," she said as we swapped our bags and hung them up next to each other in the locker. I felt the pocket with the black stone to make sure it was still there. I relaxed and breathed a sigh of relief as my fingers felt the familiar form. Maybe she didn't even notice.

Val was watching me curiously as I closed the locker and turned with her down the hall toward our first class of the day. She turned into a door and said, "This is my stop. I'll see you at lunch."

I rested easy in class that morning. In the cafeteria I grabbed my loaded lunch tray and headed toward the table where Richard, Val, and I sat the previous day. Richard was seated with his back to me as I approached, and Val was looking at him as they discussed the previous day's ride. I heard Val say, "I think the ride was a good training course. It has all the right elements and isn't too rough or dangerous. It's close to the house, letting us train longer because we don't have to ride or drive somewhere else."

Richard responded, "It isn't tough enough to get us ready for the regional event. We need something more technical."

"Hi guys," I said as I set my tray down next to Richard's. "What's going on?"

"We are trying to decide where the best training trails are for our next race," Val said looking over at Richard.

"I think the trail you showed us yesterday would work great, but Richard thinks it lacks technical difficulty."

"Well, there is a more technical ride in the canyon, but it's about a mile or two longer, and the trail isn't groomed," I said munching on my lunch.

"Really!" Richard responded enthusiastically. "That may solve our dilemma. We could ride the more technical loop a couple times a week and the simple loop on the other days."

"I don't know Richard," Val responded with concern on her face. "I don't think either of us can risk an injury right now."

"Oh, don't be such a girl. We're not going to get hurt. We'll just be careful," Richard said.

"If you hadn't noticed, Richard, I am a girl, but I guess it won't hurt to check the new trail out before blowing it off," Val said. "How do we get to it?"

"Just follow the same trail we took yesterday and take the right turn at the top. It goes up a little further and joins the trail again about a half mile further down, just before you come out on the stream. The trail is just a loop, so there isn't much chance that you will get lost."

"Why don't you come with us?" Richard asked. "You did a pretty good job of keeping pace for us yesterday. We could use some training competition to improve our times."

"I wish I could, but I have some stuff to get done," I responded, thinking of the room in the rock wall. "I could ride with you to the fork to show you were it is if you want, but I don't know if I have time to do the full loop."

"Sounds good," Val responded. "Let's meet at our place again at the same time."

I showed up at Val's a couple of minutes earlier. I saw Richard and Val pulling their bikes out from among the moving boxes that cluttered the garage.

"I see you found your pump," I said as I jumped off my bike.

Val looked up and smiled. "Yep."

We rode off this time with Richard in the lead. He rode us at a pretty rigorous pace. When we reached the fork in the trail I was dripping sweat and breathing heavily. I stepped off my bike and turned back down the trail as Val came around the corner. I couldn't help but notice that the exertion had put some color in her cheeks. Despite her tussled hair beneath her helmet and the beads of sweat rolling down the sides of her face, she was very attractive. Her jersey was zipped down just enough to catch my attention.

I looked away embarrassment as she looked up and smiled, "Good ride, Darius."

We both turned our heads up the trail as Richard's back tire disappeared behind a tree.

"I better get going before he gets too far ahead," Val said between breaths. "I'll see you tomorrow."

"See ya."

I watched her until she disappeared around the same tree that Richard had just ridden by on his way up the trail, noticing that she looked as good from that angle as she had coming up the trail. Then I pointed my bike down the trail toward the rock wall and focused on what lied ahead.

When I reached the wall, I placed the stone in and turned it.

CRACK.

The doors opened and I stepped into the dark. Once I was inside, I felt around for the hand impression on the side of the door. I put my hand in and casually said, "Lights."

Nothing happened, so I tried again a little louder.

"Lights."

A third time I tried, this time shouting.

"LIGHTS!"

Nothing but darkness.

I rested my head against the door, wishing that the lights would just turn on.

The room instantly illuminated.

My heart pounded. Somehow the room could read my thoughts. I decided to test this new theory. I thought silently, "Turn the lights off."

The room went black.

"Turn the lights on," I thought again, and the lights came back on.

I wasn't sure why it had worked previously. I guess it had something to do with the level of concentration. When I casually attempted to do things there was no response, but when I concentrated, everything seemed to work according to plan.

Now that I had mastered the door and lights I began to explore the room in earnest. Something wasn't quite right about the situation, but I couldn't figure out what it was as I wandered throughout the room. When I looked behind me, I saw footprints from my dirty shoes. It dawned on me that there was not a speck of dust or dirt in the place this time. It was completely clean. That seemed odd since the last time I was there the place was covered in a thick layer of dust. How did it get cleaned?

As if in response to my question, a small door opened from the opposite side of the room. Out of the dark opening burst a silent robot—four or five inches tall and twice as wide. It cleaned up of the footprints with a small rotating broom that circled beneath it like a street cleaner. Once the last speck of dirt was clean it zoomed across the room to the open cavity and disappeared into the darkness. Silently, the opening closed and all was normal again. My jaw hung loosely in awe of the spectacle. *Seriously? A robot cleaner.* My initial entry to the room must have triggered some sort of self-cleaning mechanism that had gone dormant over the years. Nobody would believe it. Then it dawned on me. I could probably never tell anyone about this place. It was secret for a reason.

I walked over to the twelve desks that were facing the shiny wall. Each desk was on a swivel of some sort and could turn 360 degrees. There was also a shiny square on every desk that was about twelve inches square. Next to each square was a hand indentation like the one on the doors, the black stone, and on the desk in the other room. I sat down in one of the desks and placed my hand in the indentation. Nothing happened. There were a few compartments on the desk that would not open by mind control or physical contact. One of them had a similar image of a set of headphones.

I walked over to the shiny wall. There was another hand imprint and another headset compartment next to the shiny element. I paced around the room. Each hand imprint was next to the shiny rectangles found on each wall, but there were no headsets next to the other shiny surfaces.

I made my way around the entire large room before entering the smaller room. I put my hand on the indentation just inside the wall and thought, "Turn on the lights."

The room illuminated. I was beginning to feel desensitized of the ability I had to turn on lights with my thoughts. It just seemed so easy, so natural. I looked at my watch; it was getting late. I knew that I should go, but I wanted to try one more thing before I left.

I sat down at one of the desks in the smaller room, placed my hand in the indentation and thought, "Open the headset compartment." To my surprise the small compartment popped open to reveal a set of futuristic headsets. They were black with inlaid silver designs. They must have been wireless because there were no cords or plug slots. I instinctively put the headset on my head. I waited for a moment, expecting something to happen. When nothing happened, I put my hand in the indentation on the desk and waited.

Suddenly, the shiny substance on the wall in front of me instantly lit up, displaying an image of me sitting at the desk with the headset on. In the image I could see and hear myself describing what I saw on the screen in front of me. Image after image flashed on the screen. The screen went blank, and an image of my mother and father flashed on the screen.

"How did you do that?" I yelled out as I stood and backed away from the desk. The screen flickered out, but nobody answered the question.

My hand shook as I hesitantly threw the headsets on the desk and walked backward toward the exit. *How did the room get a picture of my parents? How did it get an image of me doing something I hadn't yet done?*

None of it made sense. I couldn't understand how all of this was happening.

I placed my hand on the indentation near the door and thought, "Open the door."

CRACK.

The door slowly opened, and I walked outside as the sun slipped behind the west hills. I grabbed my bike and sped home.

For the next two days I went to school, ate lunch with Richard and Val, and then went on a bike ride with them in the afternoon. I then hurried straight home to catch up on my homework. At least I used homework as my excuse not to return to the Rock Room. I still couldn't understand what was happening.

Friday morning I saw Val waiting at the locker.

"Hi Darius," she said. I pulled off my pack and hung it in my locker. I noticed her staring and asked, "Is there something wrong."

"What was that?" she asked as she looked at me.

I noticed that she had black rings around her eyes as if she hadn't slept in days. Maybe the trail was too technical and she was getting worn out. Or maybe she was just up late doing homework.

"Are you okay?" I asked with some concern in my voice. This surprised me because when I normally asked these kinds of questions they always sounded insincere.

"Yeah, I'm okay. I just haven't slept well lately," she answered.

"Or, maybe you're training too hard?"

"Maybe, but I haven't trained any harder lately than I have in the past."

"Then what could it be?"

"I have been having strange dreams lately," Val said looking into my eyes.

"Really?" I responded, avoiding her glance. "What about?"

"Uh," she hesitated and then blurted, "you."

I looked up as red crept into my cheeks and my ears burned. No girl had ever told me that she was dreaming about me. Let alone a pretty girl that shared a locker with me. In fact, I could not recall a time that a girl even casually talked to me at school. Now I was having a conversation with one of the prettiest girls at school about how she was dreaming about me. Life was funny sometimes. One day you were completely invisible. The next day some girl was dreaming about you.

"Before you get any funny ideas, let me clarify," she backtracked.. "I saw you in one of my dreams wreck on your bike and fly into the river," she said, obviously noting the surprised expression on my normally emotionless face. "You were okay, but had to hike around to get back to your bike."

"Well, that is a crazy dream," I responded, then tried to change the subject. "I once had a dream that my older brother got hit in the head by a frying pan. I think it was a result of watching too many cartoons."

"Darius, don't try and change the subject," she said. "This dream wasn't like any normal dream I've had in the past. It was almost as if I was there in real life."

"Well some dreams are pretty realistic," I responded, trying to rationalize what I knew was occurring.

"Not like this one. I saw it three times at 1:00, 3:00, and 5:00 a.m. I know because I woke up and checked the clock."

"Wow that sounds pretty disturbing," I said, turning to walk down the hall toward my classroom.

She followed in silence until she neared the door of her classroom and then said, "Can we talk after school about the black thing you keep in your backpack?"

"What black thing?" I asked knowing perfectly well what she was talking about.

"Don't play games with me. I'll meet you at your bike after school."

At that she turned into the classroom. I watched at the door until she sat down. I turned quickly in the direction of my class and picked up the pace. I could sense trouble when the dreaded bell rang. I slid into my seat in time for the reprimand from Mrs. Williams, "That is two times, Mr. Shannon. One more and you'll have detention."

"It won't happen again," I muttered unconvincingly as I opened my books.

The day dragged on as I played out the conversation I was expecting to have with Val. I couldn't come up with a good story to explain the dreams or the black stone. I knew what Val was going through and didn't want to patronize her by playing dumb. The only option was to find out how much she knew before deciding what to do next.

After school, I waited by my bike for a few minutes before I saw Richard and Val walking toward me. Richard grabbed his bike on the other end of the rack and said, "See you later," as he mounted and rode down the street.

"You want to go to the park where we can have some privacy?" Val asked as she unlocked her bike.

"Sure."

The conversation during the ride was limited to a few trivial comments about classes we had in common and the homework we were working on. When we reached the park Val led me to a remote bench. We laid our bikes on the ground and sat down next to each other. I was looking at the ground in front of me and Val was looking out across the park. An uncomfortable silence was broken by Val turning toward me and saying, "Is it really true?"

"What?" I inquired.

"Darius, I'm not in the mood. I need to know if it is all true."

"Well, that depends on what 'it' is," I responded.

She looked at me for about a minute with frustration, anxiety, and weariness showing on her face. "Okay, I'll start from the beginning and tell you what happened," she stated, lacking enthusiasm and apparently energy. I empathized with her since not too long ago I'd been through the same ordeal.

"That sounds like a good idea."

She looked relieved to have someone in which she could confide her secret. "On Monday when our bags got mixed up I opened one of the pockets in your backpack and found a shiny black stone."

She looked up to see my reaction, but I returned a blank stare. She continued, "I pulled it out to look at it more closely. I must have stared at it for an hour before I was interrupted by Richard when he barged in the room."

"Did he see it too?" I interrupted with concern in my voice. Rachael, Val, and now Richard had now all seen the stone. My secret was getting to be less of a secret every day.

"I'm not sure," she responded. "I dropped it back into the bag as the door opened. If he did see it, it was only for a second."

"Okay, there's not much we can do about that," I said despite the feeling in my gut that I should be more concerned about the situation.

She continued, "That night the dreams began."

"Of me."

"Yes, of you falling off your bike. At least that is what I dreamed of the first night."

My interest level rose dramatically. "So there was more than one night of dreams?"

"The dream repeated three times, as I mentioned before. It was so real," she wandered off in thought.

"So, what else happened?" I asked impatiently, knowing the inevitable outcome.

"The next night I had another dream. In this dream I saw you turn off the trail on your bike and ride to a rock wall and stop. It also repeated three times. I haven't been able to explore the turn-off yet, but does it exist?" she asked, looking at me as I moved dirt with the toe of my shoe.

"Sort of," I answered without looking at her.

"Sort of? How does it sort of exist?"

"Yes, it exists," I replied still not looking up.

"Good, because I thought I was starting to go crazy."

"Is that all that happened?" I asked, hoping that she had not had any other dreams.

A sharp and knowing glance from her assured me that it wasn't. I began to well-up in anxiety at the thought of what transpired. Now there was someone else aware of the secret.

"You know that it isn't. In the last two nights I saw something that I'm having a hard time believing," she paused to check my reaction.

"Really, what did you see?"

"I saw you open a door in the mountain with the black stone. Last night I saw you enter and look around inside a large room and a smaller room," she said as she turned to look at me.

"Wow, that is pretty unbelievable," I laughed unconvincingly. "Now I can see why you hesitated to tell me about it."

"Is it all real?" she asked again.

"Well," I whispered after a brief pause and an uncomfortable laugh. "I'm not really sure what I should say. This is all starting to sound a little crazy."

"You definitely need to start saying more than you have been up to now."

The time slowly clicked by as I pondered how to deal with the situation. *What could I say? What should I say? What did I really know about Val? Could she be trusted with this knowledge?* Richard was certainly not the best person to leak this to and Val and Richard were twins.

"Well?"

"Yes," I relented. "It is all true."

"Take me there."

"Right now?" I asked, trying to think of some excuse to avoid going before I could think this through. If I took her there at that moment, I knew that there would be no turning back. She would be drawn into the thing in the same way I was. I was certain that my fears were not only for her safety but also for my own. If others got word of this they might not understand.

"Yes, and don't give me any lame excuses about homework or chores or anything else."

I thought it over and realized it was too late for me to deny it. She would probably follow me there anyhow, so why not just take her.

"Okay, let's go."

She smiled. "I knew you would be reasonable."

We strapped on our packs and rode our bikes out of the park toward the canyon. Forty five minutes later we took the turn-off and made our way to the rock wall.

"How do you make it open?" she asked as we approached.

I told her the story in its entirety of how I had reached this spot. I also, in some embarrassment, told her how long I'd struggled to get the door open. Finally, I explained how I found the rings and then commented, "So once I had the rings I just put my hand on the stone like so and..."

CRACK.

Val jumped back with a start and let out a short scream. I laughed lightly at her surprise and she smiled and hit me on the arm.

"I bet you jumped too the first time it opened."

"Actually, I didn't. I was too overwhelmed with the whole series of events to even doubt it would open. So when it did, I wasn't too surprised."

"I can't believe it really worked," she muttered as we walked into the room.

CRACK.

We stood silently in the dark, Val with her hand on my arm, gripping firmly. I liked the sensation of her standing next to me, so I hesitated to turn on the lights. I figured the suspense would enhance the experience.

"How do you turn on the lights?" Val whispered.

"I'll show you," I said lamely, before realizing that we were in complete darkness. I turned and placed my hand in the indentation and thought, "Turn on the lights."

Instantly the room illuminated.

"How did you do that?" Val asked, squinting her eyes at the brilliance as she stared at the wall where I held my hand. "I don't see a switch anywhere."

"It's actually kind of weird how it works. I just put my hand in the indentation and I think about what I want to happen."

"No really, how do you do it?" she prodded.

"That is the truth," I said. "I take you to a secret room carved into a mountain, open a door with a rock and you still don't believe me?" I turned the lights out with a thought, leaving us in darkness for a moment before turning them back on again.

"Cool, let me try," she said as I backed out of the way.

She placed her hand in the indentation. Nothing happened. She did it again, closing her eyes for good measure.

"Why doesn't it work for me?" she asked.

"I'm not sure," I said a little embarrassed. "It works fine for me."

"I can see that. But why can't I make it work?" she said as repositioned her hand in the indentation.

As I stared at her hand I could see the indentations in the wall from where the rings slid in and out. "You need the rings to make it work."

"Well how do I get them?" she asked. We were only a few inches apart, and my heart started to pound.

"I don't know," I responded, taking a step backward. "Maybe we can find some more outside or in here."

We wandered around the rooms, speculating the uses of each object in the place. She was fascinated by the desks and the shiny wall segments.

After a while I said, "We better go. We don't want to have to find our way out of here after dark."

"Okay," Val said in disappointment. "I wish I could come back tomorrow, but Richard and I have a race on the other side of the valley. I'll be gone all day."

"We could come back on Monday after school."

"That sounds like fun. Monday it is."

We rode home in silence as each of us ruminated on the experiences of the afternoon. As we approached Val's street I said, "See you Monday."

"See ya, Darius." She turned up the street and headed toward her house.

CHAPTER 5

I was out the door early and headed to what was now called the Rock Room. I entered and turned on the lights after the door had shut behind me. I wandered around, examining the space. I spent some time analyzing the patterns on the walls and floors. There was little repetition of images or patterns and everything connected fluidly and with an exact precision. In fact, the lack of flaws in the space was the most jarring feature.

After some time, I wandered into the small room with the desks. I looked at the headset and slipped it on. *Here goes nothing.*

I placed my hand in the indentation and thought, "What is this used for?"

The images of myself flickered onto the screen. In the image I could see myself talking to the screen as my memories flashed by. This continued for a few minutes as image after image flickered on the screen. I saw me and Rachael at the beach when I was seven, sand up to our chins followed by an image of me and Jim throwing around the football when I was ten years old. The images fluttered by until I realized that it wanted me to describe what I was seeing.

For the next several hours, I vocalized whatever image flashed onto the screen from my imagination. I felt like I had been talking for hours when an image of Val flashed on the screen.

I stammered, "Well, that is Val." I felt heat in my cheeks as I said it, embarrassed despite the fact that there was nobody to hear me talk.

The screen continued to flash images until my arm began to cramp and my mind ached. I drew my hand from the indentation on the desk and removed the headset.

I stood up and rubbed my backside with the palms of my hands, cursing whoever designed the furniture without any padding.

It was three o'clock, and I needed some lunch. I grabbed my pack and located my peanut butter and jelly sandwich. I walked around to stretch out my legs as I ate and wondered why the Rock Room would put me through such an exercise.

The little cleaning robot followed at my heels, cleaning up the crumbs that fell from my mouth with each bite. It scurried along in silence doing its job thoroughly. The place was immaculate despite the dust and mud from the trail that I'd tracked in each visit.

"Why don't I ask the Rock Room why it is making me do all of this description of my memories?" I said as I turned and tripped on the robot, falling to the floor.

I put on the headset and placed my hand in the indentation. I thought, "Why do you want me to describe the images that are displayed?"

"To learn," responded the Rock Room through a clear strong voice in my thoughts. It was a perfect, penetrating voice like the ones you hear speaking on movie trailers. It made me want to jump into action whenever I heard it. All of this talking with the mind was like having a conversation with myself without saying anything.

"What? To learn what?"

"Language," was the response.

Of course. The Rock Room was teaching itself English. The room looked centuries old, so whoever was previously using it probably didn't speak English. The room could communicate with me if I just taught it the language.

With new resolve I went back to work, teaching the room how to communicate in English. I worked until a voice spoke again in my thoughts, "Darius leave. Dark is come."

Somehow the strange voice, the Rock Room, and the telepathic controls didn't seem to be that unusual to me. I merely glanced at my watch and noticed the late hour. Any reasonable adult would have discounted the whole experience by ignoring the dreams. But a youth was quick to believe and open to learn. The vicissitudes of life have not tarnished and tainted a normal youth, opening the mind to a whole new world of opportunity.

"I'll be back on Monday with Val," I communicated to the Rock Room.

"Good, learn fast with two," it responded.

Hanging the headset, I grabbed my pack and raced out the door and down the canyon toward my house. As I came off the dirt trail I noticed Mr. West's car parked in the lot. I looked around but didn't see Mr. West, so I continued through the parking lot and onto the road.

Sunday seemed to drag on slowly. My mother had strict rules about going out on Sunday. She said that it was the only day that the family could spend time together. Somehow this didn't stop Jim from having his friends come by on occasion. I sat downstairs on the couch staring at the ceiling. I was thinking of questions I would like to ask the Rock Room once it could comprehend sufficient English. I was looking forward to having Val's help. The only problem was that she did not have any rings. The Rock Room was obviously designed to house more than one person, but there was no indication of how others were to communicate with the system. I pulled on my rings, trying to dislodge them with the intent of sharing them with Val.

"What are you doing?" asked Rachael.

"Nothing," I responded without flinching from my current position.

"Where did you get those rings?"

I thought for a moment prior to responding. I didn't want to lie since it was likely the question would be repeated in the future by others so I merely said, "In the canyon."

"Where in the canyon?"

Should I tell her the location? I struggled with how to answer but figured no harm could be done by being truthful. "Just up the trail from the bend at the river."

"I thought so," said Rachael as she turned and strolled out of the room.

Monday morning finally came, and I raced to school. I wanted to be there before Val so I could talk to her before class. As I turned the corner of the empty hallways I saw Val waiting at the locker. "I thought you might be here early," she said as I hung my backpack and grabbed my books.

"Yeah, I wanted to talk to you before school about the Rock Room."

"I was hoping to do the same thing," she responded.

"You first," I said.

"Okay," she said, pausing to gather her thoughts. "I had another dream."

"Really," I responded in surprise. I hadn't had any more dreams after I visited the room and just assumed it would be the same for Val.

"Well, actually I had two dreams," she corrected. "One on Friday night and one on Saturday night."

"So you were dreaming about me again?" I asked slyly.

"Stop teasing. This is serious," Val retorted a little playfully.

"What happened?" I asked, trying not to sound too interested, but unable to restrain my curiosity further.

"The one on Friday started with the two of us looking around the room. You put your hand on one of the handprints in the bigger room, and a drawer popped open to the right."

"Was there anything in the drawer?" I asked.

"I don't know," she said. "I woke up."

"Well, I guess that is something," I said, disappointed that she hadn't at least made an effort to peer into the drawer.

We both stood for a moment in silence as other kids started passing by in the hallway.

"What about Saturday?" I asked to encourage her to tell me more.

"I'll have to tell you after school or we might be late to class."

"Not again," I said in alarm as I shut the locker and started at a brisk pace with Val tailing at my heels until she reached her classroom.

"See you later, Darius," she called as she glided into the room.

I picked up my pace as the halls cleared and the anticipation mounted within me. I rounded the turn into the classroom and slid into the nearest chair with a sigh of relief a moment before the bell rang. Mrs. Williams wasn't in the classroom. In fact, nothing in the classroom looked familiar. I looked around and realized that I was in the wrong classroom.

"Oh no," I said as I grabbed my books and ran out the door, a little too slow to miss the class erupting into laughter at my mistake. The students all looked older and were probably friends with Jim. Just my luck. As if Jim needed any more ammunition.

I sprinted down the hall. As I slowed my pace, the silence was irritating. I hustled to my chair and tried to avoid contact with anyone. A few giggles were heard in the room but were silenced by stern glance from Mrs. Williams. She then turned her full focus toward me.

"I guess you will have the luxury of thinking about what time school starts during detention," she said.

Good grief.

At lunch I told Val and Richard about what had happened that morning. Val looked disappointed.

"I guess you'll miss the ride today," said Richard grinning broadly. "You really went to the wrong classroom?" he asked incredulously as he laughed again at my humiliation.

"Don't remind me," I said, mortified by my mistake and disturbed that I would have less time at the Rock Room after school. I chided myself for being so stupid. It irritated me that I continued to make such brainless mistakes.

"I wish I could have seen it," said Richard. "I bet it was hilarious," laughing again at the situation.

"Shut up, Richard," said Val with a stern look. "It's not funny. Now Darius won't be able to help us train, and you need all the help you can get after Saturday's race."

CRAIG WOLL

Richard gave a wicked look to Val, his demeanor instantly changing. "That was just bad luck."

"Oh really. Dad said that it was due to a little premature celebrating," Val retorted.

Both looked at each other for a few moments before I changed the subject to avoid an escalation in the argument. It was the first time I'd seen them lose their cool at the same time. Val was usually very level-headed until Richard did something she disapproved. For some reason she would always get really riled up about the little irritations caused by his actions. Maybe it was because they were twins and their minds were similar. Or maybe it bugged her that they shared so many characteristics in common.

"I think I might be able to catch up with you guys if I head straight for the canyon after detention," I said to ease the situation.

Val looked over with a knowing eye and said, "Okay, we'll get started and hopefully you can catch up."

Richard was still fuming as he picked at his lunch. "Sure, sounds fine," he said as he eyed the fake mashed potatoes in disdain.

After detention I mounted my bike and sped toward the canyon. I reached the rock wall and saw Val pacing in front. The treaded path in front of the wall showed that she had been there for some time.

"What took you so long?" she asked.

"I got here as fast as I could."

CRACK.

The door opened and we both entered the room. Val walked straight over to the wall and said, "This is the wall from my dream." Her mouth gaped open as she saw the little automatic sweeper move across the room. It had rained over the weekend, so we tracked in a little mud.

"What is that?" she asked.

"I don't know. It's just some robot that cleans up the room. It came out the other day when I was in here."

"Why didn't you mention it before?" Val asked.

"I didn't think it was important."

"Boys are so weird," she said.

"I get that a lot," I said as I examined the wall. "I don't see any drawers here."

"That's because you haven't put your hand in the handprint and opened it yet," retorted Val in a sarcastic voice.

A little annoyed, I put my hand on the wall in the indentation and thought, "Open the drawer," doubting that anything would happen.

I sprang back in surprise as instantly a drawer opened beside me. Val giggled at my nerves. She hadn't even budged because she was sure of what would happen. Both Val and I peeked into the drawer. After peering in for a moment, I looked up. Val and I were standing across from each other over the drawer. Our faces were only an inch or two apart. Our gaze held for a moment before I straightened up quickly and said, "I wonder what it is."

"It looks like a box."

"I know that, I meant, I wonder what is in it."

"Let's find out," Val said as she lifted the box and turned it over in her hands.

The palm-sized box was made of a very fine wood and inlaid with gold designs and letters that matched those found throughout the room and on the various objects. There was a latch on one edge of the box with a tiny mechanism to unlatch it.

Val unlatched the lid and slowly opened the box. Inside were two rings. They were identical to the rings I was wearing.

Val pulled them out of the box and began to admire them.

"Maybe we should put them back," I said with some concern. "We don't know what the Rock Room is capable of doing. They could be a booby trap."

"Don't be ridiculous," said Val as she placed the rings on her fingers and admired them. "These are for me."

"Now at least I can open the door," she said.

"Actually, you can probably do a lot more than that," I commented.

"Really, what else can I do?" she asked, whirling around to face me and then looking down at her hand to admire her new hardware.

"I'm not sure of everything, but you can turn on the lights, open drawers, and..." I paused, not knowing how to describe how I'd been teaching the room.

"That reminds me of the Saturday night dream," Val said, cutting me off as she walked toward the smaller room. "I saw us sitting at these desks and talking to the wall. We were wearing those headsets, and our hands were on the desk like this…" She placed her hand in one of the indentations at the desk.

The glossy area on the wall immediately lit up with an image of Val talking about the images. She pulled her hand away in shock. "What was that?"

"That's what I wanted to talk to you about this morning" I said. I took a seat at the desk to the right of Val.

"You saw it too?" she asked.

"Yep, and more."

"What do you mean?"

I told her of my Saturday visit and of my brief conversation with the Room after I had been teaching the language for a few hours. I included as much detail as I could so that she would understand the process.

"I wish I would have been here," Val said quietly.

"It's getting late," I said as I looked up from my watch, "but we might have time to teach the Room a little more English."

We sat at the desks and began describing the images that we were both seeing. After an hour of talking to the room, we heard the voice say, "Enough for today. Come back tomorrow."

We left the Room and followed the worn path from the rock wall to the trail. The sky was darkening as the sunset faded slowly from the horizon.

"Beautiful," sighed Val as she emerged first onto the trail and stared across the valley at the horizon.

"Yes," I agreed staring at Val, her face glowing in the fading light.

Val turned toward me for a moment, then turned away in embarrassment.

"Let's go," she said quietly, "It's getting dark."

I merely followed her.

CHAPTER 6

Val and I spent our afternoons riding and teaching English to the Rock Room. We didn't see much of Richard over the course of the week. He was reclusive and started sitting with Dallon Johnson and Tommy West during lunch. Dallon was the quarterback for the freshman football team and was very popular at school. He was the one that emerged from the car that nearly killed me the first day of school. Tommy West was like an abnormal growth stuck to Dallon's hip. Their athletic prowess and good looks were their main tools of attraction. They drew in admiration and outright worship by most of their followers. Richard was also a natural leader and not too bad looking of a kid. This alliance drew in even more kids and their gang of followers grew each day.

On Friday during lunch Val and I were deep in conversation over what to do next with the Rock

Room. It was learning so fast and could now speak English back to us in near perfection.

"I think we should ask the Room what to do next," Val said.

"I think you're right," I said glancing up in time to see a group of people closing in around us. Richard and Dallon were in the lead and each sat on opposite sides of Val. Tommy sat next to Dallon. I was now staring across at four people, but they weren't paying much attention to me as I finished my lunch.

Val looked perfectly calm as she glanced at Richard. "Hi Richard."

"Hey Val," said Richard uncomfortably, trying not to look at me.

"Richard and I wanted to know if you were coming over to my place with everybody. We are having the last pool party of the season," said Dallon looking over at Val with one of his winning smiles. The other girls in the room were scowling.

"Sounds like fun," she responded, then looked at me. "I assume Darius is invited as well."

"Sure," Dallon responded coolly with a less than friendly glance at me. "Any friend of yours is a friend of mine."

The bell rang, signifying the end of the lunch period and the crowd dispersed. Val and I headed over to the tray return, fighting the crowd to avoid being tardy to our next class.

"Why did you get me invited to the party?" I asked a little irritated at the thought of having to mingle with a group of kids that would openly demonstrate a lack of interest in my presence. "They obviously don't want me there."

"Well, I wanted you there," she responded avoiding my stare. "It will give us a chance to talk some more about what to do with the Rock Room. And besides, we need to get out and meet more people. It will look suspicious if the two of us are always going off alone together into the mountains every day. What do you think people will start saying?"

"Okay," I said, sulking over Val's response. I knew she was probably right, but I was starting to think that she might actually enjoy spending time with me alone in the mountains. It was the first time I had really spent any significant time with a girl that was not related to me, and I hated to think that I would now have additional competition for her time.

I had an unsettling feeling as I rode toward Dallon's house. He and his crowd did not mingle well with people of my station. I had been a witness to multiple humiliations and a few painful reminders that someone did not easily interfere with his entourage.

As I walked up to the front door of the house, a resurgence of foreboding waved over me. Never before had I felt so strongly that I should leave this one alone. For once in my life I intended on following the premonition. As I turned around to leave, I ran straight into Val and Richard.

"You weren't thinking about leaving were you?" said Val with a knowing eye.

"It won't be a party without you," Richard piped in sarcastically.

"That's enough, Richard," said Val, giving him a sharp look as she rang the doorbell.

The door opened before the bell quieted and Mr. and Mrs. Johnson walked out. Mrs. Johnson yelled back into the house, "We'll be back by eleven, so don't get too crazy."

Mr. Johnson turned to the three of us at the door and said, "Everyone else is out back. Just go straight through the kitchen and out the French doors."

"Thanks," we responded, entering the house.

I looked around and realized that I was way out of my league. The entryway opened up into a winding staircase that headed to the second floor. Paintings and expensive furniture adorned the various rooms on both sides of the entry. Our run-down house with faded furniture and worn carpet was nothing compared to what I saw at Dallon's house.

"Come on, Darius," Val urged me with a tug of my arm toward the kitchen.

As we opened the doors to the backyard we were just in time to see Dallon performing a front gainer to the delight of his gang of followers, the majority of which were girls. The giggles and applause reverberated off the house and filled the yard with the chimes of exuberant admirers.

Dallon pulled himself out of the pool and was surrounded by a few of the most daring of the group. I couldn't help but notice that Dallon was built like a Greek God. He had chiseled features that were accentuated by his summer tan and the glistening water dripping off his body. I hoped that Val wasn't noticing the same thing. I might have even felt a tinge of jealously as I looked down at my scrawny build.

"Hey Rich and Val, I was hoping you'd show up soon," Dallon said with a smile, ignoring me. "There are chips and soda on the table. Get on your suits; the water is great."

I had worn my suit so that I wouldn't have to change, but Val had her pack and went in the house to change. Dallon approached me near the table and said casually, "So are you and Val a thing?"

"No!" I responded a little defensively.

"Good, then you won't mind staying out of the way if I ask her out?"

"Go ahead," I said trying to contain the feeling that was welling up inside me. I wasn't sure if it was jealousy or anger. I looked around and realized that this may not be the best time or place to do something stupid.

"Anything look good over here?" asked Val as she neared the table with the food.

"Yep," responded Dallon with a sly smile. "Now that you showed up."

"Try the dip," I said, nodding my head toward Dallon.

"What was that?" Dallon asked in surprise. "Did you just call me a dip?"

"I don't know, do you see any other dips around here?" I quipped defiantly despite the staggering odds against me. This was probably not one of my finest moments.

Dallon approached me confrontationally. As he neared me, Val intervened, "Grow up you two."

I settled down and found what felt like a safe corner of the yard. There were kids everywhere, and not one of them stopped to talk to me. Val had been whisked off by Dallon and his posse. They were making her the center of attention, primarily because Dallon was focusing all of his charms on her.

Val glanced uncomfortably in my direction a few times, but as the party rolled on, her natural good nature took over and she was soon laughing and enjoying herself. There was a dichotomous reaction from me as I spiraled into a funk of self-pity. I imagined her becoming friends with Dallon and then never speaking to me again. Richard had already gone down that path, so it was logical to me that she would soon follow.

I was staring so intently in the direction of Val and Dallon that I was startled by a warm sensation oozing from my head and dripping down my face. I jumped up and shouted in time to see Tommy and a few others running off with an empty container of nacho cheese. The whole place erupted in laughter as everyone turned to ridicule me. My last glimpse before turning to go was that of Val suppressing her laughter at my predicament.

"I'm out of here," I said as I turned and walked toward the house.

As I neared the door I clearly heard Dallon ask Val, "Why do you hang out with that loser?"

My heart sunk into the pit of my stomach, and I didn't even blame Dallon because I was always asking myself that same question. I opened the door and went through the kitchen toward the front door. The site of the entryway brought back the recollection of the premonition I had as I had approached the house. If only I had listened I wouldn't have created enemies with the most influential kids in the freshman class.

As I rode my bike home, I reflected on how miserable of an experience I was likely to have in school now that all the most popular kids hated me. And to be honest, I didn't blame them. *Who was I anyway?*

CHAPTER 7

Saturday I arrived at the Rock Room early and alone. I opened the door and sat down at my usual desk. I looked over at the empty seat next to me and for the first time realized I might have blown my friendship with Val. I didn't feel much like teaching the Room English, so I just sat there ruminating on the previous night's experience, becoming more and more depressed as I relived the moments in vivid detail over and over again.

"Why did I get so angry?" I thought, remonstrating myself for my lack of restraint.

For the first time the Room responded without the use of a headset or my hand in the indentation. The screen flickered and illuminated an image of Dallon looking at Val. The clarity was incredible. I could see the smile on Dallon's face and Val, as usual, was beaming back.

"Great, so now I'm jealous," I said.

"What is 'jealous'?" the Room asked out loud.

Surprised at this new development with the Room, I temporarily forgot my worries. I looked around to see if there were any speakers but couldn't locate any. They must have been imbedded in the screen or behind a panel somewhere.

"Why didn't you talk before?" I asked.

"I did. What is 'jealous'?"

"Of course you did in my mind, but why didn't you say anything out loud?"

"What does 'out loud' mean?" the Rock Room questioned again.

I thought for a moment, not sure how to teach it the proper meaning of the phrase. "It means talking in a way in which I can hear using my ears," I finished lamely.

"I did not need to speak 'out loud' while you had the brain receptors on and your hands in the hand readers."

"Brain receptors? Hand readers? Is that what you call them?" I asked, starting to get excited again.

"That is what I call them in your simple language," was the Rock Room's response. "I do not yet know better words in your language."

"What do you call the black stone I found that opens the door?" I asked. "And what do you call these rings and these desks and the screens?" I continued without taking a breath.

"You must ask only one question at a time," the Room responded. "There will be time for all of your questions once Val gets here. Until she comes, what is 'jealous'?"

"I don't think..."

CRACK.

The door opened and Val walked in followed by Richard. His eyes grew large as he looked around at the place.

"What are you doing?" I asked in alarm. "I thought we were going to keep this a secret." Now I was really mad.

"Wow, this place is incredible," said Richard. "Exactly like I saw it in the dreams."

"You had the dreams too?" I asked. "But you never touched the black stone?"

"Tell him Richard," said Val looking at the floor in shame and embarrassment.

"A couple of weeks ago I walked in on Val while she was examining something. She hid it and I didn't think twice about it. Then the two of you kept going off on your own and not coming back until late, so I got a little curious. I hid off the trail when you rode by and followed you from a distance."

"You were spying on us?" I asked in disbelief.

"Not exactly. I just wanted to make sure Val was okay," continued Richard unconvincingly. "The first time I followed you I thought you had just ridden out of the canyon before I could catch up, but then I watched you coming down the hill while I was looking out my bedroom window."

"So you followed us more than once?" asked Val. "You didn't mention that before."

"It wasn't a big deal. Do you want me to finish my story?" he asked.

"Yes, keep going," I said. This was answering some of the eeriness that I felt about being watched. It had been growing recently and maybe it was just due to Richard's constant spying on us. In some ways it was a bit of a relief.

"I caught a glimpse of you as you left the trail on the second day. The spot was easy to find as I rode up. It was starting to wear into an alternate trail."

I took a mental note to hide our tracks in the future so we couldn't be so easily followed. If Richard found the path, it was only a matter of time before someone else found it and stumbled upon the Rock Room. In fact, it would probably be necessary to leave the trail at various locations to never wear one spot too thin.

"I followed the trail to the rock face but didn't see you anywhere. I looked around for a few minutes and even called your names. I noticed the black stone on the wall and examined it for a while. The markings were incredible."

"Did you actually touch it?" I asked.

"Yes. I even tried prying it out from the wall to take it home, but it was stuck too strongly."

"Tell him about the dreams," nudged Val.

"I was getting to that," said Richard, annoyed at all the interruptions. "That night, after touching the stone, the dreams started. They showed me the rock wall opened and this room. I also saw a drawer open over there," he said, pointing at the spot where Val had gotten her rings from.

"Did you see anything else?" I asked.

"Yes, I saw all three of us sitting at the desks over there and watching things on the screen. I also saw..." he paused, then said, "never mind."

"You can't stop mid sentence," Val said excitedly. Richard had obviously come to a portion of the story she had not already heard.

"It's kind of weird, but I also saw your little sister. What was her name again?"

"Rachael?" Val and I said simultaneously, looking at each other in surprise, forgetting for a moment the awkwardness of all that had transpired in the last twenty-four hours.

"I guess that makes sense," I said.

"What do you mean?" asked Val. Now she was the one with the questioning glance.

"Rachael touched the stone before I knew about all of this. She is probably having the same dreams we all had," I responded.

"So why isn't she here?" asked Richard.

"I don't know," I answered. "She touched it before you or Val, so I'm assuming she has already had a number of dreams. I've been so busy with school and trying to teach the Rock Room English that I haven't really seen her for a while."

At that moment, a soft tapping could be heard just outside of the door. This was the first and only time that we had ever heard any noise coming from the outside.

"What was that tapping noise?" asked Val.

"It is Darius's sister, Rachael," said the voice of the room.

Val grabbed my arm at the sound of the voice. "Darius, who said that?" she asked.

I was rather enjoying the physical contact and delayed a few seconds in answering. "That is the voice of the Rock Room," I said. "It started talking out loud this morning just a few minutes before you arrived."

"You better let your sister in before she breaks the black stone and locks us all in here," said Richard with some concern. He must have realized that he might be trapped with his sister and me for eternity inside the middle of a mountain.

I opened the door, and Rachael stood there with a stick in her hand. Her mouth dropped open in awe as she looked into the room. I looked down in her face and noticed for the first time the black rings around her eyes. It was an obvious by-product of the dreams and subsequent lost and restless sleep for numerous nights. She probably had it worse than any of us due to the amount of time from when she touched the black stone and the time she actually entered the Rock Room.

"Just like the dreams," she said with a sigh of relief. She leaned against the entryway before entering the room.

"Are you coming in or not," I asked curtly as I moved over to let her pass.

CRACK.

The door closed as Rachael entered. The four of us stared at each other for an uncomfortable few moments. Richard and Rachael were still in a state of awe, while I was thinking about what to do next.

CHAPTER 8

"Well, what do we do now?" I asked.

"How did you find this place?" Richard asked.

"How did you get those rings?" Rachael followed up.

"And when did the Rock Room started talking?" Val asked.

"The room talks?" asked Rachael with excitement in her eyes.

"Yes, and it does more than that, doesn't it Darius?" answered Val as she turned her gaze on me.

I saw that I was not going to be able to reverse course, so I started from the beginning. I wasn't into my story more than a few minutes when Val interrupted me, "Should we sit down?" she asked, pointing to the chairs in the large room that faced the shiny wall.

"Good idea," said Rachael. "My legs are killing me after the ride up here."

"You came up here on YOUR bike?" I asked, surprised at her determination.

"Yes."

"But you don't even have any gears," I said in disbelief. "How did you get up the canyon?"

"I walked when the pedaling got too hard."

I was still shaking my head in astonishment at my sister's fortitude in getting up the canyon as we approached the desks and sat down.

"Cool, they swivel!" exclaimed Richard as he turned his desk to face Val and I. It was surprising that everything was still in perfect working condition. There was not even a tiny squeak from the chairs as we moved around in them.

Rachael sat next to Richard and I began again. There were pauses for questions and clarifications as I proceeded to the moment that we opened the door for Rachael. Then Val jumped in and told her story from the moment she touched the black stone at the house to the moment the room spoke prior to Rachael coming. Richard repeated his story for the benefit of Rachael. Rachael looked at them all and explained how she had touched the stone a few weeks ago and had been bothered by strange dreams ever since. She looked exhausted.

"What now?" Val asked, looking at me.

"I'm not sure," I said as I walked over to my pack and got some water and a granola bar for Rachael.

"Why don't we get Rachael and I some rings?" mentioned Richard as he looked down at my hand.

"That's a great idea!" chimed in Rachael, forgetting the food for a moment.

"Okay, we can try, but there were only the two that I gave to Val last time we opened the drawer."

Val arrived at the location first and attempted to open the door. We stood around her in silence for a few moments as she appeared to be concentrating deeply. She raised her head and blurted out in frustration, "Why won't the drawer open?"

"Only the master of the room has access to this location."

We all looked around, trying to determine what this new insight meant. I finally asked what everyone was thinking, "Who is the master of the room?"

"Darius."

"But why?" I asked incredulously. "I don't even know what that means."

"You were the first. You were the one that was chosen."

The others turned and stared at me. I, for one, did not feel like a chosen one. The night before was one of many experiences that testified to me not being the chosen one. Jim was the chosen one. Dallon was the chosen one. Richard was the chosen one. Val was the chosen one. I could not reconcile in my mind how I could be chosen for anything.

After an awkward silence and not knowing what to do, I placed my hand on the wall and opened the drawer.

The drawer contained two boxes this time. Val lifted them out and handed one to Rachael and the other to Richard. They each opened the box and found the rings inside. They put them on, and while Richard and Rachael were examining the rings, Val and I headed toward the desks in the smaller room.

"I don't understand why I am the master of the room," I whispered.

She looked at me and said, "You were chosen."

We continued in silence, then put on our brain receptors and placed our hands on the readers. The screens lit up and images began flashing before us.

From the other room we could hear Richard say, "Come on, Rachael. Let's go see what those two are up to. I don't trust Darius with my sister," he said jokingly. Rachael giggled.

Rachael and Richard approached us cautiously. I motioned for them to sit down in the remaining desks and pick up the headsets. They placed them on their heads and mimicked Val and I by placing their hands in the indentations.

The past was forgotten for a moment as I said, "I'm about to find out what we are supposed to do next."

The four of us stared at the screen as an image of each of us seated in the large room appeared. We had a desk, and something too small and clouded to be seen was being projected on the glossy surface of the wall in the larger room.

The headsets emitted directly the voice we had heard earlier in the room. It told us that we must now learn to use our minds.

"What does that mean?" asked Richard, confirming to each of us that we had heard the same thing.

"It means that up until now you've only used a small fraction of your mind. From now on you will be learning to use progressively more and more of your minds until you have mastered your potential," replied the Room.

"How long will that take?" asked Val.

"Eternity," responded the Room.

"Eternity," we all whispered as we thought about the expansiveness of the word.

"But you will achieve the first level of mastery in a much shorter time," the Room clarified.

Without thinking I blurted, "Why us?"

"You chose to listen when you needed to hear."

"Huh," I muttered. "I'm not sure I understand what that means." In retrospect, I really did not understand the magnitude of the commitment I had made when I put on the rings.

"The very fact that you admit that you do not understand shows that you are ready to learn. If you listen to the things that are taught, you will gain the most precious of all things: Wisdom."

"Now I'm really sure I don't understand," I mumbled.

"This room has been sealed for many centuries as calculated on your planet in rotation around your star." The Room continued, "The stone you found was hidden from mankind in order to preserve it. It was meant to be destroyed, but one of great courage had the wisdom to preserve the stone against the advice of the Council for someone like each of you to find."

"But seriously, why us?" asked Richard.

"I do not know all things, but there is great power stored in the stone. This stone has a power that has not dissipated despite never having been replenished in more than 7,000 of your Earth years. It is attracted to good and finds an owner that is unlikely to abuse the power that it holds."

"But all I did was hit it with my bike."

"Darius Shannon, I do not know the answer to all things, but soon you will have someone that may answer your questions. I must now help to prepare each of you to begin your training."

"Training?" asked Rachael. "You mean, like going to school?"

"Yes. There is much that you must learn if you choose to become like those that have mastered the mind."

"When do we start learning?" I asked.

"Now," said the Room. "But you must not sit at these locations again until you have reached the first level of mastery. Now that your language has been learned, you will become students and sit at the desks in the Training Room."

As the voice ended, the screens went blank, and the headsets no longer appeared to function. We tried to get them started again, but after a few minutes, we all got up from our seats and walked into the larger room. I was the last out of the room and heard a light whoosh of air behind me. I turned in time to see the room seal off as if it had never been there. In fact, on further inspection I could not even tell there had been an opening. The only indication that anything existed behind the wall was the strategically placed hand indentation near the old opening. As a test, I placed my hand in the indentation and attempted to open the space again. Nothing happened, so I followed the others.

We sat in the front four desks of the Training Room, placed the brain receptors on our heads, and put our hands in the readers. The large glossy wall in front of us shimmered to life.

Richard read the top line, "The Code of the Mind Legion."

"What is the Mind Legion?" asked Rachael.

"The Mind Legion is the organization that commits to preserving and spreading the precepts on which power is predicated."

"That clears it up," quipped Richard with a chuckle. "I didn't understand a word of what he just said."

"It looks like the Code of the Mind Legion is a set of rules that the Mind Legion follows," I said as I scanned the listed items.

"Yes, in some ways that is true," reinforced the Room. "You will learn soon that it is not just a set of rules but an established order."

"A lot of these things seem like common sense. It's almost like some sort of religion or something," said Val.

"The Code of the Mind Legion is the basis of universal truth. This is why it has so many similarities with religions of your world. Its precepts are those that preserve life and happiness for all humans. It is also a means of developing great power," responded the Room.

"What do you mean by power?" asked Richard. "Are you talking about superhero powers?" he asked with another laugh.

"I do not understand what is meant by 'superhero' powers. Explain," the Room responded.

"You know, the ability to fly, command the weather, punch through brick walls, run faster than a speeding bullet, that kind of stuff," answered Richard with a smile.

"Yes," was the Room's reply.

Richard's smile vanished and silence prevailed as I daydreamed of what that meant. I imagined that I would soon be filling the trophy case at home with my wild victories in sports. I did not know what the others thought, but this was the beginning for us of that eternal struggle in man to subdue pride in order to obtain greater wisdom.

I broke the silence and asked, "Are you saying that if we keep this Code you can teach us how to do all those things that Richard described?"

"No," responded the Room.

"So you are saying that we cannot obtain super powers?" asked Val.

"No," responded the Room. "You can obtain great power."

"Then which is it?" asked Richard impatiently. "It can't be both ways."

"I am merely stating truth. I cannot teach you how to do those things that you described. My job is to teach you the Code. Another will be responsible to teach you how to follow the Code and harness the power."

"Another?" I asked. "Who?"

"That is not yet determined," the Room responded.

"Are there more powers we can learn from this other person?" asked Richard excitedly.

"Yes."

"Like what?" asked Val.

"To read minds, to place thoughts in other people's minds, to become invisible, to walk through solid walls, and many more things," the Room responded.

"What else?" demanded Richard as excitement boiled up inside of him.

"The Code says that you cannot run until you have first learned to crawl and walk."

For the rest of the day the Room answered questions and reviewed the Code of the Mind Legion. We were amazed at how quickly the time passed.

"The day is ending, so I give you my final admonition before you leave. These things that are taught in this room are only for the chosen. You are under obligation to keep secret the Code and the training you receive. A diminishing of power directly proportional to the magnitude of your error will be withdrawn from you if you break this or any rule in the Code."

The screen went blank as a signal that the training was finished. We all removed the brain receptors and stretched our stiff joints as we headed toward the door.

"I hope we learn how to use some of those super powers soon," said Richard as we walked out into the clearing outside of the room.

CRACK.

The door shut, and I replaced the black stone in my backpack. We rode down the trail and out of the canyon in silence. Our thoughts were our own, but I guessed that each of us imagined what the future might hold.

As Rachael and I walked in the door, I said, "Mom, do you think we can get Rachael a mountain bike? She seems to really enjoy riding in the canyon."

CHAPTER 9

At lunch on Monday Richard sat by Val and I. We leaned close together, discussing in quiet tones our experiences in the Training Room. Richard was the first to sit back and caught a glimpse of Dallon and his group of friends sitting across the cafeteria talking, laughing, and pointing at us.

"Oh boy, I smell trouble brewing," said Richard as he scanned the gathering crowd.

"Don't do anything stupid," said Val. "The Code said something about the turning of a bitter enemy to trusted friend leads to power and prosperity. It also said that provocation is the absence of mind control, and the absence of mind control degenerates light."

Richard and I just looked at her as if to say, "How did you remember that?"

"What? Weren't you guys paying attention?" Val retorted at our stares.

"You don't need to worry about me," I commented as I glanced over at the crowd. "Those guys are huge. Any one of them could make me wish I was never born."

Richard winced in guilt at the jeers they were throwing at us. "Cheesehead" was one of my favorites. Even though it wasn't overly creative, it had a nice ring to it.

I continued to ignore the escalating commentary. Partially because they were all bigger and stronger than I was, and partially because of the worried glances from Val. After one particularly harsh comment, I rose and walked toward the group. The silence in the room grew thick as anticipation heightened at the impending catastrophe.

"No, Darius!" whispered Val.

Dallon rose and approached me with an arrogant strut. "Are you ready to finish what almost got started on Friday?" he asked in a menacing tone.

"Dallon, I just came over to apologize for what I said on Friday. I was out of line and obviously offended you."

"So you are scared. Maybe you should get your girlfriend over here to protect you from me."

"No, Dallon. I'm not scared, and Val is not my girlfriend," I said calmly "She is free to decide who she wants to hang out with."

I felt a thrill of strength sweep over me as the anger of the situation was diffused. The crowd felt the tension in the room disappear and began to disperse. Dallon was reticent to let the issue go but saw that the demeanor of the crowd had changed and was astute enough to sense that the timing was not right. He just turned to his groupies and said, "Let's get out of here. This loser isn't worth my time."

When I turned back toward our table, Richard and Val were gaping at me in disbelief. I walked over, grabbed my tray, and took it to the tray return, and walked out of the room.

As I passed Mr. West near the exit of the cafeteria, I heard him whisper, "Well done my boy."

After school Val, Richard, Rachael, and I met at the room to continue our instruction. We entered the room and sat at the desks in front of the glossy wall.

"So what are we going to learn about today?" I asked as I looked around at our tiny group.

"Today you will each be assigned to a master and will become apprentices in the Mind Legion," said the Rock Room.

"Masters? Mind Legion? What are you talking about?" I asked in confusion. Up until to this point we had never really learned much about the purpose of the Rock Room or any of the events that had transpired over the last few weeks.

"The Mind Legion is the organization that built this room and everything that you have seen since you entered here. All those that put on the rings and enter into the training of the Mind Legion must be assigned a master until they are sufficiently trained to proceed independently. You become an apprentice when you are assigned your master."

"How is that possible?" asked Val. "Are there other people here that are part of the Mind Legion. I mean, will our master be somebody we might know."

"No, there are no longer masters of the Mind Legion here on Earth. They were removed many thousands of years ago. However, a master does not have to physically be here to take on a new apprentice," replied the Room. "They can appoint a small part of their mind to assist you in your apprenticeship."

"They do what?" asked Richard.

The Room continued, ignoring Richard's question. "You may notice that each wall in the room has a screen, a receptor, and a reader in front of it. There are twelve such walls in this room. To your left is Station #1. This will be Darius's training station. To his right will be Val, then Richard, and finally Rachael will use the final station along that wall. Go to your assigned location, put on the receptor, and place your hand in the reader."

We all arose and shuffled over to our designated locations. We placed the receptor on our heads and put our hands in the reader.

"What happens next?" I wondered in silence as we all looked around in anticipation of how the training would proceed.

The Room responded vocally to my thought so the others could hear. "Your mind will be analyzed and mapped, and a master will be assigned to assist you in capitalizing on your strengths and identifying your weaknesses."

Suddenly, a jolt of energy burst into my head. I stared blankly at the wall as a sensation I had never felt before permeated my brain. It was as if a tiny energy pulse was traversing the synapse.

"What's happening?" I asked, suddenly scared.

"Your mind is being analyzed, and a map is being recorded. Each map is stored in the archives of the Mind Legion," the Room replied.

It seemed like hours transversed as thoughts and images flickered in my memory, but the process only took a few minutes.

I leaned forward against the wall when the process ended to steady myself. I turned to look at the others and saw Rachael and Val sitting on the ground looking around. Their eyes were slightly glazed and they seemed deep in thought. Richard was still standing, but leaning against the wall for support and comfort.

"That wasn't so bad," said Richard as his legs wobbled and he sunk to the floor between the girls. Val and Rachael giggled at Richard's attempt at bravado.

"What happens now?" I wondered as I looked around.

"In a few moments a perfect 3-D replica of your master will appear in front of you. The image will have full access to the master's mind power. It must be taught your language before you can communicate by voice," responded the Rock Room.

"But that could take weeks," said Val a little exasperated.

"Yes, it could if they did not have access to the things that you have already taught me. They also will access the mind map that was made and is now stored in the Mind Legion archives. They will learn in a matter of minutes because they speak the universal language that is the root of all languages in every world in every galaxy. They are masters and require little teaching to master any language. Their minds have been perfected through the ages, and they will easily find the patterns in grammar and pronunciation."

From the corner of my eye I could see each of the screens begin to flicker. In anticipation, we all turned to see who would be our Master. Val and Rachael squealed in delight as they learned that their Masters were female.

"I thought it would be a man for some reason," said Val, "but I'm glad that it isn't."

"Me too," said Rachael, glancing over at Val.

"Did you hear that?" I asked.

"Yeah," answered Richard. "Somebody was calling my name."

"Yep, I heard my name too."

"Me too," responded the girls in unison.

"What do we do now?" Richard muttered.

"Answer it I guess," I said.

"You are correct," said the Room, "but you must put your hand in the reader since you are all new to speaking through the mind. Ask the Master his name, and then ask him what you must do next. Wait patiently as your Master analyzes your mind and constructs your language."

We obeyed the instruction without questioning it. Everything seemed natural to us in the innocence of our youth.

After a few minutes a rich voice entered my head, "My name is Kallikrates. I am Chief Captain of the Mind Legion."

My heart thrilled at the sound of his voice, and I sat silent for a moment, soaking in the depth of character in it. I soon remembered my instructions and asked, "What should I do next?"

"Begin living the Code," was the simple response in a slight accent that I had never heard before.

"What does that mean?" I asked doubtfully.

"Do all that is written in the Code," said Kallikrates. "Remember this: the Code only works if your intentions and actions are completely aligned. It is not enough to merely know the Code and do what it says. You must truly believe and feel that what you are doing is right."

"I don't know if I understand," I responded. I didn't think that I was sufficiently qualified to keep the Code. In fact, I wasn't sure that anyone could keep the Code.

"You are correct. You will not understand until you live it and believe in it. Once you have done that for some time you will begin to understand," was the response.

The image disappeared, and each of us removed our hands from the reader and replaced the receptor on its hook. We looked around and waited for the masters to return.

"It is late, and you must go," said the Room. "The masters also need some time to discuss your situation and to review your mind maps before they proceed with your training. The distance from Earth to each of them is a long one, and they must recover and prepare for the prolonged effects of the training. Return tomorrow and we will continue your instruction. Remember the words of your masters and you will soon learn to be like them."

Chapter 10

Val, Richard, Rachael, and I spent our afternoons in the Training Room on the pretext of being on long bike rides. The summer turned to fall, and the days began to shorten. We went through life as if in a dream as we suspended our previous reality in hopes that the new reality would become permanent. At times we pinched ourselves as a reminder that night was over and we were dawning on a new day.

The regimen became automatic for us. Each weekday we entered the room and sat at the desks for some simple instructions on the Code. This lasted for fifteen or twenty minutes. Usually an aspect of the Code was shown to us on the screen. It might be something about showing kindness in the face of rudeness or earning trust by keeping commitments with exactness. The list seemed endless. We had about a minute to memorize it, and then we repeated it back to the wall in cadence. When all of us had the Code memorized, the screen showed us some event from the life of one of the great Masters demonstrating how the Code should be applied. At times, Kallikrates would flash on the screen and we'd see his chiseled chin and flowing golden hair. There was always a sparkle in his steely eyes as he performed some feat. I would glance around to see if the others recognized him. They never did. I wondered if their Masters were sometimes shown.

After viewing the great events from the life of a Master, we would swivel in our desks, face the person next to us, and recite the memorized section of the Code. We would explain in our own words how it was to be followed in our life. Once that was completed, we each went to our assigned wall and worked with our master for about an hour to fully learn how the Code specifically applied to us. During that time the masters answered any questions that we had. They also gauged our readiness and assigned us some task to complete related to the topic of the day. They never forgot to validate whether we finished the task. I marveled at their exactness.

About a week after Richard and Rachael had joined Val and me in the Training Room, we were each asked to perform our first big task. We were to use telepathy to communicate with our Masters by removing our hands from the wall and communicating directly with them. As the lesson progressed, we could hear Richard voicing our common frustration, "I just can't do it."

I was concentrating so intently on the phrase that I was trying to convey telepathically that I didn't hear Val sigh with relief as she successfully mastered the task and was praised by her Master.

I tried it again, "Can you hear me?"

A silence followed, and I looked up to see a smile on the projected image of Kallikrates's face. "Well done," he responded telepathically. "It took me more than two weeks to learn telepathy. I was too thick-skulled to trust my Master."

I smiled and turned to see Val smiling back at me, and Richard and Rachael were still struggling in front of their screens. Suddenly Richard jumped and let out a whoop as he pounded his fist in the air, "I got it."

Val and I laughed as Richard looked over with a smile. Rachael broke down into tears as she failed again. She dejectedly removed her receptor and walked out the door with the rest of us. Val put her arm around Rachael and said, "It will come, just don't give up."

"I know," said Rachael. "I just wanted to get it as fast as you guys did."

"My master said that it took him over two weeks to learn telepathy," I said in hopes of lifting Rachael's spirits.

Richard laughed and said, "Mine did it the first time he tried."

The first few weeks the tasks were very simple, like speaking telepathically. As time progressed, the difficulty of the tasks increased and so did the failure rates on each of the tasks. Sometimes it took two or three weeks of practice to master the next task. The Masters encouraged us to continue following the Code as we learned it and to practice our tasks in secrecy.

The days were getting shorter and so were the training sessions as we attempted to get home before dark. One day as we began our training, the Room indicated that we each needed to open a drawer near our training wall and return with what was found within.

I approached my wall and used the reader to open the drawer. Inside there was a black stone slightly smaller than the palm of my hand and made of the same material as the stone used to open the Training Room door. I picked it up and noticed that it had an indentation for my thumb and pinky with corresponding indentations for the rings that I had on. On one side there was a shiny silver circle that was about the size of a quarter.

"What does this does," I said as I looked at the stone.

Kallikrates popped on the screen and said, "It is a training stone. You must use it to train when you cannot come to the Training Room."

"How does it work?"

"Put it in your hand with your palm up. The silver circle should also be pointing up. Now you must use telepathy to communicate through the stone."

I noticed that the others were receiving similar instruction from their masters as they held their stones in the palms of their hands.

"When you pass the word 'training' to the stone it will start where you left off in the lessons," said Kallikrates.

I focused on the stone and thought, "Training." The stone sent a two-foot holographic image out in front of me of the next section of the Code that I needed to learn.

"Well that should be subtle enough to keep a secret from everyone."

Kallikrates laughed at my joke. He was hard to predict at times. There were moments when I felt like he was my best friend and at other times he was my most demanding coach. At times, he would sternly put me back in my place or correct one of my human errors. But it was always clear that he was focused on my development above all else. Every word of advice and counsel was directly focused on my advancement in the learning and following of the Code.

I turned and saw that the others were seeing a similar image.

"What else can this stone do?"

"If you hold it sideways, perpendicular to the floor, and think of the name of one of your companions, you can telepathically communicate with them through the stone. It acts as a signal booster and can carry the message from world to world when your mind is strong enough," said Kallikrates.

Without consideration I turned my hand and thought "Val?"

The image of Kallikrates disappeared as my hand turned. "Yes, is that you, Darius?" Val responded in awe as she turned to look over at me. Her eyes glimmered with the realization of something new and amazing.

"Yep, if you turn it sideways like this we can talk to each other using the stones," I responded.

Val turned back to the wall and appeared to be in deep concentration.

"What else can it do?" I asked Kallikrates.

"That is all that you can do with it for the time being. In a few more months we can explore other features of the stone."

For the rest of the day we practiced using the stones, foregoing our regular instruction on the Code. We learned the etiquette of communicating through the stone. Access to the stone could be blocked by us or limited to one or many participants in a conversation. Each task demanded complete concentration and many failures before we were able to master even the basic power of the stones. Most importantly, we could now use the stones to extend our training sessions beyond the room and to communicate with each other telepathically without a brain receptor or direct contact.

Those days were some of the best of my life. I was learning at a pace that I never before could have imagined. The training was creating a phenomenal expansion of our natural abilities. Not only were we able to better perform the tasks learned in the Training Room and through the stone, we were seeing the success in all aspects of our lives. Each of us excelled in school, outstripping our peers in all subjects as we learned to master more and more of our minds. We also saw an increase in physical capabilities. I was a member of the wrestling team, following in my brother's footsteps. As I mastered elements of the Code, I grew in strength and speed and slowly worked my way up to the varsity squad. Richard experienced a similar success with the basketball team. He had barely made the freshman cut and was backing up the varsity team by the end of the season.

This new success did not come without its challenges. Dallon was becoming more and more upset at my athletic prowess. Richard did his best to keep Dallon in check since they both played on the basketball team. I knew that if I got out of harmony with Dallon or any others it would cloud my concentration and lead to a reduction of power. Kallikrates must have known what I was going through and gave me the following advice, "Negative feelings are cancerous to your progress. They start out subtly and imperceptibly change you until they overcome you bit-by-bit and destroy your mental capacities. Power and light cannot exist in the same space as hate and anger."

I solved my dilemma using a simple method. I avoided Dallon at all costs.

CHAPTER 11

Four rain-soaked jackets lined the wall near the entrance of the Rock Room. The water dripped slowly from the jackets to the floor sending a soft percussion throughout the open space. A small panel opened on the far end of the room, and a tiny wheeled robot scooted to where the water was gathering. Three small legs appeared from beneath the robot as it elevated to the height of the jackets. A larger tubular appendage extended and applied hot air to the surface of the jackets for several minutes until the dripping stopped. The robot lowered to the floor, and a straw-like appendage protruded from a circular encasing and silently sipped up the water from the puddles near the door. The appendage retracted, and the robot sped across the room toward the far wall. A wall raised and closed behind the robot in perfect precision. Silence filled the room.

A scan of the room revealed the four of us with headsets on and our hands resting on the wall in front of us. Each of us appeared to be in silent conversation with ourselves. Every so often our lips would form words even though no audible sound came forth. We had grown accustomed to the silence since we could converse with each other through the stones any time we wanted. We still used the handprints so that we could focus our concentration on other tasks than telepathy.

During this particular practice session I was working with Kallikrates on some simple telepathy and mind control techniques for the third time that week. I had been struggling, and the intense training sessions were beginning to wear on me. The others were noticeably fatigued as well. Not the physical fatigue associated with most exertion, but mental fatigue. We were concentrating for longer periods of time than our minds were accustomed and like any other part of the body, it was feeling strained.

"Are we ever going to learn anything fun?" I asked impatiently to Kallikrates, hoping for respite from the grueling tasks.

"What do you mean by 'fun'?"

"I mean things like flying or walking through walls or superhuman strength. Up until to now we have just worked on improved memory and simple telepathy tasks. Don't get me wrong, these are pretty neat, but they don't seem overly useful."

Kallikrates contemplated for a time and asked me a penetrating question. "What makes you think you are ready for such things?"

CRAIG WOLL

"Well, I don't know," I said, becoming slightly perplexed. I knew that I needed a good answer if I was going to get anywhere. "Maybe it's just the fact that I've been able to use telepathy without any problems for over a month now. I'm also able to recall from memory anything that I hear or read. It seems like that shows that I have learned to control my mind."

Kallikrates began to chuckle at what I thought was a flawless case.

"What's so funny?" I responded, reddening as a twinge of anger and embarrassment rose up within me. "I'm serious about this. I think I'm ready for something bigger."

"I'm sorry, Darius. I should not have laughed. It is just that you brought back memories of someone that said that same thing many years ago."

"Well, what happened to him?"

"His master allowed him to attempt to use his powers to walk through a wall."

A few moments of silence ensued before I plucked up the courage to ask again, "What happened?"

"He broke his nose," Kallikrates chuckled as he pointed to a spot on the bridge of his nose where it leaned slightly to one side.

We both laughed at the imagery. It was amazing how Kallikrates was able to diffuse with ease and style any situation. He conjured up remedies and stories that seemed to always teach the proper principle and change the focus to the real matter at hand.

"So, when will I be ready?" I ventured to ask as we both prepared to continue.

"That is hard to say. It is not common for an apprentice in their first year to attempt any difficult mind control. The results can be disastrous. I got off easy with merely breaking my nose. Had I actually been partially successful I could have potentially rematerialized in the middle of the wall. In all likelihood, such an action would lead to death or serious injury."

"Why did your master allow it to happen? Didn't he know that you could kill yourself?"

"Yes, he knew the potential for injury. At the same time, he knew that his primary job was to teach me. At the time, the one lesson I had not learned by heart was humility. I had consistently outperformed my peer apprentices and felt that I was somehow better than they were. The broken nose was merely a lesson to prepare me for much greater challenges."

"Well, is there anything that I can learn that's more active than talking to Rachael from across the room using my mind?"

"Yes, there is one thing that I can begin to teach you that you might consider 'fun.' But if I do so, you must promise that you will not use the gift outside of the Training Room until I have given you permission."

I perked up and immediately responded, "I promise," intending to do exactly as he said.

"This task will require the combination of several simple tasks that we have worked on up to this point in the training. They are foundational stones upon which most of the future tasks you learn will emanate. Tasks build on tasks in the mind until you can perform something appreciable. Even before following the Code you consciously and subconsciously arranged tasks in meaningful patterns to accomplish your desires. Since we began training, you have now learned how to take those patterns and refashion them into new abilities. If you take a perfect memory and combine it in the right way to the ability to communicate telepathically, you can watch anything kinesthetic and communicate it back to each part of your body to repeat exactly what your memory captured."

"I'm not sure that I understand what you mean by that," I responded in some confusion. It was a case where I knew the meaning of the words, but I had not captured the essence of the statement.

"You will simply be able to copy any movement that you observe in another person."

"You mean that I can learn to do anything that I watch?" I asked as my mind began to race through the possibilities.

"Yes. I am going to show you a movement on the screen. Once it disappears, I want you to copy that movement in its exactness."

The first visual was of someone doing what appeared to be sign-language. I attempted the hand movements and was only able mimic the first few signs before becoming confused and asking to see it again. This continued for some time before I was frustrated at my inability to mimic the sequence.

"I thought you said that I would be able to do this," I said after failing again to mimic the behavior.

"The power of the mind is only unleashed as the physical, mental, and emotional laws are followed, and only if that power is obeyed with exactness. You must be in harmony in body, mind, and relationship. Any element of disharmony with one of the laws associated with a task will disrupt your ability to master the task. Since this task requires more use of your physical body than previous tasks, its success is predicated on your exactness in following the physical elements of the Code. Can you recall what some of those elements include?"

"Yes, the Fifth Point of the Code requires that the mind and body must be properly rested."

"And, what time did you retire last night?"

Last night, I had put in a movie at around midnight and fell asleep on the couch sometime after that. I responded timidly, "It was pretty late."

"What else does the Code teach us about maintaining control over the body?"

I was now beginning to feel uncomfortable as I realized what was happening. "The Eighth Point of the Code says that we must eat only until satisfied, and to eat nothing that leads to pain, discomfort, or inability to control the mind."

"How well have you fulfilled this aspect of the Code?" Kallikrates questioned, knowing the answer.

"Not so well," I responded quietly, looking down as I took in the subtle rebuke.

"Are there other Points in the Code that correspond to the physical?" Kallikrates asked.

"Yes, the Thirteenth Point of the Code says that in order for the body and mind to stay in harmony they must each be exercised daily." I scrutinized my feet, not daring to make eye contact as I anticipated what was coming next.

"And how often have you exercised your body in the last month?"

"Well, since wrestling season ended, I haven't been as consistent as I probably should."

"Your honesty is encouraging, my young Darius," said Kallikrates with a smile. "Few there are that are able to master the physical requirements of the Code in their first few years. You show a great understanding and merely lack determination in following through with what you know. Once you have taken that knowledge and learned to apply it, you will obtain great wisdom and power."

"How long does it take to master the physical?" I asked, finally mustering the courage to look in the friendly and concerned face of the master.

"That depends on the individual. In your case, I believe it will not take long. And once you have mastered all or part of the physical points in the Code, you will begin to see immediate results. The Code is always looking forward, not backward. The memory of your past mistakes will serve as reminders, not definers."

I rode home in silence from the Rock Room thinking about what I had learned. I was frustrated and angry for failing to complete the task. Val and Rachael respected my silence as they listened to Richard ramble on about how his master held the time to proficiency record for demonstrating some of the key skills they were now learning, and how he would teach Richard some of his secrets that were not in the traditional training philosophy.

Rachael and I put our bikes in the garage, hung our jackets outside the door, and slipped off our wet and muddy shoes prior to entering the house.

"Hi you two," said our mother. "There are a few pieces of fried chicken on the table or leftover tuna casserole in the fridge."

We raced toward the table and I had a chicken leg in my hand before remembering the words of Kallikrates about following the Code. My mother and father stared at me in utter amazement as I put down the fried chicken and walked toward the fridge. Both of their heads turned on queue as I walked by. Neither spoke or chewed the half-eaten food in their mouths. Rachael slowly set down a piece of chicken she was raising to her lips as she watched me go by.

As I placed the tuna casserole in the microwave, I turned and looked at them. "What?"

"I was only joking," responded my mother. "There is plenty of chicken."

"Are you cutting weight again for wrestling season? I thought it was over," asked my father between bites.

"I'm just trying to watch what I eat so I feel better," I responded, turning again to the microwave as it chimed.

After dinner I noticed that I wasn't feeling lethargic or uncomfortable like I normally did when I ate large quantities of fried or fatty foods. I took a mental note of the fact and went on with the evening. At about 10:00 p.m the family sat down to watch a movie together. I got up and headed toward the stairs.

"Where are you going?" asked my father curiously.

"I thought I would get to bed. It's been a long day."

"Your mother bought the fixings for banana splits. Are you sure you don't want one before heading to bed."

"No thanks," I said with a genuine smile.

Rachael watched me curiously and then said, "Me either, I'm going to bed too."

"Suit yourselves," said our confused father. "Leaves more for the rest of us."

Rachael followed me down the stairs. "Did you learn something today that is making you do this?"

"Yes and no," I responded. "Yes, I learned something today, and that's why I started watching what I eat and how much rest I get. That's just part of following the Code. But no, it doesn't feel like I'm being forced to do this. At first I really regretted not having the fried chicken or the banana split, but now I feel better than I would have had I eaten either. It's kind of weird, but I want to follow the Code more closely."

"Yeah, me too," said Rachael.

I woke up a few minutes before my alarm and shut it off so it wouldn't wake Jim. I got showered and dressed and ate a good breakfast. On my way to school I stopped in the park and found a secluded spot so I could practice the last task that Kallikrates had given me. I pulled the training stone from one of the pockets in my pack and turned it upside down, telepathically summoning Kallikrates. He appeared in front of me and presented me with a few simple tasks that I was easily able to master.

"You are finally learning to live the Code," said Kallikrates.

"Yep, it is starting to make sense now."

"I see," said Kallikrates. "You have learned a valuable lesson from the Code. Learning is much more than just reading, hearing, studying, or observing. True learning is only seared into the mind when it is lived. Persistence in the face of opposition is the key to developing the trust within you that is needed to open the secrets of power that are already in your mind. It is unusual for one as young as you to learn this lesson. Only time will tell if you can continue to follow the Code with the same intensity as you have for the last few days. Many apprentices have shown similar spurts in learning only to recede in the face of a real test."

For the next few weeks I worked hard to become proficient in mimicking the movement of others and practiced often.

One afternoon Kallikrates said with a slight smile, "Are you ready to have some fun?"

"About time," I said, beaming with delight at the prospect. I finally felt exhilaration, knowing that I had trained hard and had earned an opportunity to do something great.

Kallikrates put an image of a man doing a type of martial arts on the screen. I mimicked the increasingly more complex moves with ease. After an hour of training, I was able to perform the majority of the basic moves and was enjoying the exertion. I looked around as I sensed a change of atmosphere and an unusual silence enveloped the Training Room. The others were all staring at me in wonder.

"Cool," said Richard. "How did you learn to do that?"

"Basically, I'm learning to copy any movement that I see someone else do."

"Well, I wouldn't want to mess with you after watching that," Richard responded longingly. "I gotta learn that task." He turned back to the screen and began what appeared to be an intense discussion with his master.

The next day at school I saw Richard and Dallon in the hallway. It had been months since we had crossed paths, mainly due to my diligence in avoiding a confrontation. But today felt different. A sense of foreboding washed over me, but I continued down the hall because no perceivable danger was before me. I tried to pass without making a scene. Dallon had his back to me and could not see my approach. Just as I came up alongside of him, a door swung open beside me and knocked me solidly into Dallon. The odds of this scenario were so small that I deemed it impossible despite the premonition that I had felt.

The contact with Dallon had scattered his books across the hallway floor. A group of seniors walking toward us laughed hysterically at the accident. I looked up from the scattered mess in time to see Dallon's face turn red in fury. He wasn't used to looking foolish and he obviously didn't like the sensation. He turned on me in his rage and swung his fist straight at my face. Without even thinking, I dodged the fist and grabbed Dallon's arm while turning my hips into his body and throwing him over my back.

Dallon lay still for a moment, dazed at what had occurred and probably wondering how he had been thrown on the floor. Realization hit, and he sprung from the floor like a cat, charging straight for me. I threw him again, and Dallon got up more slowly but no less enraged. Before he could make another charge, Mr. West grabbed Dallon and Mrs. Williams grabbed me.

"Both of you come with us," said Mrs. Williams holding onto my arm in such a way that I was half-dragged and half-carried down the hallway.

I was surprised to see Mr. West walking down the hall in similar fashion with Dallon. Both teachers had scowls on their faces. I was unsure of whether they were scowling at the incident or the unpleasantness of having to work together to solve the problem.

It was well known in the gossip circles that Mrs. Williams and Mr. West were not on friendly terms. Apparently they knew each other at college or some other place before coming to work at the same school.

The Vice Principal exited the office just as we approached. "What's going on here?" he asked, looking at the two teachers with a seasoned eye and then at us.

I breathed a sigh of relief as Mr. West cut in on Mrs. Williams. "These two were practicing some wrestling moves in the hallway."

"Fighting inside the school?" the Vice Principal asked incredulously, looking at us for some explanation.

"He started it," said Dallon, pointing at me.

"I don't care who started it," the Vice Principal said flatly. "I'm finishing it, and you are both suspended. Come into my office so we can call your parents."

"Is that necessary?" asked Mr. West.

"Yes!" responded the Vice Principle and Mrs. Williams in unison.

The result of the fight and the phone call was a one-day suspension followed by two weeks of being grounded to the house after school and on the weekends. I thought I could use this time to train but found that all my tasks were much sloppier, and I was unable to do some tasks that I'd previously mastered. It was as if I took two months backward in my training.

"Kallikrates, what is happening?" I asked after several failures in my training.

"You broke your promise and failed to keep the Code," was his disappointed response.

"I don't understand. I was just defending myself."

"Do you think that avoiding a little physical pain is worth breaking your promise to not to use the skills that were taught?"

"Well, when you put it like that, I guess not. But what was I supposed to do? Let him punch me in the nose?"

"Yes, if it means keeping your promise and following the Code."

"How do I get back to the level of performance that I had before the fight?"

"You have to rectify the pain that you caused as a result of your decision. If it were easy you would never learn. This is your broken nose."

"How do I rectify the pain?"

"I cannot tell you how you must proceed in solving your own problem. You must exert some effort if you want this to be a lasting learning experience," Kallikrates replied.

Upon returning to school after the suspension I was eating lunch with Val. Dallon walked behind me and whispered under his breath, "You're going to pay for what you did."

Val looked at me with concern. "What are you going to do?"

"I don't know yet," I said deep in thought, wondering if I really was going to have a real broken nose experience.

A few moments later I rose from the table and walked toward Dallon.

"Wait. What are you doing?" asked Val in alarm.

"I'm going to take care of this once and for all," I said.

The crowd around Dallon quieted as I approached. The slow and subtle whispering sound of voices could be heard. "Fight! Fight! Fight!" they chanted. It was as if everyone knew it was going to happen, but nobody wanted a teacher or administrator to intervene.

The students that were seated near Dallon's table began to creep in closer to get a better view of the proceedings. Others hurriedly passed the word that something was brewing.

Dallon turned with a smirk on his face. "Came to apologize did you?"

"As a matter of fact, yes," I responded.

"Well, go on. Everybody is listening now. Let's hear your apology."

"I'm sorry for throwing you like I did after I bumped into you the other day. There was no excuse for my behavior. I'm also sorry for avoiding you all the time while I'm in school. You've never done anything that justified my actions."

Dallon was speechless after my apology. He literally just stood there staring at me. Finally after a long period of silence he said, "Are you serious?"

"Yes," I said with a little more sincerity as I felt the situation might be diffusing.

The crowd backed off as Mr. West approached. "Is everything okay over here?" he asked, scanning the situation.

I turned to Dallon to see how he would respond. "Yeah, there's no problem. Darius was just about to tell me how it was that he threw a kid twice his size."

Mr. West eyed me for a few seconds and said, "Is that true Darius?"

"If Dallon says so, then it must be the truth," I responded, catching a quick glimpse to see if Dallon was sincere. He was tough to read, but I was not feeling too much anxiety so I thought I would let the situation play itself out.

"Okay, I guess I'll have to take your word for it," said Mr. West as he turned to leave at the sound of the bell.

The crowd cleared, leaving the two of us alone. Dallon turned to me. "Do you really think you could teach me how to do throws like that?"

I smiled in relief, and with a nod I said, "How about you meet me after school in the wrestling room and we can practice for a few minutes. I can't stay long because I'm technically grounded by my parents for the next couple of weeks."

Dallon grinned and commented, "You got off easy. I'm grounded for the next month." He paused. "Once you teach me those moves, there won't be any protection against me."

"I'm hoping I won't need it," I responded with a smile. "I try not to fight with my friends."

Over the next few weeks, Dallon and I trained after school and our past differences slowly faded. It was a little awkward at first, but we soon found that we had common interests. I also noted that I had regained all the skills that I had lost. In fact, I was a little surprised at the increase in capabilities that I felt as I repaired the relationship and aligned more closely to the principles of the Code.

CHAPTER 12

Time turned from a constant progression to a variable progression. The days and weeks passed as if they were an instant in time. Instants felt like days and weeks. I often pondered over this phenomenon. During my training regimen I found myself periodically referring to clocks to see how much time had elapsed. In the moments that my mind and body were completely aligned I could absorb knowledge at a rate that far exceeded my prior capacity. I would complete entire lessons in as few as five minutes while thinking that I had spent hours in concentration. This gave me additional time to contemplate and practice on my own. In some sessions I would think that I had only been working for five minutes when in reality I had been absorbed for three hours. Before I knew it, Spring was upon me. The flowers were blooming, and the smell of freshness filled the air as the April rain washed away the winter.

Val, Richard, Rachael, and I began to refer to our small group as the Earth Mind Legion or EML for short. Over the winter months and into the spring we found ourselves spending less time in the Rock Room and more time using the training stones for our lessons. This gave us less time to observe each other's progress, so we would try and communicate with each other every day about what we were learning. I often felt like Richard was withholding some information about his lessons. He would sometimes snicker at Rachael or Val as they would express excitement over some task they had mastered. He often spoke in generalities about his training.

The training stones made communication possible between us during our times of separation. At school, we put our hands in our pockets, grasping the stone and sending a telepathic signal to one another without appearing suspicious. There were a number of interesting developments that occurred to each of us as we concentrated intently on the telepathy. Rachael had to concentrate the hardest due to distance. On one occasion, Val and Rachael were in a discussion and the signal cut out on Rachael's end of the line. It took Val several minutes to reestablish connection. When she did, Rachael would not talk about the break in communication. Later we came to find out that Rachael had followed someone into the boy's locker room and literally ended up in the showers before she realized her mistake. This provided comic relief for us whenever someone else would drop a connection. In most cases it was simply a minor occurrence of bumping some unsuspecting students or running into a wall.

"This isn't working," stated Richard flatly one day at lunch. "We're all too busy coordinating joint training sessions."

"What do you mean?" I asked.

"Well, for starters there is only one way into the Rock Room that we know of, and it requires the use of the stone to open the door. That wouldn't be such a problem except that there's only one stone, and you are the self-appointed keeper of it. That means that whenever one of us wants some privacy with our master we have to find a closet or an empty room."

"I know," said Val, looking timidly at me to gauge my reaction. "Mom thinks I'm getting depressed because I spend all my time in my room with my door locked. One day I was sitting with my back to the door going through some practice. She silently opened the door and watched me for a few minutes before asking what I was doing. I slipped the training stone in my pocket. I had to tell her that I was just practicing something. She sat down beside me and asked if everything was all right. She must think I'm going crazy."

"What can we do?" I asked. "There's only one way into the Training Room, and there's also only one stone."

"I've been thinking about that," responded Richard. "What if we were to place the stone in a safe location near the entrance? That way we could all go to the room at our convenience until school gets out in June."

"I don't know. What if someone found the stone? Remember what happened to us when we touched it?"

We all sat in silence, recalling our own vivid experiences after touching the stone. The memory of the dreams and the compulsion that overwhelmed us at the time rushed clearly into our memories with near perfect clarity. This was one of the most difficult aspects of improving the power of our minds. Our memories became clearer, and our mistakes could overwhelm us if we dwelled on them for any extent of time.

Richard was the first to break the silence. "It's not as if anything is going to happen to it. You said before that it had been buried there for thousands of years."

"That's true, but I'm still uneasy about it. Let's think about where we might put it for safe keeping," I said, folding my milk container into a tiny square with my fingers and thinking about the proposition of leaving the stone somewhere. I continued to have the impression that I was being followed whenever I went to the Training Room. I would often sit silently observing my surroundings, but I had never seen any trace of evidence that my suspicion was true. I assumed I was just being a little paranoid, but I still felt uneasy about leaving the stone behind. If we lost it, there was no way of entering the Rock Room.

"Why don't you ask the Training Room if it has a suggestion on where to hide it," said Val thoughtfully as she nibbled on her lunch. "Boys are never willing to ask for directions. I bet the Room could tell you how it was done in the past. This can't be a new problem if this location has previously been used for training by the Mind Legion."

In a rush of reality the suggestion hit us as the only feasible solution to our dilemma. "That's a good idea," Richard and I said in unison under our breaths, ashamed at not having thought to simply ask. Val had a knack for logic and practical thinking.

That afternoon at the Rock Room, everyone turned and looked at me in expectation. Not knowing what else to do, I placed my hand in the imprint near the door and vocalized my thoughts, "Is there a place near the entrance that we can hide the black stone that opens the Training Room door?"

An image of the outside of the Training Room splashed on the screen near where I had placed my hand. It showed a cavity that would open on the rock wall.

"Let's try it out," said Richard enthusiastically.

CRACK.

The door opened and we searched for the spot on the rock wall. Richard was eager to find the location and began to show some frustration as the minutes ticked away. After some time combing the rock back and forth, Rachael called out to us, "Over here, I think I found it."

We trudged through the overgrowth and approached the location from which Rachael called. She put her hand flat on the surface of a rock that had a slight discoloration of the shape of a hand with two rings on it. The wall slid over, revealing a crevice that was slightly larger than the black stone.

"Way to go Rachael!" I said enthusiastically as she beamed back at me proudly.

I pulled the stone from my pack and was about to place it inside when Val stopped me and said, "Don't you think we should make sure that we can all open the crevice before you put in the only key to our entering the room."

It was sometimes aggravating how sensible Val was about everything. She had excellent foresight. It usually irritated me when she thought of something that was plainly logical that I had overlooked. I pulled the hand holding the stone back and replied, "You're probably right, as usual."

Each of us took a turn testing our ability to open and close the crevice various times. Once we were certain that it would open, I placed the stone inside and we tried again one by one to open the cavity. Since I was the last to try on the second round, I pulled out the stone before shutting the opening again.

"Now that we solved that dilemma let's get back to our training," I said as I took the stone with me toward the door of the Training Room.

"Wait a minute," said Rachael. "What if someone is already inside the room and someone else arrives? How do they get in? We've been pulling the stone from the door as we enter to keep it hiddent."

This was another perfectly logical query. Once again it irritated me that I hadn't thought through the problem in enough detail to work out these minute details. But it made sense that Rachael would think of it. She, of course, was the first to experience this problem, and the others had experienced it as well. I was oblivious to the problem since the stone was always in my pack. Usually the person outside just made a telepathic connection with one of the others inside the room.

"What do you propose we do?" I asked shortly, placing the stone in the wall and opening the Rock Room.

CRACK.

"I don't know. If I had the answer I wouldn't have asked the question," she responded with some irritation as we entered the room.

Val stepped in to diffuse the situation before it escalated into a teenage sibling argument. "Darius, why don't you ask again what we can do?"

I grudgingly conceded my possession and placed my hand on the previous location from inside the room.

"How does someone from outside get in if others are already in the room?"

An image flickered on the screen and showed the inside of the room. There was a spot marked on the wall about six or seven feet off the ground with the same symbols as those found on the black stone. It was located several feet from the entrance. A hand was placed on a palm pad below the symbol and a door slid sideways, revealing a cavity in the wall slightly larger than the stone.

We walked over to the location in silence and looked up at the markings above our heads.

"You know, I've looked at these markings a hundred times and never once gave any thought to their significance until today," I said as I place my hand on the wall.

Like fulfillment of prophecy, the door opened and we all crammed to peer into the cavity. It was the same cavity we had seen from the outside. It opened from each side as a resting place for the stone.

We went through the same ritual, at Val's request, as we had on the outside. We all opened and closed the cavity with and without the stone. I was the last, and once I reopened the cavity, I closed it and left the stone. My pack felt uncommonly light, and I glanced back after walking away feeling somewhat empty, as if I had left a part of me behind.

The next day at lunch I looked up to see Rachael running toward me. I knew something wasn't right because she went to the nearby middle school and had never joined us for lunch. As she approached, Val and Richard turned to see Rachael heading toward us.

"What is it?" asked Val as Rachael approached.

"I lost my stone," said Rachael in a panic. "I checked everywhere in my room and my locker and my backpack. I can't find it anywhere."

Val put an arm around her as she broke into tears. "It will be okay, Rach. We'll find it."

Richard was a little more pragmatic and asked in a tone of authority, "When was the last time you used it?"

Rachael wiped her eyes. "I think this morning when I was getting ready for school. I called Val to ask her advice on something."

"That's right," said Val.

"So the stone is somewhere between here and our house," I thought out loud. The others looked at me blankly.

"Darius is right," Val chimed in. "It has to be somewhere between your school and home. Most likely it's just sitting in some dark corner of your room."

"Did you stop anywhere or talk with anyone since you last had your stone?" asked Richard.

"Just my Mom and Jim," she replied. "He gave me a ride to school in his car because I was a little late."

"Where do you normally keep the stone?" I asked.

"In my pocket."

"What about today?" asked Val. "You don't have any pockets in that skirt you are wearing."

"Well, when I wear a skirt I usually put it in my backpack or jacket," Rachael responded.

"Have you checked there?" I asked.

Rachael looked at me as if I was crazy or stupid. "Of course. I looked there first."

"Well, there's nothing we can do about it now. We can all help you find it after school," I said.

"Okay, I just hope I'm not in trouble for losing it," Rachael said with a worried look on her face.

Rachael was always self conscious about the EML. She was younger and had less life experience. The tasks were hard for all of us, but she was by far the hardest worker. Every night after dinner she would go and practice in her room, and every morning she was up before me practicing. To lose her stone must have felt like another failure.

"Don't worry, we'll find it," said Val, trying to comfort Rachael as we walked with her to the edge of the school property.

The four of us retraced Rachael's steps and searched for the stone. After several hours of unsuccessful searching, we sat dejectedly on our couch in the living room.

"Maybe we should start again from the beginning," offered Richard.

We all grunted at the thought of retracing our steps again.

"We could ask the Training Room if it knows how to locate a lost stone," said Val.

"It's almost dark and it looks like rain," said Richard. "Let's wait until tomorrow."

I looked at their faces and felt an urging to solve the problem immediately. A thought came to my mind that I voiced immediately, "Maybe we can ask one of the master's through our stone."

I pulled out my stone and looked around to make sure nobody was watching.

"Not here!" said Val. "What if somebody walked in? Go to your room and try there."

"I don't think my room will help. I don't have a door," I replied.

"Well then go to the bathroom or Rachael's room," said Val. She paused, and her forehead crinkled. "You don't have a door? How come I never knew that?"

"I'm a little embarrassed about it. There was a door on the room, but when we put in new carpet several years ago the door wouldn't open or close, so we took it off and placed it in the garage."

"Weird," said Richard as he and Val started laughing.

I got up and left before they started inquiring further about the predicament. "I'll just go into the bathroom," I called back as I walked down the hall to hide my complete humiliation.

"Kallikrates," I thought as I passed into the bathroom and closed the door.

An image flickered and appeared from my stone. It was Kallikrates. For some reason no matter how many times this phenomenon occurred, it still impressed me. "Are you ready to begin training for today?" he asked.

"Not exactly. We have a small problem. Rachael has lost her training stone and we have been unable to locate it."

"So it looks like we will be training today with a real world experience," he said with a smile and a bit of excitement in his voice. Obviously he was relishing this opportunity to move from theoretical into reality.

"Is there a way to find a lost training stone?" I asked with some relief as I noticed that he wasn't angry.

"Yes. I was wondering when one of you would finally lose the stone. This task will be more difficult than your previous tasks to this point. It requires you to isolate an object using your senses from all other objects that surround it. At your stage of training and level of mind mastery, I think that the object would have to be within a few feet of you to feel it."

"Well, how do I sense it?" I asked not fully understanding what he was talking about.

"Every object is comprised of tiny molecules that are broken into tinier pieces. These are joined together in patterns that emit a very small amount of electromagnetic energy. Each object has a distinct pattern. It is a little bit like a fingerprint. There are no two exactly alike until you get to the atomic level, and even then the sub-atomic particles can often leave a distinct trail."

"So I'm supposed to be able to sense that pattern in her stone?" I said in consternation. "Maybe we should have Val do this. She's the one that's good at sensing things."

"Yes, Val does have an aptitude for sensing feelings and emotions. This, on the other hand, is merely an object. The pattern from this object will have a pattern slightly aligned with Rachael's pattern since she has so much of her mind and DNA in the stone. This will help differentiate it from other stones even though their pattern is very close to that of her stone."

"But, how do I sense it?"

"Look at the stone in your hand. Can you see it?"

"Yes."

"Close your eyes. Good. Now can you feel the stone in your hand?"

"Yes."

"How do you know it is the stone?"

"It feels like the stone, and I have held it thousands of times."

"Excellent," said Kallikrates. "Now put the stone on the counter."

"But you will disappear."

"Do you really think that the Chief Captain of the Mind Legion will disappear if you put down your stone? Even the most junior of the Great Council can control an apprentice stone from even this great a distance."

I opened my eyes and set the stone down. To my surprise, Kallikrates was still there. "Why have you always disappeared when I take my hand off of the training stone?"

"Because I would never break the Code by staying when I am no longer wanted and/or needed."

"So since I want you here, you're able to maintain the hologram even when I'm not holding the stone."

"Yes, something like that."

"I learn something new every day."

"Good, now back to work. Close your eyes again. Can you feel the stone?"

"No."

"Why not?"

"I'm not holding it."

"True, but can you sense the stone?"

"I don't know what you mean."

"Keep your eyes closed, turn in a circle five times, then stop."

I obeyed. This felt like a five-year-old birthday party. Next I was expecting to be told to pin the tail on the stone. Instead, I was facing the wall when I stopped.

"Where is the stone?" asked Kallikrates.

I concentrated, then turned around and pointed at the stone.

"Well done. You pinned the tail on the stone."

"How did I do that?" I asked, realizing that Kallikrates had read my memory of playing pin the tail on the donkey.

"You have a relationship with every object in this universe that goes beyond the simple senses that you have trained over a lifetime. As you develop that relationship, you will not only be able to locate objects, but you will also be able to manipulate objects when it is necessary."

"How do I find Rachael's stone?"

"In the same way you located yours. Ignore your normal senses and focus on the pattern that the training stone carries. Rachael's stone will emit a signal that is very similar to that of your own stone. This signal will differ from every other object in the environment. Concentrate on that signal, and when you can sense a second signal you will find Rachael's stone nearby."

"Hey, are you done in there?" shouted Jim as he knocked on the door.

I grabbed the stone off the vanity and Kallikrates instantly vanished. I opened the door and Jim rushed past me with his belt already unfastened.

"You might want to close that door before it gets ugly in here," said Jim as he unfastened the top button on his pants.

I closed the door, shaking my head in disgust as I walked over to the couch. The girls were staring at me, waiting for some explanation while Richard was watching sports on the TV. He hit the mute button as I approached. I was concentrating on the two new stones that I faintly sensed as I entered the room and got nearer to Val and Richard. The patterns were similar to my own but still distinct enough to know they were not my stone.

"Well?" asked Richard.

"Let's retrace her steps one more time," I said.

They all groaned at the prospect.

"How are you going to find it?" Rachael whined.

"It's tough to explain, but basically I can feel your stone."

The others looked at me in wonder as they followed me around the house and out the door into the garage. As I passed the passenger door of Jim's car, I stopped and opened the door. I could sense the stone, but after several minutes of reaching around the seat and behind the cushions, I emerged and said, almost to myself, "I know it's in there. I can feel its signal, but I can't seem to locate the stone."

"So, you're telling us that you can sense it here, but you can't find it?" asked Richard in disbelief. "What happened to it? Did it somehow disappear?"

"Leave him alone, Richard. Maybe it used to be here and it left some sort of trace of itself on the seat," Val said without much conviction.

"I know it's here somewhere" I defended myself. "I just can't seem to locate it."

Rachael was reaching around the seat and putting her hands behind the cushions and underneath. She pulled out some stale French fries, a few pennies, and some other food items that were unrecognizable. Val looked a bit nauseous as Rachael kept pulling older and more interesting forms of food from the seat.

The rest of us were turning to go inside the house in final defeat when we heard Rachael squeal, "I found it!"

"What?" we all said in unison.

"You really found it?" Richard asked again in disbelief.

"Yes, I can feel it with my fingers," grunted Rachael as she reached in between the seat cushions. "There was a small tear in the fabric that it must have slipped into somehow. The hard part is that I can touch it, but I can't seem to get a good grip on it."

Richard reached over and released the lever next to the seat. It quickly reclined back. Rachael scrunched her face into the reclined seat while her backside ungracefully rose up into the air. After settling back down, she reached into the seat again and retracted her hand. She backed out of the car and punched Richard in the arm as she turned to show us the stone in her hand. "Thanks Richard! I never would have been able to reach it without your help."

Val and I looked at each other and busted out laughing. Rachael had an old French fry stuck to her face. Richard was all smiles as he rubbed his arm, "Glad I could be of service," he said with a smirk.

CHAPTER 13

Mr. West became an avid fan of ours. He even shook hands with Rachael one afternoon before his run in the canyon. He commented to her that he hoped to see her in his class next school year. We were always running into him, and he was always excited to see us. In contrast, Mrs. Williams seemed to be seeking opportunity to critique and sometimes embarrass us in public.

One morning prior to class, Richard and Val were attempting to coax me into joining their racing team. "Come on, Darius. You have to give it a shot. We have a race next weekend not too far from here," said Richard.

"But I don't have a jersey or any equipment," I responded as I adjusted my English book from one hand to the other.

ANNALS OF THE MIND LEGION

"You can wear Richard's jersey from last year, and I'm sure we have some old stuff lying around the garage," pleaded Val.

"Maybe I'll try it out so long as you two will quit pestering me," I finally said in exasperation. Deep down I was looking forward to an opportunity to spend more time with Val. This just gave me another good excuse.

I turned sharply into Mrs. William's class and sat down in my usual seat in the front row. She had assigned seats at the first of the year, and after my perpetual tardiness she felt that I should be closely monitored.

Mrs. Williams was distributing a quiz to the class and left a pile on my desk to pass down the row.

"What's this?" asked John Bates when I turned to hand him the quiz.

"It looks like a quiz," I said turning to face forward again.

Mrs. Williams abruptly grabbed the quiz off of my desk and ripped it into pieces, throwing it into the garbage can near her desk. "That will be a week of detention, Mr. Shannon. And next time I catch you cheating in class I will report it to the principal."

"But I wasn't cheating," I retorted. Anger was starting to swell through me. "I was just passing the quizzes back."

"That is enough, Darius. However, if you would like to continue I can accommodate you with an additional week in detention."

I sat gloomily through the rest of the class wallowing in self pity for the injustice that was perpetuated against me. I couldn't understand why Mrs. Williams worked so hard to make my life difficult. Maybe it was because of her dislike of Mr. West. Ever since he had been giving me more and more attention, Mrs. Williams had become more difficult.

I thought that detention would be less strenuous this time around because I had the stone and figured I could continue training while I was there. As luck would have it, Mrs. Williams was on detention duty for the week. I entered the room; she motioned me with her eyes to take the seat near the front. There was a blank notebook and a pen sitting on the desk.

"I would like you to spend the next hour writing an essay on what the result of cheating in high school will have on your future."

I nodded and began writing about how dishonesty impacted people's lives. By the end of the hour I was beginning to get cramps in my hand, and I was running out of paper. I had filled the notebook with my thoughts on the topic, using the Code as my framework for the essay. When the bell rang I handed it silently to Mrs. Williams and walked out the door.

The next day I entered detention to find the same situation. Mrs. Williams signaled for me to sit down, and I trudged forward silently cursing my bad luck.

"Today I want an essay on how honesty is the foundation of a successful future."

I reluctantly opened the notebook and began writing. Surprisingly, the time flew as my thoughts cohered to the notebook in the form of an essay. Once again I took the learning from the past few months and interlaced it into my writing.

Detention for the final three days of the week was a repeat of the first two days, except the topics changed to integrity, virtue, and diligence. I proceeded to fill a notebook with my thoughts and leave without uttering a single word. Mrs. Williams would pick up the notebook and tuck it away. My mind was already racing ahead to the competition this weekend. There was no room for thoughts about Mrs. Williams and her detention.

On Saturday afternoon, I looked around self consciously at the other racers. They all had new bikes and the latest racing gear. For the second time in my life I felt embarrassed that my parents didn't make more money. My mom felt strongly about being home with the kids and had stopped working when Jim was born. Dad worked at the local packaging company as a shift supervisor. It meant long hours and hard work to earn enough to keep us fed, clothed, and sheltered, but there wasn't much left after that.

"Hey Darius," yelled Richard. "Come over here."

I made my way over to where Richard was located at the starting line.

"This is Dave Johnson. He's the second fastest racer out here."

"In your dreams," Dave responded. "If I remember correctly, you were the one reading the back of my jersey at the finals."

Richard shrugged him off. "I'll let you read mine now. It may be the last time you're close enough to make out the words."

Before Dave could respond, the announcer called for attention. I was jostled back a row or two from Richard by some older riders that looked at my worn equipment and older bike in disdain. The starting pistol sounded, and the group surged forward, leaving me to scramble into my toe clips.

Even though I had not ridden much during the last few months, my body responded mechanically to my every thought. It didn't take long to catch up with the riders at the rear of the race. By the halfway mark I caught glimpses of Richard and Dave leading the pack. I continued working my way forward, though it was getting tougher. Before long I had emerged from the group that followed the leaders. Ironically, I could now read both Dave and Richard's jerseys.

Richard looked behind his shoulder and called back between breaths, "What took you so long?"

"Thanks for waiting," I replied sarcastically, gulping in air as I persisted to exert myself.

We began to round the final turn, and I looked on in surprise as Richard extended his elbow and forced Dave off the path. I glanced back in time to see Dave lose control of his bike and go down as Richard and I crossed the finish line.

"Nice race," said Richard as we skidded to a stop.

"Yeah," I said less than enthusiastically.

"What? Are you worried about Dave?"

"You pushed him off the trail."

"Oh, that's just part of racing. Last year he did the same thing to me," Richard said with a smile as he patted me on the back. "Let's go see how Val is doing."

I couldn't help but wonder whether Richard's actions violated the Code. There are several areas of the Code that speak of harmony and integrity. I rehearsed the Code in my head and realized that what Richard had done was wrong. Did he feel a reduction in power? What about guilt? In all my time hanging out with Richard not once did I sense that he felt remorse for his actions. It worried me.

We walked our bikes back toward the finish tape and waited for the first group of girls to start coming in. We talked idly in the meantime about the race. Richard gave me some pointers on how to stay out ahead of the pack. A few minutes later Val popped around the last corner and raced across the finish line as we cheered her on. The next closest competitor didn't even come into sight until Val was walking her bike over to where Richard and I were waiting.

"Nice race, Val," I said, blushing a little with embarrassment at my compliment. I was always fumbling around with words whenever I tried to say something nice to her. I didn't want to sound like the other desperate boys that were always saying things to her at school.

"Thanks!" she said with a big smile.

"Hey Richard!" came a yell from behind us.

We turned to see a red-faced Dave Johnson walking toward us.

"Why'd you push me?" demanded Dave.

"I don't know what you mean," said Richard calmly.

I watched Val as she turned a suspicious glance toward Richard. Her brow creased and she sent a clear and silent message of disapproval to Richard through her actions. He shrugged off her scowl and faced Dave.

"You pushed me off the trail," stammered Dave, too angry to control his voice.

"It's just part of the race, Dave. Don't take it personal" replied Richard as he stared down Dave.

"Were you scared I was going to beat you?"

"Dave, you have an active imagination."

Dave clenched his fist and swung at Richard's face, but he wasn't quick enough. Richard had grabbed his fist with his left hand and was holding it there in a vice like grip. Dave struggled for a minute, and then sent the other fist into the fray. Richard grabbed Dave's left hand while he spun into the punch, and threw Dave over his shoulder onto the ground.

A group of riders held Dave back as he prepared to charge Richard.

"Come on guys, let's get out of here," said Richard as he picked up his bike and turned his back on Dave.

"This isn't over," Dave yelled.

Richard ignored the comment and kept walking. Val and I looked at each other in shock and followed Richard.

"What were you thinking?" whispered Val as they walked through the parting crowd.

"Don't worry about it, Val," Richard sneered.

"Don't worry about it? What does that mean, Richard?"

"Everything is fine. Nobody got hurt."

"Nobody got hurt this time, but what about next time?" Val retorted.

"I'm old enough to handle myself," Richard spat.

We approached Val and Richard's father at the car.

"Way to go you two!" their father exclaimed with a broad smile. "You get better every week. And we'll keep our eye on you, Darius. Second place is not bad for your first race."

Val was silent on the drive home. Her displeasure with Richard's behavior during and after the race showed on her face as she watched Richard and her father talking in the front seat in animated voices and rising enthusiasm. I reached over and touched her arm to get her attention.

"You have to let it go, Val or it will affect you more than him," I whispered to her.

"I know," she mouthed. Her eyes looked sad. In that moment, I inched my hand nearer to hers, but I was too embarrassed to follow through and hold it.

She pulled her training rock from her bag and motioned for me to do the same. When I had a firm grip I immediately heard Val's voice in my head as she began a telepathic conversation.

"I'm worried about Richard," she said.

"Why?"

"He's just so competitive. I'm afraid that he might take it too far someday."

"What should we do?"

"I don't know that there is anything we can do. I just hope his master is helping him understand that the Code is more than just a set of behavioral rules. You have to want to follow the Code because of a love for the good it allows you to do, not for the power it helps you attain."

"I know," I said, wondering if I really did know. "I think I learned that lesson the hard way. Maybe we can have our masters contact his master to express our concern."

"That's a good idea. I assume all the masters are high-ranking members of the Mind Legion and all know each other."

"I hadn't thought of that. In fact, we have been so busy all this time that I don't think that any of us know who each other's master is."

"That's not exactly true. I know that yours is Kallikrates and that he is the Chief Captain of the Mind Legion."

"But how? I never told you."

"My master knows yours quite well."

I could feel a change in the telepathic stream. It was only a slight variation, as if Val was embarrassed or unsure about how much to say.

"How does she know Kallikrates?"

"Everybody knows Kallikrates," was her response.

"But how does your master know Kallikrates? And why would Kallikrates tell her about me."

There was a pause in the conversation, and I sensed that Val was uncertain about whether she should respond openly.

"You're holding something back. I can sense it," I said. "If I'm not meant to know something, I won't violate your trust by demanding an answer."

"See. That's exactly why I hesitated. First off, you are so far ahead of the rest of us in our training. I still struggle to talk telepathically through the training stone, and you are already sensing deeper feelings and nuances through the telepathy. Second, you ask me a reasonable question, get no answer, sense my discomfort, and withdraw the question. You not only understand the Code better than the rest of us, but you actually follow it. In fact, I don't even think that you struggle to follow it as if it was just natural to you."

"I don't know, Val. You give me more credit than I deserve. Anybody else would do the same thing."

"That's the thing, Darius. Nobody else would do the same thing. That's why I hesitated to answer. My master says that you are different than all the apprentices that she and Kallikrates have ever met, and they have met thousands."

"I'm sure there are others that have been as good or better than I am. Maybe they just haven't spoken with enough masters."

"Darius, they run the Council of the Chief Captains of the Mind Legion. They talk to all the masters."

I was dumbfounded. I had never been the best at anything. I was lucky most of the time, before becoming a member of the Mind Legion, to be above average in anything. I was just a normal kid.

The silence lasted a few minutes as I thought about Val's comments. The conversation was starting to make me feel uncomfortable. I never liked talking about myself, so I took the conversation in a different direction.

"What do you mean 'they' run the Council of the Chief Captains of the Mind Legion? I don't really know anything about the Council, and I didn't know that anyone besides Kallikrates helped run anything."

"Don't you ever ask Kallikrates why we are doing all this training and what the end goal is?" asked Val.

I could tell that my face was heating up again as Val looked at me. I had been operating on blind faith for so long that I was past the point of curiosity regarding certain questions. "Actually, no, I've never asked those questions. I probably should have. Maybe I was just afraid that I might not like the answer. It all just felt good to me."

"Well, I don't think it's my place to answer those questions. You should ask Kallikrates," said Val with finality.

I sensed that the conversation was over, so I sat pondering what other questions I should ask Kallikrates when I had some privacy.

Chapter 14

After church on Sunday I grabbed my training stone and looked around the house for a place to talk with Kallikrates. My room was not an option because there was no door, and I might run the risk of being seen or heard by someone else in the family.

"Whatcha doin?" asked Rachael from behind me.

"Uh," I paused. "Nothing," I lied, then winced and corrected myself, "I was looking for some place private."

"Why?"

"So I can ask my master some questions."

"Can't you just talk to Kallikrates telepathically?"

"What did you just say?"

"Can't you talk to him telepathically?"

"No. How did you know his name?"

"You've got to be kidding. Everybody knows his name. He's the Chief Captain of the Mind Legion."

"Who are you two talking about?" asked my mom as she approached.

We both fell awkwardly silent as we tried to think of a response. The Code is very particular about altering the truth, and neither of us wanted to deal with the consequences of breaking one of its most important aspects.

I sighed and said, "We were talking about Kallikrates, Chief Captain of the Mind Legion."

"Oh, well that sounds interesting. I just came down to see if you two wanted to go with your father and I to the park."

Rachael and I stared at our mother in disbelief. "Sure," I said, figuring that my questions could wait until tomorrow when I could go to the Training Room and have access to more privacy.

"Can you believe that?" asked Rachael as Mom made her way upstairs. "She wasn't even fazed, and you practically came right out and told her all about the Mind Legion."

"I know. I guess it just pays to follow the Code."

"When you talk to Kallikrates, ask him why you are so weird," Rachael said with a giggle.

"What's that supposed to mean?"

"You'll see."

I was a little confused and quite eager to discover what Val and Rachael were referring to with these comments.

At the park we threw the Frisbee around for a while. Ever since I was a little boy, I had enjoyed going to the park with the family and throwing the Frisbee or playing on the jungle gym. I was too old at the time to go down the slides and play on the old see-saws, but I still loved to throw the Frisbee with my dad. There was something therapeutic about it.

"Hey, Darius," someone yelled from the other side of the park.

The Frisbee glanced off of my head as I turned to see who was yelling. I turned in time to see Dave riding over toward me on his bike.

"Hi, Dave."

"You tell your friend Richard that payback is coming next weekend."

"Sure thing. Anything else I should tell him?"

"No," said Dave hesitantly, fidgeting with his shifters.

"Well if there isn't anything else, I'm going to get back to my game of Frisbee."

"Um," stammered Dave. "There is one other question that I had."

"What's that?" I asked.

He looked around nervously to make sure nobody was listening. "Do you know if Val is dating anybody?"

That was not what I was expecting to hear. The blood rushed to my face. "I don't think so, but you'll have to ask her."

"Okay thanks," said Dave as he turned and rode off.

"What was that all about?" asked Rachael as she wandered over to see what was going on.

"Nothing much," I said as I picked up the Frisbee.

"Who was that?" she asked.

" Dave. He was at the race yesterday."

"He's cute," Rachael said, staring after him. "Maybe I should start racing too."

I threw the Frisbee to my dad effectively ending the conversation. Rachael's last comment didn't make me feel any better about my conversation with Dave.

The next day I rode straight to the Training Room after detention. When I entered the room I saw Richard sitting there talking to his master. I had noticed that Richard was working very hard with his master. His competitive nature did him well in learning new things. I was sure that he would soon be surpassing me in what he could do with the powers.

"You're here earlier than usual," said Richard as I approached him.

"I had some questions for my master."

"I'm sure that Kallikrates will have some answers."

"So you know who he is too?"

"Everybody knows who he is. He is the Chief Captain of the Mind Legion. You don't mean to tell me that you never asked him about why all of this exists."

"Not yet," I answered, embarrassed that I obviously had not been asking the same questions as the others. "I ran into your buddy Dave yesterday at the park," I stated in an attempt to change the subject.

"Oh yeah, what did he have to say?"

"He said that he was planning something special for you next weekend at the race."

"I'm not surprised, but it's not like Dave to send threats through a messenger. Did he say anything else?"

I hesitated briefly before answering, "Actually, he was wondering if Val was dating anybody."

Richard smiled and said, "He's always had a crush on Val."

The conversation ended and we both went to our normal wall screen in the Training Room.

"Hello Darius," said Kallikrates as his image appeared on the wall. "What's on your mind?"

I responded telepathically, "I have a few questions."

"Go ahead."

"Why does everybody know who you are, and I don't know who any of their masters are? And why does everyone keep saying that I'm different? And why do we have these Training Rooms here?"

"Is that all?"

"No, I've got a lot more questions, but these will do for now."

"I was wondering when you were finally going to start asking some important questions. Questions themselves are excellent catalysts of learning. They show humility, thought, and interest. They also expose your level of readiness for knowledge. Wisdom is the byproduct of many questions asked and then acted upon. Rather than continuing with a lecture, let me provide you with some simple answers and then we can go into more detail in our future lessons."

"That sounds all right."

"First, the Mind Legion is an organization compromised of participants from all across the universe. Each planet that is inhabited has representation in the Mind Legion Council. This representation is two-fold. First they are given a vote in the Council, and second they enforce the decisions back at their planet. The Chief Council is led by the Chief Captain of the Mind Legion in partnership with his wife."

"Isn't that you?"

"Yes it is. And it is a grave responsibility. Trillions of lives are impacted across the universe by the decisions made and supported by the Chief Council. Each planet has its own Council that is led by the Chief Captain of that planet. This Chief Captain is also a representative in the Chief Council for that planet."

"So the representatives in the Chief Council and Chief Captains of each planet are the same person?"

"Not exactly. The Chief Council and Chief Captain are also partnerships. It is always a husband and wife, except in rare occasions where one partner has been lost."

"How could one of the partners be lost?"

"There are two ways. First, they can die. Second, they could turn from the Code."

"So who is your partner?"

A broad smile came across Kallikrates face as he responded, "I thought you would never ask. She is my favorite topic of choice, but it is not our way to give our most precious thoughts to those that are not sincerely interested. Her name is Salvina. She and I have led the Chief Council together for many years and have no secrets between us. Her mind is open to me even now, and I sense that she has told your friend Val that you are my apprentice."

"She is Val's master?"

"Yes, and there is no better in the entire universe. Your friend Val will be well taught and will become one of the greatest Mind Masters Earth has seen."

"Are there others here on Earth?"

"Not anymore. They were lost many years ago."

"How?"

"That is a story for another time. All elements of the past will be unfolded to you in their proper time and place. Your mind is like a young fruit. It will mature in its time and season. As it matures you will be ready to learn much more."

"Okay, I think I understand," I said, not really fully understanding. "Why do people keep saying that I'm special? I've always thought of myself as just an ordinary kid. In fact, I've never even had many friends until Val and Richard came along."

"Darius, I have been a master for many years. In all that time I have had thousands of apprentices selected by the Training Rooms to work with me because of their capabilities. Only the very best are given to the Chief Captain for apprenticeship. In all these years I've never seen your equal."

"But, I'm nothing special," I contested.

"That is not true. Your mind has exceeded any other I have worked with. You are able to sense other's feelings and thoughts. You have mastered most of the basic powers and even many intermediate powers. I'm afraid to teach you more because without a firmer foundation in the Code, there is risk that your mind could be used against the Council."

"I'm sure that others have learned just as quickly."

"No, others do not learn as quickly, at least not all the elements. Some are more adept at individual elements, but not at applying all of them."

"So what does all of this mean?"

"It means that you must take great caution. Your stewardship is great because you have been blessed with a gift that none other has. It will be your choice to use that gift to benefit the Council and the universe or to oppose the Mind Legion. This choice is given freely to all that learn of the Mind Legion."

"Are there some that oppose the Mind Legion after learning the Code?"

"Yes, there are many, and I am afraid that their numbers are increasing at a more rapid pace. There are even those on the Chief Council who can no longer be trusted. Those that leave the Mind Legion become

Mind Thieves because the only way they can attain power once they begin breaking the Code is to steal it from others."

"How can that be?"

"We are not sure. The methods of the Mind Thieves were hidden or destroyed after the Great War. I was just a Chief Captain of my planet and a junior member of the Council at that time. It was a dark period for the Mind Legion."

"Was that when the Mind Legion were lost from Earth?"

"Yes."

There was silence for a minute or so, then the sharp crack of the door to the Training Room opening.

"We will continue this discussion another day," said Kallikrates. "It is time for your group instruction."

CHAPTER 15

Rachael and I rested our bikes against a tree near the rock wall early one morning in the first days of June. School had been out for several days, and our training was picking up again. Both of us turned at the sound of a broken twig as Richard and Val walked into view in the clearing.

"Good morning," I said as they neared.

"Good morning," Val responded as Richard maneuvered his bike into position near his regular parking spot.

I opened the door and we all stepped into the room and wandered over to our seats in the group training section. Once we sat down and looked forward a voice immediately began speaking, "We have now covered the written elements of the Code. The next phase of your training requires that the Code sink into your very self and become one with you."

We turned and looked at each other. Over the past several months we had each learned from experience that in order for us to learn and develop we had to keep the Code. Each of us now questioned internally what more could be done.

"You may have noticed that to each of you have been given some ability that exceeds that of your peers. This is a product of the neurological patterns that you were born with and have developed over your short lives. You must now help each other understand how to perform what easily comes to you."

"You want us to teach each other how to do things we have learned?" I asked tentatively.

"Yes, it is the only way for each teaching to sink into the core of your mind and become permanent. One of the most difficult lessons of the Mind Legion is to learn that you cannot fully gain something without first giving it away."

We looked at each other somewhat uncomfortably as we contemplated giving away the secret to mastering the tasks enabled by our power.

The first couple weeks of this new training regime were very difficult for all of us as we tried to articulate and perform those things that were natural to us. Over time we learned that each of us required special attention from the designated instructor. We also needed to spend more time trying and less time talking about the task. Underlying it all was the realization that the only way to master performance was to find and follow the piece of the Code on which the ability was predicated.

As the summer progressed we all learned how to best help each other. In addition to refining and perfecting our skills, we also grew to appreciate the individuality in one another. Unfortunately it didn't start out that way. Richard was really hesitant to open up and share with us his particular ability. He took pride in his dominance and was often impatient. "What do you mean you can't do it?" said Richard hotly to Rachael one afternoon. "It's so easy."

"Maybe for you Richard, but for the rest of us this is difficult," shot back Val.

"Well, just try harder," he insisted. "It will come to you."

The task was to elevate a penny a few inches off of the palm of your hand to demonstrate the control of an object in its environment. This was Richard's favorite ability. He had rapidly learned to master the task and was soon working on bigger and bigger objects. When it was just the four of us, he would sometimes levitate his bike for a few seconds. Usually he exhaled as he let go in response to the level of exertion it required.

Val and Rachael were really struggling to perform the task. They had both failed to perform in the three sessions that Richard had run.

"What do you think about when you are elevating the objects?" I asked with real interest. "I just can't seem to master it," I continued as my penny levitated shakily above my hand.

"Well, I guess the best way to describe it is that I spend less time concentrating on the object itself and more time on the surrounding particles. I can just sense that the object is surrounded by them even though they are not visible. Then I visualize those tiny objects working together to support the elevated object."

"What did it take to get to the point where you could elevate the bike?" I followed up, still focusing on the penny in front of me.

"Well, my master told me that once I showed respect to all the elements in the environment, it would expand the trust they have in me, and they would work for me if my requests were not unreasonable. It seemed weird at first, but I started paying attention to each object's purpose and tried to avoid abusing it."

"Richard. That's really amazing," said Val, turning toward him. "It's almost harmonious in the way you talk about it."

Richard's moment of glory was interrupted by a squeal of delight from Rachael. "I got it. Look. It's floating." She beamed at us, her penny floating above her hand. Then she spun the penny in circles.

"Once you get the trick of it, there's not much to it," she said as she made the penny perform various maneuvers.

Richard seemed disappointed to see Rachael and later Val and I master the task. It must have been hard for him to give up his superiority in that area.

It was a long debate for me to decide which task would be most helpful to the others. I was torn between two. The first was the ability to master the movement that was observed in another. The second was the ability to locate objects that were hidden from view. These two skills were unique to me. The others had tried and

CRAIG WOLL

succeeded to some small degree in completing the tasks, but they were far from mastery.

I consulted Kallikrates on which one was more important to teach. He responded with a question, "Which one will help them most?"

"It was really helpful to know how to locate objects when we searched for Rachael's stone."

"Yes, that is true. Why are you hesitant then to choose that task?"

"I don't know," I said, hanging my head in shame. "Deep down I feel that it would be better for them to master movement that they see, but..." I paused, not sure of how to proceed.

"But, you don't want to give up something that makes you special,"

"I guess so."

"Will you lose the ability if you teach it to others?"

"No."

"Then why do you hang on to it?"

"I suppose it is because this is the first time that I've been noticed for my skill. What happens if I give it away?"

"You will become great."

"How so?"

"Only the great can give away their most precious gifts with no expectation of recompense. Only the great realize that their power is enhanced by the network of trust established between their friends. Only the great care more about others than themselves."

I pondered his words for a moment, seeking to understand, attempting to change the way I felt. In the end I knew that there was only one choice: Give away my most precious gift.

The training was hard. I strove to show them and explain to them things that were hard to articulate. The progress was slow and tempers flared, but in the end there was satisfaction in seeing them rise up to the challenge. My heart swelled inside as I watched Rachael perform a master level ballet sequence. We clapped and cheered as she finished. I looked over and saw a tear streak the side of Val's face. She turned to me and smiled before wiping it away and putting her arms around Rachael to congratulate her. Rachael was beaming and even Richard patted her on the back with a grin of appreciation.

One afternoon, after Rachael taught us how to accelerate the growth of a wildflower, we sat around in the room joking and enjoying ourselves. Suddenly, the Room spoke and we grew silent.

"You have performed well your tasks of training others. In one month's time it will have been one year since you were each admitted into this training facility. If it is the will of the Council, you will be asked to take in your first apprentice at that time. Each of you must begin looking for a worthy pupil. They must be trustworthy and have demonstrated potential to learn and excel."

"Why do we need apprentices?" I asked with concern. "Don't we still need to learn more?"

"You will continue to be trained by your master until you become a master."

"But why don't the new people get a master like ours?" Val asked.

"Good question," I whispered to her.

"The first year training is normally performed by a senior student. In this case, you were the first, and it required a master to step in and perform the duty."

"Does that make us second year students?" Rachael asked.

"No, your training with the masters has allowed you to move ahead at a more rapid pace. In one month's time you will be considered third-year students."

"Does that mean we keep working with our masters?" asked Richard.

"Yes, in the third year all students are given a master that is either on the Great Council or the individual councils found on each planet."

"How soon do we need to decide on the apprentice?" I questioned.

"You must decide by one month from today. I caution you to speak nothing of this with the apprentice you are considering. I do counsel you to speak with your master about who would be a worthy candidate. They have selected many and know what attributes are necessary for this to be a success."

"At least we get to keep training," said Richard in relief.

"Your training will only continue if the Council agrees to allow Earth to continue regenerating the Mind Legion."

"What?" we all asked in surprise, and then we all began talking at once.

"Hold on," I said. "Do you mean there's a chance that we may not continue our training?"

"That is correct."

"That can't be. We've come so far. They can't just shut us down," I responded despondently.

"The decision will be that of the Council," said the Rock Room with finality.

We left the evening concerned and morose at the thought that this could all be over in just a few short weeks. *What more could we have done? What more could I have done?* I couldn't bear the thought of parting with Kallikrates. He was like a second father to me. His counsel and wisdom was the thing that kept me going. *How could I go back to being just a normal kid again? What about Val?* The EML was what kept us together.

I tossed and turned all night thinking about what could be next. My mind would race from thoughts of apprentices to thoughts of going back to how things were. Kallikrates was not much comfort. He was elusive on the topic of the decision but welcomed discussions on new apprentices. I dozed off only to be awakened by a wet finger in my ear. I swatted away Jim's hand and turned over before I fell back into sleep with Jim's jovial laugh in my ear.

CHAPTER 16

In a few days it would be one month since the Rock Room had informed us of the impending decision by the Great Council. The suspense was killing us. We were not only unsure as to whether we would continue our training. We were also unsure who we should select as our apprentice. All of us had narrowed down our apprentice choices with our masters to two or three likely candidates, and now we were merely waiting to hear if we would proceed with training.

Val and Richard had left for a long weekend with their family. They were going to spend a few days with a relative at the beach. Rachael was spending the day with a friend she was considering as an apprentice. That left me alone and somewhat lonely. For the first time in the past year I didn't really have anyone to talk with about the Mind Legion. I fumbled with my stone for a few minutes, debating whether I should call Val and talk to her for a while. Finally, I just put it in my pocket and walked into the garage.

I jumped on my bike and sped toward the canyon. I might as well get in some alone time at the Rock Room with Kallikrates. I was nostalgic as I rode the trail and remembered the events that led to so many changes in my life. I questioned what I would do if all that I had worked for was taken away. I tried not to dwell on it too long because it made me depressed.

The door opened under my hand, and I put away the stone like I always did. I turned in time to see a panel open and one of the small robots scoot across the floor toward me. It was holding something. It screeched to a halt within a few inches of me and extended a robotic arm, holding a spherical object. I took the object and inspected it. The robot scooted away and disappeared behind the panel.

The object was shaped like a marble and seemed to be made from the same material as the black stone we used to open the door. I walked toward the panel where I normally conversed with Kallikrates, staring at the object in my hand. It was heavy for its size and seemed to emit some sort of energy that was almost imperceptible. As I neared the monitor on the wall, a chair emerged from the floor.

This was the first time that a chair had come out in the year since I'd been in training. Obviously it was intended for me, so I sat down. The chair was simple, but had armrests that extended beyond the reach of my fingers when I sat back in it. And unlike other chairs in the Rock Room it was malleable and formed to my shape. Near my fingertips there was a small half-spherical indentation.

Kallikrates emerged on the screen and began to speak, "Darius Shannon. Today is the first day of a new life for you. You have been selected as the first Captain of the Mind Legion in the regeneration of the Earth. Your duties will be many, but before you accept or reject this opportunity, there are many things of which you must be made aware. I alluded to the history of your planet and of a great tragedy that occurred here. All of this must be made known to you so that upon accepting or rejecting this offer you will be fully knowledgeable to the risks and responsibilities it entails."

I sat up in awe, unable to answer. A train of thoughts ran through my head. *Me, Captain of the Mind Legion? How?*

Finally I was able to speak and said, "Does that mean that we get to continue training?"

"Yes."

"Woo hoo!" I yelled out unable to contain my enthusiasm. I'd been so worried for so long that it just felt natural.

Kallikrates smiled and continued without breaking stride, "The Council debated this topic for many days. There are those that feel you are too young and too unprepared to move the Mind Legion forward on Earth."

"I'm not sure that I disagree with them," I responded soberly.

"Cerys was in favor of the decision. He felt that you and the others had demonstrated great promise and ability."

"Who is Cerys?"

"Cerys is one of the most respected members of the Great Council. He will likely take command of the Council when I am no longer Chief Captain."

"I think I like this guy."

"Your friend Richard has tremendous admiration for Cerys."

"How does Richard know him?"

"He is Richard's master."

"Really? I never knew that," I said. "What about the others on the Council? Did they think it was a good idea?"

"There were some who agreed with Cerys. There were others that felt a foreboding in relation to this decision."

I could see that Kallikrates was weary and pensive so I asked him, "What about you? How did you vote?"

His eyes lit up and filled with compassion as he stated, "I was the first to endorse you as Captain and urged that you and the others be allowed to continue training."

"Thank you," I whispered.

"I have no doubts that you can weather the storm, Darius."

"But? I can sense a but in there."

"You are astute," he responded. "But I fear for your safety. I've sensed a shift in the fabric of power over the past year. There are things being hidden from me. To hide something from me requires great energy. I dare not say more on speculation. I must learn more before making a judgment. There is a source to these discrepancies and I must find it."

This was the first time that Kallikrates shared with me his thoughts and fears. I could sense his concern and it made me shudder to think that the greatest member of the Mind Legion was vulnerable.

"Is there something that I can do to help?"

"I'm sorry, Darius. This is a big day for you and for the Mind Legion here on Earth. It is no time for worry or concern," he continued with a smile. "There are many practical affairs that must be arranged if your training is to continue. As I stated, you are asked to be the Captain of the Mind Legion here on Earth. We cannot compel you to accept this offer. We also cannot complete the initiation until you understand more fully the responsibilities and the history of this planet."

Kallikrates pointed at the small sphere and went on, "You were given a small sphere that you must now place in the indentation on the chair you are seated in. This sphere contains the history of the Earth as taken from the mind of its last Captain and merged with the memories of those that witnessed the events as members of the Council."

I looked up at Kallikrates then down at the small sphere, I placed the sphere in the indentation and

Kallikrates disappeared and the screen began to flicker before me.

CHAPTER 17

The screen in the Rock Room came alive as the tiny sphere was placed in the spot near my hand. The image was sharp and clear. A face emerged before me of a man. His lips were moving as if he was talking to me but I heard nothing. There was an odd sensation that filled my body and mind. I felt like I was being dragged from my seat into the scene that was being portrayed. Somehow I could sense the melancholy in the man's face and a tiny bit of depression swept over me as I tried to relax.

What was happening? How could I be feeling this sensation?

Finally, the audio kicked in and I heard the voice of the man. The tone matched the feeling that had engulfed me. It was morose and serious. I could not understand a word of what he was saying. It was clearly some other language. The longer I stared at the face the more signs of stress and sadness appeared.

After some time I began to notice his surroundings. He appeared to be capturing this message in the very spot that I was sitting. The designs matched those in the Rock Room perfectly.

When curiosity overcame me I blurted out, "Why can't I understand what he's saying?"

"He is speaking in the language of the ancients. It is the first and most perfect of languages. It is the only method to be used in preparing historical documentation," said the Room in response to my question.

"Can you translate it for me?" I asked somewhat concerned that I might have to first learn a language in order to understand the recording.

"Yes."

"Well then, let's start over and translate it into English so I can understand," I remarked, sitting back and thinking it would be much more pleasant if I had some popcorn and a drink.

The image of the man reappeared. He was not old but he looked worn. His skin was dark, like the native tribes from this region. His hair was long and black and pulled behind his ears in a pony tail. His teeth were straight and white and he had a few wrinkles around his eyes and the corners of his mouth that made me think that he was prone to smile. At this time he was not smiling. In fact, there was no humor in his countenance. His voice was rich and deep as he spoke.

"If you have activated this sphere it means that you have been chosen to be the first of the Captains of the Mind Legion on Earth since the time of the Great War.

It is my pleasure to congratulate you on this distinct honor and responsibility. I hope that you find the courage to accept the offer once you understand fully the implications of your decision.

"I am the last Captain of the Mind Legion on Earth. As such, it is my responsibility to ensure that the history of what happened here in my generation is not lost. I am hunted, and since I do not know when I shall be found and my powers vanquished, I make this record in hopes that someday the Council will see fit to allow Earth to once again practice the Code and reestablish the Mind Legion. You are now listening to me, so it is apparent that the first step in renewing Earth's status has begun."

The screen flickered and showed events as the voice of the last Captain of the Mind Legion on Earth spoke in an intense and passionate tone. He was moderator to the proceedings of the historical recording that I witnessed. At times I would see and hear the dialogue of individuals but much of the recording was narrated by this man.

"Many years ago, the Great Council discovered a small planet on the outskirts of their domain. It was the first new planet in many generations that had been found that was worthy to sustain life. The Council had great debate and many divisions over whether this planet should be explored with the intent to expand the dominion of the Great Council.

"Earth had very unique features that were not common among planets known at that time to the collective minds of the Great Council. One of the primary elements that attracted their attention was the distance of Earth from its sun. A secondary feature that caused them much debate was the quantity of light-collection stones found on the planet. Neither one of these elements alone was enough to warrant attention, but together they combined to make Earth look very interesting.

"The light-collection stone allowed the planet to absorb an overwhelmingly large quantity of pure light from the sun that was located so close to its surface. There were other planets at similar or closer distances to the light source, but these planets were less densely populated with the light-collection stone.

"The Council sent out an expedition party to do additional analysis of the planet's ecosystem and to discover what forms of life existed. Their hope was for sentient beings in which they could communicate and learn the history and status of Earth. The expedition was led by the most junior member of the Great Council. Although he was young, he was blessed with unusual wisdom and purity.

"The expedition found the planet to be largely uninhabited. The climate was variable depending on the distance from poles and the elevation. The air was balanced and pure. It was cleaner and purer than any air that the expedition members had ever experienced. Within hours of arrival they were already feeling a type of rebirth and vigor. The brightest of the team understood that this was a combination of the light and light-collection stone mixed with a pure environment.

"The first few weeks were spent collecting samples and understanding the ecology. They found that there were many edible plants and fruits in abundance. They also discovered that many of the beasts were palatable when properly prepared. The humans on the planet were observed but avoided. The expedition had no desire to impact their natural progression at this point.

"The early observations were done from elaborate observatories constructed near the settlements of the humans. These observatories were built to camouflage the researchers so that neither they nor their location could be perceived. The team broke up into various sub-teams to collect data. The sum of the data was uploaded to a central location on a weekly basis and studied by the core team to better understand the people.

"It was obvious after a short time that only a few pockets of civilization were forming on the planet. Most of the population was dispersed, and they were savage and unreformed. They had not developed complex methods of communication, community, or government. A very small group of the people had discovered advantages of working together to strengthen the community and raise the standard of living for all that belonged to the group. But even those groups only had primitive language skills and almost no method for recording history.

"After two Earth years, the majority of the expedition team returned to report their findings to the Great Council. Their analysis at that time concluded that Earth would need several hundred more years and possibly several thousand years to reach a point in their civilization where the Great Council could enter and invite them to join the Mind Legion.

"The outlying observatories on Earth were closed, and only a few observers were sent to Earth every hundred years to reclassify their progress. The first of these teams to return to Earth found that an abnormally large amount of progress was made from the initial expedition. The people were now primarily forming small communities with central leadership. There was still a lot of violence and a lack of strong verbal and written communication, but those areas were advancing.

"By the second visit following the initial expedition, it was reported to the Great Council that the people had now formed preliminary governments and were beginning to record histories. In addition, art and refinement was showing up in a few communities.

"The Great Council began sending observation teams to Earth every ten years and finally gave approval to their youngest member to return again for more pervasive observations. He arrived with a small team, and they learned the language, mannerisms, and customs of one of the more advanced societies on the planet. They mingled with the people as if they were one with them.

"In a very short time they learned that the humans of Earth possessed great love of family and intense desires to learn and develop. They also observed a very emotional people who often bickered, quarreled, and even killed each other over minor differences of opinion. This was something most of the observers had never experienced nor imagined.

"The Great Council member on Earth communicated his desire to provide the people with knowledge and wisdom that would help refine their culture and curtail the violent emotions."

Images of violence and intrigue filled the screen. In one case an observer from the Mind Legion was killed without reservation while wandering in the forest near the observatory. His murderer looked over him without a trace of emotion before walking away as if nothing had occurred. One man was shown conspiring against his father to obtain the leadership of the tribe. He slowly administered poison to him until he eventually died of, what others thought was natural causes. Case after case of conflict and suffering passed before me.

In my heart and mind I sensed that there was much anger and disagreement. I was startled by the power in which the feeling washed over me. I was used to viewing movies and suspending reality to be entertained. In this case, the emotion dragged me into the story. It was so strong that I couldn't help but feel a part of what happened. I swallowed a lump in my throat as I watched on, my eyes not blinking.

"These depictions were captured by the Mind Legion, and were communicated through a direct link to the mind of those involved. It is impossible for them to capture in accuracy the events without capturing the emotion," the voice said.

"The Council requested a reconvening and ordered the observation team to return and share their findings in person with the Council. This was unusual because the telepathic method of communication was commonly used between worlds for simple conversations. As it turned out, this was not a typical conversation. The question of expansion to developing worlds was one that the Council considered to be of great importance."

The screen flashed and transitioned to a new place that I had never before seen. There was a large room filled with men and women. They were proud and wise looking. Their faces shone and many of the men wore beards. The women were beautiful with flowing hair, slim figures, and bright eyes. Their clothing was black with bright silver designs around the collar and at the edges of the sleeves. The room was oval in shape and at one end sat the oldest and wisest looking of the group. His hair was white but his face was young barring some deep set wrinkles that hinted of his age. He sat alongside his equal in presence. She was a stunning older woman. Their chairs were slightly higher than the others that circled the room. Ornate stone pillars rose in the background. The light emanating from the inlaid designs found on them. Suddenly, it hit me. This was the Great Council. The Chief Captain of the Mind Legion was the man in the elevated chair. I looked him over in awe.

A man stood from the left of the Chief Captain and spoke in a firm voice, "We cannot populate Earth with the Mind Legion. It will be too difficult to control the happenings on the planet. At that distance the images and feelings will be too faint. We will not be able to ascertain whether there is descent amongst those that are trained."

I felt a great longing to see them open Earth as an outlying station of the Mind Legion. I was dragged into the history and felt compelled to side with those that were for expansion and to oppose those that wished to maintain things as they had been. At times I nearly came out of my seat in an attempt to counter some point made by one of those that was in the Great Council meetings.

A younger man stood and said, "I know that I am the junior member of the Council, but I wish to speak. I am willing to rescind my seat at the Council and manage the affairs of Earth. Our planet is old. We were one of the first planets to join the Mind Legion many thousands of years ago. When I became Captain of the Mind Legion for the planet and received the history, it contained a reference to how the planet came to receive the Code. At that time, this same discussion was had among the members of the Council. One of those members offered to take responsibility for the planet, and we were given a chance. Our planet now prospers and peace permeates every heart. I cannot imagine what might have happened to us had the Council forbid this action."

Something about the tone in his voice and the features on his face gnawed at my memory. Who was he? At that moment a flash of understanding entered my mind. Kallikrates. It was Kallikrates that fought for Earth. So he was the one that made it happen.

"There is wisdom in your words. Although you are young, you show great promise," said the elder man with a smile. "We will allow you to take the Code to Earth on one condition."

"Anything that you desire," Kallikrates responded.

"You will remain on the Great Council."

A smile of gratitude and relief lit up Kallikrates' face. "It would be my pleasure."

"Do not feel honored by the request. It comes as a protection for you and for Earth. We want to be close to you so that we can measure what transpires on a regular basis."

The Council adjourned and the next sequence showed Kallikrates speaking to a man and a woman outside of a makeshift shelter. There was something familiar about the scenery. The shape and cut of the cliff behind the shelter looked surprisingly like the entrance to the Rock Room.

"What was Kallikrates doing on Earth?" I asked, leaning in to get a closer look at him standing outside the Rock Room so many years ago.

"He was training the first generation of the Mind Legion," responded the Rock Room.

"I was asking a rhetorical question," I said in exasperation. "Can you stop the historical movie thing for a minute and rewind to the part where Kallikrates shows up on Earth?"

During the course of our conversation I had lost track of what was happening and didn't want to miss a thing.

CRACK.

The screen went blank, and the chair I was sitting on disappeared. I crashed to the floor and turned to see who had entered. From my vantage point, all I could see was a silhouette blocking the sun as it descended into the western horizon. "Hey Darius, what are you doing on the floor?" asked Rachael as the door shut and her face became visible.

"Well, I missed the chair as I went to sit down."

Rachael laughed and shrugged it off. I decided not to elaborate because the look on her face made it obvious that the conversation was now going to change direction.

"What do you think a good apprentice is like?" Rachael asked me inquisitively as she walked across the room toward the desks and handed me the small sphere that had rolled across the floor when my chair disappeared.

"I don't know," I said, slipping the sphere into my pocket and sighing in relief that Rachael hadn't demanded an explanation of the sphere. "I guess they would need to be trustworthy and be willing to work hard."

"It's just so hard to choose. Every time I think I found somebody that would be great, I notice some weakness exhibited in their behavior."

"I guess I know what you mean," I said. "I've been struggling with the same thing."

"Take Sally Jameson as an example. She seemed like she would be perfect. Everybody loves her, and she is smart and funny..."

"But?" I asked in the same way that Kallikrates always seemed to do to me.

"But whenever I get a minute alone with her, all she wants to do is talk bad about the other girls or boys at school. I just don't get it."

"And you're asking me for help?" I asked. "I definitely know less about girls then you do."

"No kidding," she chuckled.

"Hey, what is that supposed to mean?" I asked somewhat defensively.

"Well, come on," she said. "How long have you known Val?"

I could feel my face turning red as I averted her eyes. The meaning of what she said becoming immediately apparent to me. "I guess I've known her for a year or so."

"And, what is she like?"

Now I was really turning red. "She's all right I guess. I mean, for a girl."

"How do you think Val feels about you?"

It was starting to get really uncomfortable, especially because it was my sister. "I don't know. I guess she doesn't mind hanging out with me and stuff, but Val's different."

"How so?" she continued.

"I don't know," I said as the wheels in my brain were turning in an attempt to find some way out of the mess I was getting myself into. "She's easy."

Rachael looked up in surprise with a smile playing on her lips.

"That's not what I meant!" I blurted out, trying to recover.

"Well, what did you mean?"

"She's just like another one of the guys except..." I paused, trying to think of what to say next. I didn't quite know how to express what I was thinking.

"Except that she is gorgeous and smart and funny," said Rachael, eyeing me for a reaction.

"Yeah, I guess you're right," I said again. "I just don't understand why she keeps hanging out with us when there are so many people that want to do things with her."

"You really don't know why?" Rachael asked.

"No, I always wonder what she's doing. There are a lot of people out there, and you have to admit that I'm not all that interesting."

"Okay, whatever," Rachael said, rising from the desk. "I'll ask my question to somebody that can give me a useful response."

"Don't take too long. It's getting late and we need to start heading for home."

Rachael just turned and gave me the look as if she already knew that and didn't need my reminding.

Once Rachael started a mental conversation, I walked to my normal spot on the wall and began a conversation with Kallikrates.

"Hello, Darius," he said as he flickered onto the screen.

"Hey, Kallikrates," I said and waited to see if he would jump in and get the conversation rolling, but he was content to sit back and wait for me to express my thoughts. "I was wondering if we could discuss this decision I have to make about being Captain of the Mind Legion here on Earth."

I looked up at Kallikrates, hoping that he would take over at this point and say something profound. It took a few more moments to realize that I was on my own, so I continued, "I have a whole bunch of questions that I want to ask you about what that means and what I should do and..." I paused, not knowing if I should continue.

"And?" he urged me on.

"And why were you here on Earth?"

"It sounds like you have a lot of questions. The Council strictly forbids my dialogue concerning what takes place in the historical review. You must first finish the review and formulate your own opinions before I can discuss the matter with you. This is to protect the integrity of your memory of the events since the historical media is passed along with all the dimensions of memory, and if you forego the proper process by speaking with me you would only receive a one-dimensional insight."

"But how am I to understand all of this if you don't explain it to me?"

"The only way you can truly understand anything is if you come to your own conclusions through reason, logic, emotion, and hard work. If I give you the answers, you will merely be mimicking my opinions."

"Is it so bad to mimic your opinion? I mean, you are the Chief Captain. Shouldn't we all be listening to you?"

"I see that you still have much to learn. I had hoped that this one lesson would not be necessary, but for your own good I will have to withdraw my presence until you have completed your review of the history of Earth and make your decision. From this point, until you have experienced all the history and decide if you are the Captain of the Mind Legion on Earth, I will not be able to speak with you."

"No, I need you," I blurted out, forgetting to telepathically convey the message.

"Goodbye, Darius. And good luck."

CHAPTER 18

Rachael and I rode home in silence. I could sense her agitation and knew that she had felt some variance from the normal. The outburst in the Training Room was an obvious outward display of discord, but she must have felt something deeper. She had matured emotionally to a state where she could discern when not to interrupt another in deep concentration. I was in that state. I kept reliving the things that were portrayed in the historical presentation. The experience was incredibly vivid. So much so that even the slightest memory invoked a nearly equivalent emotional sensation to the one experienced earlier.

I functioned like a zombie at home that evening as I went through the motions of dinner and preparing for bed. I could not snap out of the trance. I was completely overwhelmed with my own concerns.

"Is everything okay?" asked my mother.

"No. I'm fine," I responded emotionlessly.

"I think I know what it might be," she said with the all-knowing look of a mother.

"You do?" I questioned, making eye contact for the first time that evening.

"Yes. You miss your friends."

"I do?"

"Of course you do. You have spent nearly every waking moment for the last year with them. And maybe you have a bit of a crush on Val," she said with a wink.

"Mom! I can't believe you just said that. Val and I are just friends."

"Maybe," she said smugly as she finished clearing dishes from the table.

Rachael giggled as she looked over at me.

I got up and walked out of the room. "I'm going to bed."

The moments respite from the preoccupation of my new responsibility soon ended as my mind focused in the quiet of my room. I lay in my bed and stared at the ceiling. Thoughts cruised through my memory. I saw a perfect recording of the day's events and analyzed each piece of what happened. I reached over to the side of my bed and rummaged through my backpack until my hand clasped the training stone.

"Val?" I telepathically signaled.

"I was hoping you would call," she responded almost immediately.

I had not expected a response, much less an immediate response. I fumbled to articulate my thoughts and finally just asked, "How are you doing?"

"I'm okay," she said. "What's on your mind? I sense that you are pretty agitated."

"I'm not sure I can talk about it."

"I won't breach your trust if you have promised to keep a secret," Val said with a tinge of disappointment that I could sense.

"I haven't made any promises, I just don't know for sure if I can talk about it, so I'm playing it safe," I responded lamely.

"I see," she replied slowly. "What else is on your mind?"

"Not much," was my response, but I wanted deep down to tell her I missed her. I wondered if she could sense it.

"Good night, Darius," was all she said.

I was doubly perturbed. I had a major decision to make, and I was blowing it with Val. For a little while my thoughts turned to that first ride up the canyon with Val almost a year earlier. She had been pretty then in my eyes, but now that I knew her better, she was absolutely beautiful. I couldn't help but wonder why she hung out with a loner like me.

With all the consternation of thought, I barely noticed Jim as he crawled into his bed. It was strange that he had not even tried some sort of practical joke on me. Usually he was unable to control himself. I dozed off into a fitful slumber with memories of the day on my mind.

The dreams I had that night rivaled those I had experienced when I'd first touched the black stone. They occurred in a similar fashion to the previous dreams. One hardly finished before the next identical dream began. It was like watching the same movie over and over again, but experiencing it as if it were the first time. The dreams recounted the history right up to the point that I recognized Kallikrates, and then they cut off again.

It was still dark when I dragged myself out of bed. I slipped out of my room and from the house without disturbing the family. I even took my bike out through the side door of the garage so that I would not wake anyone. By the time I reached the entrance to the Training Room, the sky was just starting to show the signs of the dawn. I took a deep breath, trying to shake the feeling that I was being watched. It was nothing—just my imagination running wild. I headed into the room, drew the sphere from my pocket, and paused a moment before loading it into position. "Let's get this over with," I said. "I need to get my master back."

I sat down and the presentation began from exactly where I had left off the day before. Kallikrates was standing near the very spot I was sitting. He was talking to two people that were obviously native inhabitants from that time period. The wall shone in all its brilliance, and I was absorbed into the story as if I'd never stepped away.

The voice said, "Kallikrates found two that he believed were worthy candidates from the settlement near one of their observation outposts. They were man and wife. They had the demeanor often sought after in apprentices. Their hearts were soft and their minds malleable. They believed in doing what was right and in helping others. For this reason they had invited Kallikrates into their home many times to converse and discuss humanity. Because of this association, Kallikrates chose experience over youth. This was a deviation from the normal selection process. In nearly all cases the apprentices are chosen from those in their teenage years. It is a time in which the human synapse is not overly developed and the potential for mature thought begins. This combination provides a fertile environment for growth, development, and bonding."

The voice was silenced for a time, and the narration ended as the scene on the screen changed to two individuals—the man and wife. Kallikrates said their names, but it was in their native tongue, and I couldn't understand. The man and woman appeared to have primitive features that were accentuated by course and callous skin. It was obvious that they were not strangers to hard work in a harsh climate.

Kallikrates called the man by name and said, "Your training now requires that you make a commitment to follow the Code."

"Of course," was the humble response of the man.

"In that case, I will give you a gift of these," Kallikrates said as he opened his hand and revealed four rings. "They are to be worn on the largest and smallest digit of the right hand. Once you put them on, they can only be removed through disobedience to the Code or complete mastery of the Code."

The man and woman took the rings and placed them on their fingers. They then admired the rings and even attempted to remove them. They then turned back to Kallikrates.

"This location must remain a secret to all but those who wear these rings. It has been prepared by the Great Council of the Mind Legion to train you. If its secret is discovered by others, it will be sealed until a worthy successor is found."

"But why must it be a secret? There is nothing here but this cliff and the trees and plants that surround it," the woman said,

Kallikrates pulled the black stone from the pouch and held it for them to see, then placed it in the wall and turned.

CRACK.

The door opened for the first time to those on Earth that would form the Mind Legion.

They entered into the space and the door closed. The image on the screen changed from being outside to being inside the Training Room. It appeared the same as it did now. I looked around to verify that everything was the same.

Kallikrates walked to the compartment on the wall and showed them how to place the black stone into the space for safe keeping. "Under no condition are you to remove the stone from this space except to open the door from the outside."

"But if the stone is in here, how are we to open the door?" asked the astute woman.

A smile emerged on Kallikrates face. "That is an excellent question. I will show you."

He proceeded to take them outside. He was careful to shut the door as he exited. They passed along the wall in front of the room until they reached the secret compartment. He opened the compartment and closed it again. Then he opened it again and explained that the door responded to his intentions, and that often the intentions are described in silent thought.

"Now you must try," he said to the man.

The man made an effort, but was unable to open the compartment.

"Would you like to try?" Kallikrates asked the woman, moving over to allow her through.

"Yes, I will try."

She placed her hand on the location and concentrated, but nothing happened.

"Very good," said Kallikrates as they both looked at him with surprise. "You must first fail so that you can later learn from the experience. The key to making anything happen is first being able to see it in your mind even when it is not visible to your eye. I want you to try again, but this time as you place your hands in the indentation; imagine the door opening like this."

At that moment he put his hand in the spot and the door popped open. He quickly closed it and signaled for the man to step forward.

The man placed his hand in the indentation and closed his eyes. The door popped open, and the woman squealed in delight at seeing the miracle. The man then closed the door and opened it several times under the direction of Kallikrates.

The woman was then signaled forward and the same process was followed. When it was obvious that they were now proficient, Kallikrates asked the man to open the main door and put the black stone away on the inside.

I was amazed to see these two people go through the same training that the four of us had experienced over the course of a year. Many lessons were truncated or skipped, but the message was clear. Everyone had to make a lot of mistakes to learn the Code. The man and woman experienced tremendous intellectual advances, and soon they were mastering many of the tasks that Kallikrates was teaching them.

The screen suddenly flashed to another scene. Kallikrates pulled the training stones from his pouch and showed the man and woman how they worked.

"I will be your first Master," Kallikrates said, facing the man. And then turning he continued, "And my wife will be yours."

"You are married?" she asked.

"Yes."

"Where is your wife?"

"She is far from here. To learn from her, you must use the screens and the training stones as I have shown you."

"But why do I need a stone?" asked the man. His brow furrowed, and he suddenly looked sad. "You are leaving us."

"Yes, it is now your responsibility to continue forward. As much as I love each of you, I miss my wife dearly and want to return to her."

"It is too soon. We are not ready," the man stammered in confusion and fear.

"No, you are ready. Do not fear. I am merely leaving you physically. We will still be in ready communication whenever you use the stones or when you are here in the room."

"When do you leave?" the woman asked in desperation.

"Today," Kallikrates said with finality and sadness in his voice.

"When will you return?" the man asked.

"It could be many generations of time as measured on your planet. And it is possible that I may never return," Kallikrates said.

The woman cried and the man's eyes glistened as Kallikrates embraced each of them and then walked across the room. A wall seemingly opened before him and he entered. The door shut, and the two were left alone in the room.

CRACK.

Rachael stepped into the room to find me sprawled on the floor in the same location as the previous day. This time she just looked at me and made a near silent "humph" and walked passed me.

I was relieved by her lack of interest because I had been so deeply entwined in the presentation that I was left dumbfounded for some time. I actually sat on the floor for a few minutes pondering what I had seen. It took a while for me to realize that I could not go on until Rachael left. I reached over and picked up the marble-like stone from the floor and slipped it in my pocket.

Rachael was sitting at one of the desks in deep thought. She looked unusually tired; she snapped her drooping head as if she were falling asleep.

"Are you okay, Rachael?" I asked in concern..

"I think so. I've just been so tired the last few days. I just can't get enough sleep, and I seem to be doing more poorly in my training. It must just be all this worrying about selecting an apprentice. I'm having a tough time deciding."

"Don't worry," I said as I walked over and placed a hand on her shoulder. "You always figure these things out."

She looked up and gave a weak smile. "Thanks, Darius."

With that I turned to leave the Rock Room.

"Hey, where are you going?" Rachael asked.

"I think I'm going to take it easy for the rest of the day. Maybe I'll go for a ride. It has been a long time since I just took some time for myself." I didn't quite know how to explain to her that I couldn't work on anything because Kallikrates wasn't talking to me until I finished with the historical experience.

"Okay, see you later," Rachael said.

CHAPTER 19

The next morning I arrived early at the Rock Room. The chair was in the same location, and I dropped into it and placed the sphere in its location. The relation of the history started from exactly where it had left off the day before.

The familiar voice continued, "Over time, and because of the unique properties of light and rock found on Earth, the progress was unlike any new development of the Mind Legion. The early groups doubled on almost an annual basis as the original two took on apprentices, and then there were four. The four took on a new apprentice and it grew to eight. From eight they expanded to sixteen, and finally from sixteen to thirty-two. This spanned over a five-year period. At this time the expansion stopped.

"This was when we learned that we must not overpopulate a single location. The maximum capacity of each facility was thirty-two members. I was the first Captain of the Mind Legion on Earth, and now I am the last."

The images flashing before me depicted group after group as they expanded into a larger collective. The feelings of growth, knowledge, and maturity filled my being with euphoria. The voice continued to provide narration throughout the experience.

After the first two people were selected by Kallikrates, there was never an apprentice older than the late teenage years in any of the predecessor groups of the first Captain. The training was of great interest to me as I observed the progress.

"In the beginning, my wife and I selected one apprentice each. She chose a female and I a male. We did not know why we chose in this manner other than that it felt and seemed like the right thing to do. The male was fourteen years old, and the female was thirteen years old. They learned much quicker than we had and seemed to naturally trust in the entire program. In contrast, we had questioned much of what was asked and disbelieved at times until proven through experience," the voice continued.

"There was genius in the selection of younger minds. They were more open to ideas and more rapid to assimilate knowledge. These two were able to select two apprentices in the following year. We also chose another set of apprentices, and that brought us to eight total members. My wife and I each had two apprentices, and the first years had one apprentice each. This pattern repeated until Kallikrates informed us that we should take no more than thirty-two into the group. This was the optimal size for learning. Any larger and some would become complacent. Any smaller and the group would become stagnant.

"We were instructed to spend the majority of our time with our first apprentices and even to assign them tasks to train our later apprentices. This forced the group to work together in cohorts to train each other. Because we were often together, there were emotional breakdowns, and many times there had to be frank discussions to repair hard feelings. Fortunately, any disharmony became evident in performance, so the apprentices that were driven to succeed often repaired any issues in a relationship before we needed to intervene.

"As each of us took on additional responsibilities we learned and developed our skills and our relationships. Kallikrates stayed in close contact for the first five years of development. We spoke with him nearly every day, and received counsel from him whenever we reached some problem we could not solve on our own.

"In the fifth year, as all thirty two of us were training together, Kallikrates returned. He stepped out from the wall in the Training Room and greeted us. Our pleasure at seeing him nearly overwhelmed us as we surrounded him and took our turns embracing and thanking him for all of his help.

"He turned to my wife and me and stated that it was time for our first apprentices to start their own group. They would move to the next closest town and integrate into society. They would choose two apprentices and build a group similar to our initial group over the next five years. Later, others would break off in all directions and do the same.

"We felt great sorrow to see our young apprentices go. They were now nearly twenty years of age and had matured physically and mentally. Just prior to leaving, the two were married and left hand-in-hand without any fear that we could perceive.

"Through the training stones we maintained communication and continued to assist them in their training. We were still their masters and had a responsibility to help them with their success.

"Each year, one or two couples would leave our group and find new groups. We would maintain communication and assist were we could, but it soon became clear that our attention must primarily stay focused on maintaining our own group. We were still bringing in two-to-four new apprentices each year, and we still had the others to train.

"Twenty years after Kallikrates first showed us the Rock Room he returned again to help us organize the first Council of the Mind Legion on Earth. I was asked to be Chief Captain of the planet Earth and to take my place in the lower interplanetary Council. In this way, Earth could become a part of the collective Mind Legion.

"Our Council was formed of couples from each of the twelve established groups found on Earth. The founders of each of these groups took their seats on the Council from junior to senior with my wife and I co-leading the Council. We attended the meetings from the adjoining room to the Training Room. When privacy was needed, we could close the wall and communicate without disruption.

"These new responsibilities required us to turn over the leadership of our group to two others. They were well-trained and completely capable of the responsibility. Our new focus was on the expansion of the Mind Legion on Earth and of the integration into the interplanetary Council.

"We soon learned that the interplanetary Council was made up of Chief Captains from more than a thousand worlds. This Council reported to the Great Council and the Chief Captain of the Great Council. Kallikrates often participated in early meetings to help us learn the protocols and expectations of being a member of the interplanetary Council. His leadership was respected among all that we met. He was no longer the junior member of the Great Council, and many speculated that in time he would lead the Great Council.

"These early years were full of hard work. They were also full of tremendous happiness as our family grew. My wife and I had two young children, and they also were trained to be members of the Mind Legion. In time, they left and formed their own groups as our Council on Earth expanded and a lower Council was formed with membership composed of leaders from the new groups formulated.

"The Mind Legion was still a secret society, although there were some that noticed a trend in the affairs of humankind. In secret, the Mind Legion would influence leaders of cities and nations to adopt more humane lifestyles in harmony with the Code. They would teach, counsel, and sometimes lead the defensive wars that suppressed tyranny."

CRACK.

I fell to the floor again, and Rachael walked by without even a glance in my direction. It was like she was in some sort of trance. I shrugged it off as a girl thing and went for a walk in the nearby woods to ponder over what I had learned.

It was dark before I got back to the trailhead. I had more to think about than I had initially thought when I'd left. I rode by Val and Richard's place on the way home to see if there was any sign of life, but the lights were out, so they were either in bed or not home yet from their trip.

I pulled into the driveway and put my bike in the garage. I walked in the house and found my parents at the table eating dinner alone. They had put candles out, and there was some romantic music playing in the background. Overcoming the initial nausea associated with seeing my parents doing something romantic, I said hello and headed for the fridge.

"There's pizza in the other room," my mother said without taking her eyes off of my father. "Jim's in there eating and watching a game. Why don't you join him?"

I closed the fridge after grabbing a bottle of water and wandered into the other room.

"Hey bro," Jim said as I sat by him. "Where have you been all day?"

"Studying."

"What's wrong with you?" he asked in disgust. "Are those twins brainwashing you or something?"

"No," I laughed. "I was just interested in some local history."

"Weird," he muttered as he grabbed another slice of pizza and turned his attention back on the game.

"Where's Rachael?" I asked casually as I took a bite of my first slice.

"I dunno. She's probably talking about boys with some of her friends."

"She's not here?" I asked with some alarm.

"Nope, I haven't seen her all day."

I wandered into the other room in time and saw my dad lean over and kiss my mom as he headed for the freezer. This was a ritual for them every few months. They would order pizza for us kids, then have a romantic meal together at home. Finances were a little tight, so they didn't get out much.

"Have you seen Rachael?" I asked, ignoring the mush going on in the kitchen.

"Yes and no," replied my father. "Yes, we saw her this morning, and no we have not seen her since."

"Are you at all concerned that she isn't home?" I asked as my father placed the desserts on the table.

"No, she asked us before she left if she could spend the night with a friend. Since we were planning our romantic dinner ALONE tonight we thought it was a good idea."

"Oh," I said, taking the hint from my father and feeling somewhat relieved as I left the room and finished the game with Jim.

CHAPTER 20

I found Rachael sitting at a desk in the Rock Room with her head down as if she was asleep. I looked at my watch and saw that it was barely 6:30 a.m. I assumed that she must have left early to get to the room before me. No wonder she was tired.

I reached down and put my hand on her shoulder to wake her up. She didn't budge, so I shook her a little bit and called out, "Rachael, it's me Darius."

There was still no movement, so I shook harder and with some alarm called out, "Rachael, are you okay?"

She moaned a little before sliding off the chair. I caught her before she hit the floor. I laid her down next to the desk and tried to arouse her, but she wouldn't wake up.

Panic set in. What should I do now? How could I get Rachael help without revealing the location of the Rock Room?

As I paced the floor trying to think of some way to help Rachael, I noticed that I had reached into my pocket and was fiddling with the Training Stone. Without thinking I grasped onto it and thought out "Val?"

"What's wrong, Darius?" was her immediate response.

"It's Rachael. She's here in the Rock Room and I can't get her to wake up. I think she's been like this since yesterday," I blurted out.

"I'll be right there," Val responded.

I continued to pace the floor and open and close the Rock Room door as I waited for Val. Every few minutes I would tap Rachael and try to elicit some response. A few times she groaned or seemed about to wake up, but then she would pass back into unconsciousness. I grasped my stone desperately and tried to call Kallikrates for help. There was no response.

CRACK.

Val ran in and went immediately to Rachael. She bent over her and attempted to wake her. She did so with a more tender and feminine touch than I had. Her method brought Rachael closer to consciousness, but still she couldn't be aroused from her comatose state.

"Have you called Kallikrates?" Val asked.

"No," I said not knowing how to elaborate on the response. I couldn't tell her about being cut off temporarily from his assistance. "I thought of you first." This was true and seemed to do the trick.

Val smiled at my response and blushed. "It's okay. I'll talk to his wife."

I stood idly by as I watched Val go through a silent conversation with her Master. A few times she glanced over at me with a little shock and then went back to whatever conversation had been transpiring. At one moment she looked over at me with a grateful and a radiant smile. Pride shone on her countenance and then once again back to business.

Several minutes transpired, but it seemed like ages before Val began poking and prodding Rachael while still maintaining communication. She then began searching Rachael's pockets for something.

"Where is her stone?" she asked me audibly as she continued searching.

I snapped out of my daze, picked up Rachael's backpack, and began searching. In one of the side pockets I extracted the stone and handed it to Val.

"Thanks," she responded, then went immediately back to work.

Val placed the stone in Rachael's hand, and Val placed her free hand over Rachael's to make sure that she had a full contact on the stone. Val held perfectly still and looked at Rachael's face, her brows crinkled in concentration. Rachael began to stir a little, and then her eyes popped open.

"What are you doing here?" she whispered weakly when she saw Val. "I thought you weren't coming home until tomorrow."

"Rachael, it is tomorrow," Val said, squeezing her hand a little tighter.

"It is? I must have fallen asleep. The last thing I remember was Darius sitting over there on the floor."

Val looked over at me with a raised eyebrow as if to say that she wanted a full report in the near future. "Rachael, I don't know how to tell you this, but something has happened to you," she said in an empathetic voice.

"I know. I just pushed myself too hard. It's probably because I want to keep up with the rest of you," Rachael responded weakly.

"No, Rachael, somebody has tampered with you."

"What?" I gasped out. "What do you mean somebody 'tampered' with her?"

"She's so tired because there's a Mind Thief near her that has been using her as an energy source, or at least that's what my Master believes. When I put the stone in Rachael's hand, she was able to run some testing on Rachael's mind."

"What did she find?" I asked.

"Nothing."

"So how is that a problem?" I countered.

"Well, if Rachael were sick or if she had over exhausted her body, there would be mind traces. According to my Master she has had her mind tapped and erased. That's the only thing that would leave no trace."

We sat in silence for a few moments. Each of us was deep in our own thoughts. So far this Mind Legion had been like an after-school club. We would get together after school and on the weekends and learn new and interesting things. Now it was immediately clear to us that this was serious business.

Val broke the silence, "Rachael, you need to sit up, and you need to eat something. Darius, can you get some trail snacks out of my pack while I help Rachael into the chair?"

I turned without responding and obeyed her request. I grabbed some snacks and a water bottle and placed them on the desk in front of Rachael. Val and I watched in silence as she mechanically chewed the food and drank some water. I was pretty sure that she would not have proceeded if we weren't there. When she had finished, we began to plan.

"I'm going to call my Master to figure out what to do next," Val said as she grasped her stone and immediately started her telepathic discussion. This lasted for a few minutes before Val turned to us again.

"Rachael's going to need 24x7 surveillance until she's back to full strength. In addition, her Master can train her in some self-defense tactics and run daily diagnostics on her to ensure no further attacks."

"Well, I guess I can watch her while we are at home and make sure she never leaves without someone else with her."

"That's a good start, but I think you have some unfinished business to take care of before we can rely on you for much," she said with a knowing eye. "I'll take Rachael to my house and then call your mom to let her know where she is. Richard and I can keep an eye on her during the day, and you can sleep on the floor in her room at night."

"Okay," I said, wanting to ask for more detail on what exactly she knew but not wanting to provoke Rachael any further.

"Rachael, sweetie, I'm going to help you to my house where I can get you well-fed and rested before heading home later this afternoon. Do you think you can make it that far on your bike?"

"I think so," was Rachael's response. "I'm feeling a little better already. Do you really believe that someone did something to me? I don't remember anything."

"Yes, I'm absolutely positive," Val said as she assisted Rachael to the door. "Darius, call me later when you can talk."

I stood dumbfounded as Rachael and Val left me alone in the Rock Room. *What just happened? Mind Thieves?* Val obviously knew something that she couldn't tell me in front of Rachael. What a horrible time to not have Kallikrates around.

Without even thinking, I walked back to my standard position and started the historical review again. It picked up where I had left off on the previous day with the same sonorous voice of the last Captain of the Mind Legion on Earth.

"As the Mind Legion grew in power and influence across this area of Earth it became necessary to expand into new regions. We did so. The Great Council was astounded with the pace of the growth and soon sent representatives back to Earth to assist in the progress. They felt that other continents and areas of the world needed to receive the same knowledge so that no single nation would rise up in too great of power over another.

"It also turned out that due to Earth's unique properties and its nearness to the sun, those who lived there for an extended amount of time could gain increasing power as the light and knowledge filled them with new capacity.

"The people of Earth and those attracted to Earth from other planets had an incredible thirst for power. This ambition in and of itself was not dangerous, but without proper monitoring it soon led to pockets of dissension from the Code.

"The Great Council began to fear that the overwhelming power amassed by those on Earth combined with their youthfulness might lead to some serious transgression of the Code and lead to a resurgence of the Mind Thieves and their secretive and destructive practices. They sent Kallikrates back to us to govern the affairs of the planet.

"I was tremendously relieved when he arrived. I had been feeling unnerved for some time about the affairs of the planet for which I was responsible as the Chief Captain. I felt that Kallikrates could bring me the answers. To my disappointment and to my great relief, he did not come with all the answers. In fact, his manner was always one of deference to my leadership. He would mentor and coach me in private just as he had done previously, but he made it a point to not take away any of my responsibilities. This meant that my burden was at times overwhelming.

"The first item of business for Kallikrates was to convince all those that were not native born on Earth to leave the planet. There was much resistance. They knew that the power they had gained on Earth would be reduced when they returned to their home planets. Many went into hiding and were nearly impossible to find.

"Kallikrates also assisted in terminating the mining operations on Earth. Many of the new settlers were harvesting the stone and transporting it to nearby planets to strengthen their people. This effort also led to infractions in the Code. The traders soon had to use deception to maintain their trade. They found ways to compensate for their loss in power due to the lies. The first thing they did was design rechargeable stones that were worn like jewelry and powered through huge generation plants created in discrete locations. Some of them developed a method for spinning thread from the black stone. It was tedious and difficult work, but those that wore the garments were able to maintain great power by increasing their capacity to store light and compensate for the reduction in knowledge.

"The final assignment for Kallikrates was to eliminate the threat of the Mind Thieves that had begun operations on Earth. This new generation of Mind Thieves had learned to collect power in giant capacitors built of the black stone. These capacitors could capture light and absorb power from those captured of the Mind Legion. In the beginning they would just steal a little power at a time from their captors to avoid being caught. Soon the Mind Legion would recognize that their members were being drained or going missing in certain regions, and they would destroy the power facilities.

"The Mind Thieves did not give up. Some of the oldest and most powerful of their society found ways to erase memories from their captors so that they could not be detected for years in certain locations. In the meanwhile, they would amass great power and begin to influence the populations in the areas where they operated. They would create wars and contention along with other civil uprisings so that the Mind Legion's focus would be on stabilization of the region instead of on detection of the Mind Thieves.

"Kallikrates and I worked tirelessly through many generations of man on Earth. We watched in disbelief as the great network of the Mind Legion was slowly dismantled by the Mind Thieves. We had to defend ourselves with protective clothing similar to the Mind Thieves. Our superior knowledge allowed us to create a more powerful fabric of the black stone that gave us an advantage for a time.

"Kallikrates maintained constant communication with the Great Council on Earth's progress. He also sent them wardrobes of the new fabric that we had designed and followed it up with instructions on how to harvest light to power the clothing.

"The Mind Legion fought back and reestablished supremacy on Earth over the Mind Thieves. At the time we believed that we had completely destroyed the Mind Thieves from off the face of the planet. Kallikrates seemed satisfied that things had returned to a stable state and he returned to the Great Council.

"I felt the weight of governing Earth on my own. We kept a constant vigilance for any sign of the Mind Thieves. They had learned patience and became even more adept at secrecy. Many more generations passed, and Earth once again began to establish peace and to develop the finer qualities of humanity.

"One day, a desperate communication came to me from Kallikrates. It was short but undeniable, 'They have infiltrated the Great Council.' I immediately knew the implication. Mind Thieves were now in control of the Great Council. I heard nothing more from Kallikrates or the Great Council. The communication of the Lower Council also ended. We were utterly alone for more than a hundred years. Not a word despite my continual attempts at communication.

"All of my time and energy was now focused on the defense of Earth from the Mind Thieves. They had been amassing power in secret and unleashed a new weapon against us to sap our power and strengthen themselves. I am banned from discussing this weapon for fear that a record of it will lead to its future use.

"We fought desperately for many generations and slowly our numbers diminished as the Mind Thieves gained greater power. Their rapid ascension to dominance eventually led to their downfall, but not before they had overwhelmed us to such a degree that only a handful of the Mind Legion remained. All of us have been in hiding since that time. A few days ago we received our first ray of hope. Kallikrates communicated with us. He informed me that through a series of events and a great war he had become the new Chief Captain of the Mind Legion and that they were now systematically eliminating the Mind Thieves planet by planet. The resistance was strong, and he was not sure if they could succeed. He said that Earth would be last since it would require the complete focus of the Mind Legion to overcome the power here.

"I told Kallikrates that I did not believe we could hold out against the Mind Thieves much longer. He despaired at our situation, and I could feel his empathy. But in the end there was nothing he could do. To attempt to rescue Earth now would lead to the complete destruction of all that had been bought with bitter blood. In soberness he instructed me to create this record in preparation for the time in which you would find this place and begin the process of rebuilding the Mind Legion.

"Now is that time. If Kallikrates or some other has begun training you, then I must assume that he was successful in destroying the Mind Thieves. You must now choose if you will take the mantle of Captain of the Mind Legion on yourself. I can attest to the great joy and wisdom that comes with this responsibility. I can also tell you that you will never feel greater loneliness or sorrow in this position.

"The Code requires that you make a decision within seven Earth days of learning the contents of this message. At the end of the seven days, the Rock Room will be sealed if you choose contrary, and the Mind Legion will wait for another worthy to lead it here on Earth."

The message ended and the screen went dark. The small stone ball was absorbed by the wall of the Rock Room. I glanced at my watch. It was 5:00 p.m. on Saturday. By next Saturday, I had to decide what I would do next. I sat for some time contemplating what I had seen and heard and felt.

I had never been a very good history student and reflected on how much more I could have learned in school had these historical devices existed. Then it dawned on me. They did exist.

Since the Mind Legion had been absent from modern history, I was unable to learn about that era, but interactions that occurred long ago were viewed and experienced as if they happened a few years ago. I saw the dawn of the Sumerian Civilization. I experienced the Akkadian Empire, the Xiao Dynasty, and the Minoan Civilization. Time and time again I watched the great cycle of formation, domination, declination, and eventually destruction. It was eerie to see it pass by so quickly. The patterns become obvious. I saw Byzantium and Babylonia rise and fall. Then there were the Romans. Theirs was a partial history since the Mind Legion was destroyed prior to the fall of the Roman Empire, but the power they attained was unfathomable. Behind it all there was always the presence of the Mind Legion. Even the great Caesar was coached and mentored by the Council.

Despite the efforts by the Council on Earth, the Mind Thieves were able to influence great leaders and destroy the greatest of all nations. I had never seen anything so tragic. I had never felt anything so sad. The weight of my decision rested heavily on my mind.

Was I the right person to be Captain of the Mind Legion? How could I know?

If I were to take on the responsibility and fail like my predecessor, what would that mean to Earth? The

Mind Thieves, if reestablished could destroy everything and everyone that I most cherished. The responsibility was overwhelming. After all, I was still just the lonely boy that happened to hit on the greatest discovery in a few thousand years. There must be others that could do a better job. In the midst of my thoughts I remembered Rachael and immediately gathered my things and prepared to leave. I had clearly stayed longer than I had anticipated.

The sky was dark when I descended the trail. Several times on my ride home I had an eerie feeling that I was being watched. Each time I had just waved it off as being scared of the dark or of being alone. Now I wasn't so sure. Maybe we were all being watched. I strained every one of my senses on the surrounding area and became even more certain that somebody was out there.

I picked up my speed and raced for home.

CHAPTER 21

Rachael was on her bed when I arrived at the house. Her eyes were open, and she was staring into the nothingness. Val was pacing the room deep in her own thoughts. I watched her as she went from one end of the room to the other. At each turn her hair whipped around her face. My heart suddenly raced. She was beautiful. There was no other way to describe her. The exertion of the situation brought out a natural color in her cheeks. Her bright eyes were filled with determination and concern.

"What is she doing hanging around with me?" I thought to myself as I stood silhouetted in the doorway of Rachael's room. I must have had this conversation with myself a million times over the last year. People knew who I was, but I didn't stand out in any way from the crowd. *So why did she choose to spend her time with me?*

It wasn't like we were alone together very often. Rachael or Richard was usually around, but Val and I just seemed to be on the same page with things.

"There you are," said Val, bursting me out of my daydream. "I need to talk to you now. Where can we go for some privacy?"

"Umm," I thought as I tried to come up with some location.

"Your room is obviously out of the question. Not only is it a mess, but there's no door. How do you survive without a door?"

I turned a self-conscious eye toward my room and noticed Jim's clothes strewn all across the floor. This included some old boxers and his athletic supporter. I didn't need to take a further look because I knew what else she had seen when she went in the room.

My face reddened in humiliation as I offered a suggestion that we go in the bathroom. I led the way down the hall and entered in enough time to kick a few soiled pieces of clothing into a corner. The rest of the mess was just going to have to remain for now.

Val didn't even look at the bathroom. Her eyes were on me as she turned around after locking the door. I started to get a little uncomfortable as I stood there alone with her in such a tight space. She smelled sweet, a little like cinnamon, making me doubly aware of how much I had sweated on my ride in and out during the day.

I finally broke the silence, "Well, what's on your mind?"

She was not amused as she crossed her arms. "What's on my mind? What kind of question is that in a time like this? There are a million things on my mind right now. We are pretty sure that we're being stalked by Mind Thieves, and you're asking me what is on my mind. I'll never understand boys."

"It was just a question," I responded hesitantly. "I had a lot on my mind and kind of forgot about the whole Mind Thief thing."

"You forgot?" she asked incredulously. "Your sister is in the other room in a trance and you forgot? What else did you forget? You forgot that two helpless girls had to ride home alone and pretend not to be scared that they were being followed or that someone would jump out from behind the next clump of trees and attack them."

"I guess so," I mumbled, feeling increasingly more guilty and starting to think that I'd been overly generous with my analysis of how well Val and I got along.

The air in the tiny bathroom was stifling. It was like someone had turned on the hot water until the room filled with steam. I noticed a bead of sweat forming on my forehead and became even more nervous of what aroma that might arouse.

Val stared at me for a few moments longer and then she broke. The tension left the room as she let go of her anxiety and the tears flowed from her eyes. She stood across from me with her face in her hands as she trembled and cried.

I wanted to do something but didn't quite know how to deal with this situation. Boys didn't have moments like this. In a feeble effort to comfort her, I reached out and patted her shoulder. Apparently that was all the invitation she needed. She stepped forward and put her head on my shoulder, and without thinking I put my arms around her and held her for a few moments as she regained control.

"I'm sorry," she said as she stepped from my arms. "I didn't mean to break down like that."

She reached for some toilet paper, blew her nose, and wiped her eyes with the back of her hand.

"It's okay," I responded. "It's been a long day for all of us."

We stood in awkward silence for another brief interval before something jumped into my memory. "Weren't you going to your house? What are you doing here?"

"When I got home I called your mom. She was a quite worried since she hadn't heard from Rachael, and her friend had called asking about her. She had been on the phone for over an hour trying different friends to see if she could locate her. I told her that everything was okay, but that Rachael wasn't feeling well. I also tried hard not to lie, but I'm afraid I deceived your mother into believing that Rachael stayed over at my house last night."

She paused and seemed to get a little embarrassed. Val continued, "Your mother insisted that Rachael come home so she could take care of her. I volunteered my services, and here I am."

"Are you staying over tonight?" I asked hesitantly.

"Of course not. That wouldn't be appropriate seeing how we are..." she paused, as if she was trying to think of the right word. Finally she finished by saying, "Seeing how we are friends and seeing how you are a boy and I am a girl."

I couldn't help but hope that maybe there was more, but she was just too embarrassed to say anything. "Richard is coming to get me. I was talking with him as you came in. He's been doing some scouting around the Rock Room. He found several locations where the vegetation is worn away within viewing distance of the entrance. He also noticed two distinct sets of tracks, one being slightly smaller than the other. He thinks it might be a man and a woman, but he's not sure."

"You guys have been busy," I said dryly.

"Yes we have," she stated flatly. "Our future with the Mind Legion depends on you."

I perked up again. "What do you mean?" I asked innocently.

"Darius, don't play games with me. You know what I'm talking about. You're making a very important decision in the next week that will determine whether we continue learning or if we will return to the way things were."

Val paused for a moment, and then trailed into a final thought, "I, for one, hope that things don't have to go back to the way they were. It would be too hard after all we've learned."

I stood in silence not knowing what to say. How did she always know what was going on? It was like a sixth sense. Whenever I was trying to keep something quiet she knew about it.

"What do you think I should do?" I asked.

"I don't know, Darius. It's a big decision to rest on your shoulders after so little time." She reached out and grabbed my hand to comfort me. Obviously, she could see worry and concern in my face. I looked into her big brown eyes. They seemed to go right through me. She leaned in a little closer.

Knock, knock, knock.

"Are you guys in there?" asked Richard. "You're not getting fresh are you?"

Val dropped my hand and wiped away the last of the tears before turning and opening the door. "Hi, Richard," she said. "We were just talking about things."

"It looks like it was pretty serious. Are you sure you were just talking? If you know what I mean."

"Richard, you know better than that," Val chided.

"How's Rachael?" he asked, changing the subject. "She looks pretty bad. I hope she pulls out of this. It's just not fair that Rachael is the one that got attacked. She's the last person in the world that deserves to be treated badly."

"Richard, if I didn't know you better I might think you are really concerned about her," said Val jokingly.

"Come on, Val. This is no time to joke around. Of course I'm worried about her and about all of us. We are in real danger."

"I know. I'm sorry."

"It's getting late," I said, looking at my watch. "You two probably need to get home and stay safe tonight. I'll stay here with Rachael. Let's meet first thing in the morning at the Rock Room and figure out what to do next."

"Don't you have some work to do alone tomorrow?" Val asked.

"I'm done for now with that. I'll explain tomorrow. I don't know if we're safe even here to discuss some things."

"I have no idea what you guys are talking about," said Richard, "but I'm sure you'll fill me in tomorrow. Let's go, sis."

I watched as they walked down the hall and up the stairs. A few seconds later the door closed behind them and I was alone. Or so I felt. For the first time in about a year I didn't have anyone to talk to.

Rachael still lay in the same position staring at the ceiling. If there was not a slight rising and falling of her chest and an occasional blinking of the eyes, I might question whether she was really still alive.

CHAPTER 22

Rachael woke me the next morning when she tripped over me on the way to the bathroom. I spent most of the night in fitful sleep as I tried to get comfortable on the hard floor. My dreams were distorted and plagued with a feeling that I could not find something that I had lost.

"Good morning, Darius," she said groggily as she trudged past me.

I rolled back over and tried to sleep for a few minutes. My mind slowly caught hold of the memories of the last few days, and I stood up and dragged my blanket back across the hall into the other room.

Jim was lying peacefully in his bed. I held my hand over his face in an attempt to get a little revenge for the many mischievous acts he had perpetrated over the years. As my hand neared his face, he snatched it and pulled me into the bed post, which I hit with a dull thud, our faces only a few inches apart.

"You got to get up pretty early in the morning to pull a fast one on me," he said.

I nearly retched from the smell of his morning breath. "What did you eat last night?" I asked as I quickly pulled myself away and faked some dry heaves.

"It might have been the chips and salsa or the onion rings," he answered pensively as he jumped up from bed.

I always admired the way Jim could just switch from sleep to being fully awake without any transition. The annoying thing was that he was naturally optimistic and chipper all the time, even when he was pulling pranks.

"I've got to get to the gym," he said as he glanced at the clock and pulled on a dirty t-shirt.

Rachael poked her head in and said, "Are you ready to go? Val and Richard will probably be waiting for us."

"Rats. We're going to be late" I said as I pulled on some socks and my shoes and followed her upstairs.

CRACK.

Val was pacing the floor and stopped to look over as we walked into the room. Richard was at his station concentrating on his telepathy with his Master.

"Great, we can finally get started," said Val matter of factly. "Richard, come on they're here."

"Okay, Mom, I'm coming."

Val looked over at Richard with eyes that could have cut through stone. She was obviously in no mood to joke around, so we got right down to business. We sat in the desks and swiveled them to face each other. Everyone looked expectantly at me.

"Uh, I guess we need to discuss a few things," I said hesitantly, glancing over at Val.

"That has got to be the understatement of the year," said Val in exasperation. "Obviously we need to discuss some things. First off, we need to get an exact accounting from Rachael of her whereabouts over the last few weeks, including any lapses in memory. Then we need you to give us a better understanding of your situation, Darius. Our masters have told us a little, but we want to hear directly from you. Finally we need to figure out how to keep these attacks on Rachael or on any of us from ever happening again."

I was relieved that Val listed off what needed to be done because I really had no idea where to start. I'd been so preoccupied with my own problems that I had not spent any time thinking about the bigger issues.

"Well, I guess that means you're up Rachael," said Richard softly.

"I don't really remember much of the last week or so. I was spending a lot of time with my friends, then coming to the Rock Room to think and discuss my plans for an apprentice with my master. About three or four days ago I started feeling really tired. I thought

I might be coming down with something, so I tried not to over exert myself."

"Do you remember exactly when you first started feeling tired?" asked Val.

"No, I don't remember the exact day. I've been working so hard to catch up with you guys that I just thought it was from that."

"Tell us everything that happened during the day when you fell asleep here in the room," I added.

"Okay, I'll try, but everything is a little blurry. Three. No. Four days ago I heard you leave the house in the morning and I jumped out of bed to catch you. I probably left the house fifteen minutes after you and started riding toward the Rock Room. I figured if you were there than I should probably be there working on something. The last thing I remember was riding toward the trail head. The next thing I knew I was standing outside the door of the Rock Room."

"What time was it when Rachael came into the Rock Room, Darius?" asked Val.

"I don't remember," I said. "I was kind of preoccupied at the time. I guess it was sometime late in the morning."

"That means there are at least a few hours of time missing. It also means that the Mind Thieves have a location nearby if they got Rachael there, drained some of her power, altered her memory, and then got her back here."

We all stared at Val in amazement. She had obviously thought this through.

"How do you know all this stuff?" I asked.

"Oh, my master has been working with me to try and solve the problem. She can't come right now because there are some urgent problems on the Council that she needs to take care of, so she has been spending as much time as possible coaching me."

A feeling of loneliness returned to me as thought about Kallikrates. It would be several more days before I spoke to him. I missed our conversations and his counsel.

"Where could they possibly put a hideout around here?" Richard asked.

"Just about anywhere," Val said. "They could be right next door to us and we wouldn't know it unless we happened to see them open the door. The place would have to be near the black stone, like the stuff you see lining the ceiling of our Rock Room, since they would need to use it like a giant battery to store the energy they are collecting. I think they're closer than we think. In fact, they may have been watching us for a year without our knowing as they waited for us to get strong enough to harvest our power."

"Why Rachael?" I asked. "I mean, why not go after Richard or you or me?"

"I don't know," said Val. "That's really a good question. I'll have to ask my master."

"We need a safe way to get to the Rock Room," said Richard. "I saw tracks all over the place around our entrance. They obviously know how we get in and out of this place."

"Maybe there's another way in," offered Rachael.

We all looked at her with a stunned expression. Why not? Of course this problem must have occurred a thousand times over the years. Wouldn't every Training Room need two entrances?

"Room," I asked. "Is there another entrance to this place?"

"Yes."

"Can you show us?"

"Yes."

"Okay, then show us already," said Richard impatiently. "What a time for this place to get a sense of humor."

A smaller entrance slid open on the wall just opposite us. There was a passageway and then two parallel tracks. On the track were little vehicles that had seats facing both forward and back. The top of the vehicle was open, but there was a compartment on the front and back to hold your belongings. The track was carefully hewn stone and trailed away ahead of us into the darkness.

"Let's try it out," Richard said excitedly.

"Maybe we should send one party out first to see if it still works," I offered. "We don't all want to get stranded somewhere miles away from here."

"Good idea," said Richard. "I'll go with Val. We can stay in communication with the training stones."

"Okay," I said.

"Come on, Val," said Richard as he climbed aboard, facing down the darkened tunnel. The only lights seemed to be those just over our head.

Val climbed in and they waited for a minute for something to happen.

"How does this work?" asked Richard as he looked around. "Oh wait, here's the palm print."

As he finished speaking, the vehicle shot off down the tunnel. The lights synchronized to the travel as they sped away.

"Wooohooo!" yelled Richard as they rode out of sight.

A couple minutes later Val called us through the training stone. "It looks like we are at the end. There's a door that Richard is about to open."

After a minute, Val said, "We came out on the last bend of the road before it heads into the canyon. We are about fifty yards from the roadside concealed behind a few large boulders. The palm print is hidden pretty well in the natural stone. We're coming back now."

Within another couple minutes, we saw the tunnel lighten gradually in the distance, and the vehicle came back into sight. Val and Richard jumped out excitedly.

"You've gotta try it out," said Richard. "It's way cool. The peak speed must be close to sixty miles per hour."

"There's another vehicle at the other end," added Val. "It looks like they are interchangeable."

"Well, I guess we now have another way to get here without exposing ourselves to the Mind Thieves. We probably need to find a way to get in and out of it without drawing any attention to ourselves."

After some lengthy discussion, we determined to never come to the new entrance in groups larger than two.

When approaching the entrance it was necessary to avoid recognizable patterns, so we had to leave the main road at different points every time. Finally, we decided that it was necessary to continue using the main entrance so we would not alert the Mind Thieves to what we were doing.

"I'm hungry," said Richard after the discussion started dying down.

I glanced at my watch and saw that it was after 1:00 p.m. "Maybe we should break for lunch?" I offered.

We went to our bags and pulled out our lunches. It had become a common practice for us to pack a lunch when we knew that we'd be spending all day in the Room.

"Oh no," said Val as she lifted a soggy bag out of her pack. "My water bottle must have leaked." She paused for a moment and then said, "I wasn't that hungry anyways." She slowly set down her bag and returned to sit down.

"Do you want some of my sandwich?" I offered.

"No, I'm allergic to peanuts. But thank you for offering."

"I guess you could have my apple," I responded.

Richard cut in before Val could answer, "How did people eat when they were training here before?"

"I don't know," I said.

"They probably brought their food with them when they came here," Val answered.

"You don't know that for sure," argued Richard. "Back then there was not pre-packaged foods and sandwich bags like we enjoy today."

"But it makes sense," she retorted. "Look around you. Do you see a fridge or a vending machine?"

Richard threw out a small piece of his sandwich on the floor. Almost immediately the little cleaning robot scooted out of an invisible moving panel and cleaned up the mess. It then turned around and headed back to where it came from as we all looked on in silence.

His point was made.

"Room. Do you keep any food here?"

"No," was the response from the Room.

"See, I told you so," said Val.

Richard looked around. "How did others get food while they were training here?"

"They used the matter converter," answered the Room.

"The matter converter?" we all said in unison.

"Where is it? And how does it work?" I asked.

"The matter converter is a mechanism that contains a certain quantity of all of the main elements found in nature. When stored in their pure form, they never go bad. These elements must be combined into the desired form to be consumed. The elements are combined by placing your hand on the device and imagining the food item that is desired. The system can process the signal from your mind and analyze the data gathered from your past experience digesting the food and determine the right combination of the elements needed to create the food."

"Let's test it," said Richard excitedly. "Show us the matter converter."

A compartment across the room opened up. Richard jumped up and ran over to see what was inside.

"It's empty," Richard said. "I'm going to try it out."

He placed his hand on the indentation point and concentrated. We all sat silently for a minute or two, waiting for something to happen. Nothing did. Richard finally looked up disappointed and said, "It must not be working anymore."

As he finished talking, a small compartment popped open. We looked on in wonder as he pulled out a piece of pizza and took a big bite.

"Wait," Val shouted. "We don't know if that's safe to eat. It could have been sitting in there for hundreds of years."

"Tastes okay to me," said Richard. He then fell to the floor making choking sounds.

"Very funny, Richard," said Val, trying not to laugh at him as he wiggled on the floor.

CHAPTER 23

All was silent in the Rock Room for a few minutes as we ate. We'd had various levels of success in materializing the items we were imagining. I was able to create some grapes that were better than average. Richard followed up on the pizza with a steak sandwich. He also got Rachael a deli sandwich with meat that looked a little strange but tasted right. Val was a little less successful when she attempted to materialize a fruit smoothie. It turns out that you have to actually have a container for your food. The cleaning robot angrily sped toward the gooey mess spilling out of the matter converter as Val apologized profusely and the rest of us laughed at the spectacle.

"Your turn, Darius" said Richard, breaking the silence that was beginning to become uncomfortable.

"Huh?" I responded as he jogged me from my reverie. "Oh right. Well, I'm not quite sure where to start."

"Maybe the beginning," encouraged Val.

I shared with them what I felt I could from the historical experience, starting from the beginning. It was a brief and unfulfilling summary since it was impossible for me to describe or transmit the emotional essence of the message that was conveyed to me. How could I express the joy I felt as I saw the Mind Legion growing in power and wisdom? It was difficult describing the despair I felt as I viewed the last Captain from Earth close his record, knowing that it had been sealed by his death.

"That explains the weirdness the last couple of times I came into the Rock Room," Rachael said.

Val looked over at us and asked, "What weirdness?"

"I may have failed to mention the part where Rachael opened the door and found me sprawled out on the floor."

"I would have liked to have seen that," said Richard.

"Sorry about that buddy, I forgot to bring my video camera," I responded sarcastically.

"Wait a minute," said Val with a mischievous smile. "Maybe there is a way to see it."

"What? No!" I said as I grasped what I thought she was going to do next.

"Room," she continued, ignoring my plea, "can you show us what happened when Rachael entered the Rock Room two days ago?"

"Yes," the Room responded as a screen flickered nearest to where we were sitting.

The image quality was near perfect as it showed how the scenario unfolded. I was comfortably seated watching the sequence of events unfold before me when the screen shut down, the chair disappeared, and Rachael walked into the room. I turned to the others in time to hear them break into laughter.

"Okay, that's enough," I said somewhat embarrassed.

"Wait, wait," stammered Richard. "Room, show us the same sequence from the next day."

The video jumped to the next day, and the whole sequence of events repeated. Richard laughed the loudest at the second occurrence, but the others weren't too far behind him. All of sudden Val stopped laughing as she watched the video.

"Oh Rachael, I'm so sorry," she said as she reached out a hand and gently placed it on Rachael's arm. "You look completely exhausted in the video."

"It looked worse than it was," Rachael said softly, but not convincingly

"Darius, how did you not notice her need?" Val chided me. "Boys are always absorbed with themselves. They just can't read body language. I'm sorry I wasn't here for you Rachael."

I looked down in shame and said, "I guess I was just a little too preoccupied with my own concerns that I wasn't paying attention."

"I'm disappointed, Darius," Val said as she moved closer to Rachael as if to support her.

My insides turned as I took the burden of guilt upon myself. I had never had so much responsibility placed on me and felt emptiness in knowing that I had not been successful. My mind filled with doubts and concerns because I knew Val was right. I had been selfish and self-centered. All my energies had been focused on my own concerns. For a time I had disassociated myself from the world. This was one of the first moments of realization in my life that the well-being of others really mattered.

My chin sunk down toward my chest as doubt filled my mind about my ability to become the Captain of the Mind Legion. I would be accountable for all of the members of the Mind Legion, including Rachael if I accepted. It seemed too daunting for someone my age. Jim or Richard could handle these kinds of things, but I was not leader, or so I thought. I kept my eyes lowered to avoid the stares that I could feel coming my direction.

"How can you take on the responsibility of all of us when you can't take care of your sister?" whispered Val as if thinking to herself.

"I don't know," I said meekly, not sure if she was making a statement or asking a question. "The truth is that I've been asking myself the same question. I mean, look at me. Do I look like the next Captain of the Mind Legion?"

"You've got a point there," said Richard.

I wasn't sure if Richard meant what he said or if he was just trying to lighten the situation. He was incredibly competitive and probably felt that he might make a better leader. In truth, I had considered him a better leader since the day I'd met him. People flocked to him. He had loads of friends at school. At the same time, he had developed some pretty decent enemies as well.

"I didn't ask for this," I said quietly as I stood and walked across the room. There was no way to put more distance between us in the confined space, so I stared at the wall and tried to be man enough to hold back the tears that were welling up inside me. I stood there for a few minutes before I felt a hand on my shoulder. I turned to look into Rachael's pleading face.

"Help me, Darius. You are the only one that can stop whatever is happening to me."

"I don't know if I can," I said in shame. "Look at the video. I didn't even notice that you were in trouble. I couldn't protect you from the Mind Thieves."

The room was quiet for what felt like a long time. We did not know what to do or say. So we just remained silent. The realization washed over us that this was no longer a game. The stakes were high. What if the Mind Thieves began attacking the rest of us? What if they had already gotten to us and we didn't know? I didn't know about the others, but I was afraid. I knew that fear and doubt stunted my reasoning and slowed my senses, but I couldn't help myself. The path ahead was fuzzy.

"Darius, Rachael is right," Val said after deep thought. "I spoke too soon. Without a doubt you know the most about the history of the Mind Legion here on Earth. You have progressed faster than the rest of us on most every task. You are the best candidate to fix the problem."

"No, I can't do it alone," I responded as Val's statements knocked me out of the stupor I was in.

"None of us is strong enough to take on an empowered Mind Thief. They could pick us off one-by-one if we try to do anything alone. We have to stick together."

"Tell us again what you learned about the Mind Thieves from the history," Rachael pleaded. "I want to know more about our enemy."

I methodically recounted the parts of the history that pertained to the Mind Thieves. I tried not to miss any of the salient points. When I stopped speaking they looked to me for more information, and all I could do was to shake my head back and forth indicating that I had shared with them all that I knew.

"So that's it?" Richard asked.

"I'm afraid so," I replied.

"What a letdown," Richard fumed. "There was obviously some effort to hide the great secret to the Mind Thieves' power. Just think what we could do if we knew what it was?"

"What could you do?" accused Val.

"Don't get all self-righteous on me, Val. You know that we could safely harness the power. We could protect Rachael."

"Come on, Richard. We'd become like them even if we used it in self defense. But somehow I doubt that your interests are wholly altruistic."

"It sounds like Kallikrates and his wife have you convinced that this stuff is dangerous. My master thinks otherwise. He says that great good could be done with the power gathered by the tools invented here on Earth all those years ago."

"I don't know, Richard. It sounds really dangerous. What if we find out the secret and it turns out that it hurts or kills one of us?"

"That's a risk we have to take if we're going to beat off this threat," he responded.

"I'm going to ask my master what she thinks," said Val, reaching into her pocket for her stone.

We settled in to wait for a response, but Val quickly turned to us with a startled look on her face. "She can't talk right now because of urgent Council business that requires her full concentration. That's the first time that she has refused to talk to me even if she was in a Council."

Richard reached in his pocket to contact his master, and then was surprised at receiving roughly the same response.

We all turned to Rachael, and after a moment, she seemed to pull out of her daze and reach for her stone. "Sorry, I've had a hard time keeping up. My mind is a mess right now."

She held the stone and at first showed no sign of anything. Slowly, frustration filled her face, and finally she threw her stone down and walked away. She stopped a few feet further and silently cried.

"What happened?" asked Val as she walked over to comfort Rachael.

"Nothing."

"It couldn't have been nothing. I don't understand why you are so upset. None of us seem to be able to talk to our Master right now. What really happened?" Val persisted.

"Nothing happened," said Rachael again. "When I communicated through the stone there was no response. I'm obviously unable to even do the simplest tasks," she continued before lightly weeping again.

"Let's test your theory out," said Richard, picking up her stone and gently handing it back to her.

Her eyes lit up as the stone rested firmly in her palm. Richard was communicating with her through the stone. She ran over and gave him a hug before backing off a little embarrassed. "Sorry," she apologized as she blushed in discomfort. "I was just so happy that it worked."

"Don't be sorry," said Richard. "I'm glad that the experiment worked."

"But, why can't I talk to my Master?" Rachael asked.

Nobody knew how to respond.

"We need a plan," Val said matter of factly as she looked to Richard and me for leadership.

In the silence, we heard what sounded like an animal scratching on the wall. "What was that?" Val and I said in unison.

"Room. What is the scratching noise?" asked Richard with an ounce of apprehension in his voice.

"I have no record that matches the noise you are hearing," responded the Room.

The sound stopped, and we sat in silence for some time in anticipation of the return of the noise. Our breathing was the only thing we could hear for several minutes. Each of us was intently concentrating on the environment to identify any anomalies. Finally, we settled down and looked around at each other expectantly.

A thought popped into my mind, and before clearing it with the others, I made a request of the Room. "Room? Do you have recordings of what occurs outside of the room?"

"Yes."

"Show us every clip from outside that includes Rachael over the last week," I continued as the thought developed into a plan.

The screen flickered, and we could see the clearing in front of the room. Rachael entered the screen pushing her bike. She placed her bike in the usual location, and then disappeared as she neared the secret compartment that held the black stone. A new visual transitioned on to the screen as the compartment opened and Rachael's face, partially blocked by the stone, filled the cavity. As she removed the stone, the screen transitioned to a new view that was similar to what you might see through a peep hole on a door. When the door opened, the screen flickered and the reverse sequence began. We could see the back of Rachael's head as the door closed behind her. Her face flickered on the screen again as she opened the cavity, and then she exited the clearing pushing her bike.

"Nothing there," Richard said as the screen flickered to life for the second time.

The sequence repeated itself two more times in nearly the same fashion. On the fourth series, Rachael stumbled into the clearing and set down her bike before walking as if she were inebriated toward the cavity. When the cavity door opened, she stared blankly at the stone for what seemed like a full minute while leaning against the wall. She finally reached in and slowly withdrew the stone. Before the compartment closed we caught a glimpse of her struggling to hold up the stone. She was leaning against the wall for some time before finally attempting to open the door. She stared in disbelief when nothing happened after the first attempt. She looked at her hand, then at the stone, then at her hand again, before reaching up and holding her hand for some time against the stone. Finally, after a visible mental effort, the door opened and she made one last effort to enter the room.

This sequence repeated itself, and then we saw Rachael and Val leaving the room together after what must have been Rachael's overnight experience in the Rock Room.

"Pause the recording," I whispered as I looked over at Rachael. "I'm sorry I didn't notice. There's no excuse for it. As I watch these recordings and think back to the last few days I realize that I have not been a very good brother. I should have known. I should have done something to stop this."

"What could you have done, Darius?" said Rachael compassionately. "None of us knew what was happening. Not even I recognized it, and it was happening to me."

"Okay, enough already with the sappiness," said Richard. "We still have a serious problem to solve here. Room, rewind to the last time Rachael entered the clearing alone. Now proceed at half speed as she enters the clearing."

We all turned to the screen to watch. Rachael stumbled in to the picture in slow motion.

"Did you see that?" asked Richard.

"See what?" Val questioned.

"C'mon, I can't be the only one that saw that. Let me bask in my own magnificence for one moment."

"That's enough Richard," said Val, trying not to smile at his comment. "Tell us what you saw."

"Better yet, I'll show you. Room, rewind the last sequence again and zoom in until Rachael fills the screen."

The screen showed an image of the opening where Rachael entered the clearing. "Now play it at one quarter speed," demanded Richard.

The image was perfectly clear as Rachael's front bike tire slowly entered. Two gasps were heard from Val and Rachael. "What did you see?" I asked, still not grasping what had happened.

"Rewind again and repeat the last sequence," said Val as she stood and walked to the screen.

The recording started again, and Val pointed to Rachael's shoulder. Then I saw it. A hand on her shoulder, balancing her. It released and withdrew into the shadow as Val stumbled out into the clearing.

We sat in silence again, taking in what we just saw. There was no doubting the visual evidence. Rachael had clearly been tampered with and then returned to us. What was more disturbing was that the person was completely aware of the recording by the Rock Room. Why else would they linger in the shadows?

Rachael leaned against Val and tears silently fell down her cheek. Never before in my life had I felt as strong a yearning as I did then to help somebody. I wanted to take away her pain at any cost.

I looked over at Rachael and calmly and firmly stated, "I won't let that happen to you ever again."

Val beamed at me and smiled through her tears as confidence sprang into all of our hearts. "That's what a true Captain of the Mind Legion would say," she spoke with admiration.

"We must do this without our masters," I stated. "There's no time to lose, and we can't wait for them. Even though they are not with us, we are not alone. Look around you. We have each other. We trust each other. We can rely on each other. Each of us has individual strengths. If we work together, we can combine those strengths into something greater than what any one of us can do alone."

"So what's the plan?" asked Richard expectantly.

"I don't know," I said and saw the confidence of the others begin to waiver. "But, together we will think of a way to beat the Mind Thieves and make things safe again."

This was the first time that we truly had to use our powers against an enemy. All of the training had been helping us understand the Code. We sat in thought as we pondered how to use our powers in self defense. The Mind Thieves were not squeamish about using their knowledge to extract power from even the most innocent.

"The plan needs to be perfect," I said at last. "We need to start our plan with the end in mind. What is it that we want to accomplish?"

"Safety for each of us," declared Val.

"Security of the Rock Room," said Rachael.

"Destruction of our enemies' power source," I added.

"Destruction of our enemy," stated Richard. "We can't be at peace until they are gone."

"Isn't that a little harsh, Richard?" asked Val.

"I don't think so," he said. "If we are safe, the Rock Room is secure, and their power source is destroyed, will you be able to sleep in peace?"

"No," responded Rachael.

"Yeah, me neither," I said.

"I see your point, but it still feels kind of harsh," Val stated.

"Look at what they did to Rachael," Richard said. "What if they had actually caused irreversible damage or, heaven forbid, killed her? Then how would you feel about destroying them?"

"I see what you're saying," she retorted. "But what about the Code? Doesn't the Code tell us not to kill? Doesn't the Code tell us to show mercy to our enemies? There must be another way."

"What if we could find a way to imprison them or banish them from Earth?" I asked. "Would that meet the criteria? That would rid us of the danger without causing us to break any part of the Code."

"I see your point," Richard acquiesced reluctantly. "But if it comes down to a choice between the safety of any one of you or their life, I'm going to take their life."

We spent the next few hours planning the details for each of the four areas that we identified. I reinforced our purpose and strengthened our resolve by explaining to the others that in the historical video I had seen what the Mind Thieves could do. They had nearly wiped out the Mind Legion on Earth at the time of the last Captain. In addition, they had almost destroyed the Great Council. Throughout this all they were manipulating governments and people to start wars and cause instability. I believed that given the resources and power that could be created if they restored their order on Earth, they would annihilate us and destroy Earth as we know it.

I spoke up at one point in the discussion to get a list of our strengths and weaknesses. "Safety is our primary goal. What are our best weapons for planning an offensive or a defensive position?"

All of us pondered the question. Richard spoke first, "I've always been good at controlling objects from a distance."

In demonstration he launched his backpack across the room, hitting the wall in a solid thud.

Val pulled a sheet of paper from her bag and crumpled it into a ball. She set it on one of the desks. "Richard, throw this against that far wall."

"With pleasure."

The paper screamed across the room and just before hitting the wall it burst into flames.

"Whoa!" I jumped in surprise. "That was incredible. How did you do that?"

Val beamed, "It was nothing. I just increased the kinetic movement of the molecules around the object until it reached the temperature of spontaneous combustion."

"What?" we all said in response.

"I made it so hot near the paper that it burst into flames."

"Cool," said Richard.

"What about you Rachael?" I asked.

She thought for a minute before looking over at my apple sitting on the desk near me. "Stand back Darius."

I immediately moved and not a second too soon. The apple converted slowly into a small tree and the roots enveloped the desk.

"Well, I guess that might come in handy." I said unconvincingly.

"I'm not done yet," stated Rachael.

The desk slowly started shaking and then was crushed together by the force of the roots. This time we all jumped in surprise. Richard clapped and whooped before patting Rachael on the back.

"Amazing," said Val. "How did I never see that before?"

"I never used it this way before," said Rachael. "I usually just flower a plant or something like that."

"Okay, I guess it is my turn," I said, walking into the open space in the room. "Stay back."

I proceeded to demonstrate a combination of kung fu, karate, jujitsu, and some other martial arts. At the end I ran up the wall and launched myself across the room, landing on the desk next to the others.

I looked around to see what the response would be. Nothing. There was silence.

"Darius, that was scary," said Val.

"I'm sorry," I said in disappointment.

"No, Darius, that is not what I meant. That was really scary. You could mess somebody up with that."

"You're the one to talk Miss Spontaneous Combustion."

A small army of the cleaning robots were scurrying around the room cleaning up the ashes and trying to free up the desk from Rachael's tree. One of the robots extended an arm with a small circular saw and began cutting the roots into small pieces while two others loaded the pieces on other robots that disappeared in the blackness of the opening in the wall. A replacement desk was escorted across the room and the old desk was whisked away, making the room whole again.

Val glanced at her watch and said, "We need to go. It's getting late, and it's not safe for us to be out after dark."

"Let's take the new exit," Richard exclaimed excitedly.

"We can't," I responded. "We were probably being watched when we came here. If the Mind Thieves are still out there, we need them to think that we are still unaware of their presence."

"You're probably right," Richard grudgingly agreed as he eyed the alternate exit. "Let's all go together and stay close to each other. Act natural so that nothing seems out of place."

Val and I looked at each other and shook our heads. Richard was always the one racing off ahead of the rest of us. He usually disregarded the group, but it was a welcome change in demeanor to see him stick with the team.

"Tomorrow we need to arrive as early as possible. Nobody travels alone," I said as I glanced around at each of the members of the Mind Legion. It was hard for me to believe that so great a responsibility was falling on us. We were still just a bunch of kids.

CHAPTER 24

I paced nervously across the Rock Room floor as Rachael patiently sat at one of the desks. She was staring at her stone and repeatedly trying to get some response from her Master. She was able to communicate now with Val and Richard, but she couldn't get any communication from anyone else. She felt that something was wrong but could not pinpoint what it was.

"Why don't you sit down and relax? Val and Richard will be here in a few minutes," Rachael said as she continued to toy with her stone. "Val said that they are at the trailhead."

"I can't relax," I said. "There's just too much at stake."

CRACK.

"Finally!" I exclaimed as Val and Richard were silhouetted in the bright doorway.

"Hey guys, let's get started," Richard said with a smile. "What's first on the agenda?"

"I thought we might practice some self defense this morning and then transition into offensive tactics in the afternoon. We don't know how long we will be able to prepare before we are forced into action."

"So why not start with the offense first?" questioned Richard. "It seems like all we do is work on defensive moves."

I really didn't have a good reason for the order, so I consented and we got started. Since we had no masters to guide us, we paired off and rotated through each partner as we practiced various attack methods.

Richard led the first task since it was his specialty. The goal was to levitate an object and then sling it toward a target set up on the far side of the room. We would use as much force as we could muster, starting with very small objects like pennies and small pebbles. Each of us was advanced enough to easily maneuver these objects, but Rachael was way behind the rest of us in both accuracy and velocity as she threw them in the direction of the target.

"I just can't do it," Rachael complained after her third failure at hitting the target with a penny.

In her frustration, she levitated the last penny in her hand and slung it with all of her force. It released just a fraction of a second too early and angled off in the direction of Richard. He was concentrating so hard on levitating his backpack that he didn't realize the penny was coming at him until the last moment. He was barely able to dodge it before it glanced off the wall to his side. The backpack fell to the floor with a crash, and he looked angrily in our direction. He laughed once he realized that it was unintended and that Rachael was the offender.

By mid-morning we tired of throwing objects at targets, and Val suggested that we take a more efficient approach of simultaneous doing offensive and defensive training. She pulled a package of tennis balls from her bag and had Richard stand near her, then sent me to line up on the opposite side of the room. His goal was to hit me, and my goal was to keep from being hit.

Richard was of course the most adept of the group at levitation and was deadly accurate. I called out that I was ready, and before the sound stopped reverberating in the Rock Room, I was laying on my back with a welt the size of tennis ball in the middle of my forehead.

"Sorry, Darius," laughed Richard as the girls ran over to see if I was okay. "It looks like I may have caught you off guard."

Val slid down to her knees next to me and placed her hand on my forehead where an obvious mark was forming. "Are you okay?" she asked as Rachael giggled behind her.

"I'm fine," I responded as I slowly pulled myself back to my feet. "I don't think that the Mind Thieves are going to wait to see if we are ready before they start their next assault.

I stood up, shook my head, and prepared for the onslaught. The tennis balls came at me in a fury. Richard was relentless. After several painful hits and a few near misses, I got into my rhythm and it became a type of dance between us. He was throwing everything he had at me, and I was dodging or stopping as much as I could. He'd get one through on occasion, but after about five minutes he could no longer hit me. After another five minutes, we noticed that the room was silent but for the sound of tennis balls bouncing off walls. We both looked over and saw Val and Rachael staring at us with their mouths open. The balls dropped to the ground and bounced or rolled away.

"What's the matter?" asked Richard.

"That was pretty cool," said Val.

"What are you talking about?" I reiterated.

"The way you two were able to control the balls. They were moving so fast we could barely see them."

"What if those were rocks or marbles or metal?" said Rachael pensively. "Do you think the Mind Thieves can do that?"

The reality sunk in. This was a life and death matter. If they had even a fraction of the skills we had and were able to surprise us, we were in big trouble.

Richard broke the silence with some very practical advice, "We aren't going to stop them by sitting around wondering what they can do. We just have to be better. That is the only option. Darius, it's your turn to be on offense."

Without even looking, I sent the first ball in his direction. It hit him right in his stomach and knocked the wind out of him before he could dodge or stop it.

"Man, that hurts," he whined once he got his breath back.

"Payback is sweet," I replied with a smile, the second ball already on its way.

We broke for lunch and continued discussing our alternatives. The one thing that we all agreed was that we needed the element of surprise on our side. That meant that we needed the fight to be on our terms and away from the public eye. The last thing that we wanted was for the Mind Legion to be exposed and shut down by the Great Council. Fortunately, the Mind Thieves needed us to obtain the power they were seeking. Otherwise, we'd all be exposed or dead.

We finished our training just before dark and then headed home as usual. It was a long day, and we were mentally and physically exhausted. The only bright spot was that Rachael was slowly recovering her energy and seemed to be nearly back to her normal self.

That night I held my stone, longing to talk to Kallikrates. I wondered if we were doing the right thing. Did we even stand a chance against someone that had so much more experience?

"Darius?"

I sat up and looked around before I realized that I was holding the stone and that someone was speaking to me through it.

"Hi Val, how are you doing?"

"I'm worried and, to be honest, I'm a little scared. Can you just talk to me for a while until I can calm down enough to sleep?"

"Sure, I'm happy to help," I responded, relieved to finally have someone to talk to about what was going on.

"My master is still not responding, and neither are Rachael's or Richard's. I really wanted her advice on what we should do next."

"It's funny you'd say that because I was just thinking the same thing."

"Darius, do you ever notice how we seem to be on the same wave length?" Val asked quietly.

"I'm not sure I understand," I answered, trying to mask the burning inside me at hearing Val say something like that.

"Boys are so dense," she muttered before changing the subject. "Do you think it's going to work?"

"Are we still talking about you and me, or are we talking about something else?"

"Boys really are strange. I was referring to our training."

"Oh…" I exclaimed in some relief. "Val, I honestly don't know."

"That's not very reassuring."

"Would you rather that I lie to you?"

"No, that's the one thing I love about you, Darius. You don't seem to be putting on a show all the time like the other boys. I've never really met anyone quite like you."

"You mean as boring as me."

"No, you're not boring. It's kind of nice to talk with someone that doesn't have some pretence. In all this time that we've been friends, you have never said anything disrespectful or deceptive to get what you wanted. I like that."

"Do you think we have a chance?" I asked.

"Are you talking about us or about the training?" Val asked slyly.

"Well, actually both."

"Darius, I honestly don't know," Val said as we both started laughing. "But, in all seriousness, I think that our odds are much better because you are on our side."

"Thanks Val, I probably don't deserve that trust, but I appreciate it."

"No, Darius, that's where you are wrong. You not only deserve it, you earned it."

"I hope I never let you down."

"I hope so, too."

"Good night, Darius Shannon."

"Good night, Val."

CHAPTER 25

Rachael and I arrived at the Rock Room and found it empty. As we entered, I immediately felt that something was wrong. The air was denser somehow with foreboding. I could sense it but could not derive the source. We were still new to the Mind Legion, so I dismissed the feeling and continued on with an ever-increasing heaviness of concern in my heart. I rationalized that it was just anxiety over the general situation.

As we waited, we ran through some basic hand-to-hand combat scenarios. Rachael would attack me and I would defend myself. In the middle of one of her attacks, I thought I heard a creaking noise and redirected my concentration. A small fist caught me square in the jaw, and I stumbled back against the wall.

"Are you okay, Darius?" she asked.

"Rachael, stay close," I commanded as I grabbed her arm and slowly circled the room.

"What is it?" Rachael whispered.

"I don't know," I whispered back to her. "Be on your guard and stay close to me."

I ran my hand along the wall, dragging it along each panel as we made our way around the room. At one point I noticed a slight temperature variation in the paneling. I stopped for a moment and listened.

We continued on a few more steps and then everything went black. I heard Rachael crash to the floor. Suddenly, it felt harder to breathe, as if something was pressing on my chest. I knelt beside Rachael in the darkness, my head exploding with pain. Stars flew by my eyes as I swooned. "Rach?" I managed to utter, but my head felt dizzy, then everything went black.

I woke up in utter darkness. I groaned as my head reeled in excruciating pain.

"Darius, are you there?" whimpered Rachael.

"Yes, I'm here," I responded slowly. "Where are we?"

"I don't know. I just woke up a few minutes before you. I didn't dare to speak until I heard you."

Some sort of rope was used to restrict my hands at the wrist and my feet at the ankle. My head was covered, leaving me in complete darkness. I tested my strength against the restraints. They were too strong or I was too weak. I listened intently for any sign of where we might be, but I was literally and figuratively in the dark. I felt fear, gut-wrenching fear. Not only fear for myself, but more so for Rachael. Then it struck me.

Val and Richard were walking into a trap if they weren't already caught.

I could hear footsteps approaching us. I kept silent hoping that there might be some value in the surprise, but it was in vain. The cover was pulled from my head, and I blinked in an attempt to adjust my eyes to the bright light. A man dressed in flowing black robes walked toward me and pulled the hood from his shorn head. He was tall and had strong features and a pleasant face. His eyes were blue and deep but narrowed a bit as he looked at me down his straight and pronounced nose. There was hardness in his face despite his pleasant demeanor. It was something beneath the exterior. He smiled in triumph as he looked on me.

I looked down. I was tied to a chair that was made of the black stone. My hands were placed over indentations like those found in various places of the Rock Room. I turned my head and could see Rachael to my right and Val to my left. That meant that Richard was directly behind me. They still had hoods on their heads, but they were on similar chairs. Each of the chairs connected to mine with black stone piping. The chairs hooked through the center directly into the ceiling.

The ceiling was covered with black rock. It had been carefully carved into a cathedral dome that seemed to channel toward a single point that was at the far end of the room. There was a small, booth shaped room with a similar chair inside. The chair connected to the ceiling like ours.

"So, you are the great Darius Shannon," the man in the dark robe drawled out in jest. "I'm not sure why Kallikrates was so impressed. You clearly lack sufficient common sense to avoid a trap when all the signs are right in front of you."

"What do you want?" I stated firmly, trying to sound confident.

"I don't think you are in a position to be asking me questions," he stated as his eyes narrowed further.

"Just leave the others alone. You can do whatever you like with me, but let them go."

"How magnanimous you are. Of course I'll let them go. I only used Rachael as bait to get to you."

"Well, now you have me. Let them go," I said as I levitated and flung a loose chair from across the room at the man.

He merely reached out his hand and the chair stopped mid-air before he hurtled it in my direction, stopping it inches in front of my face.

"Don't ever try that again. You can clearly see that my powers far exceed yours. Next time I might not be so generous."

I looked around and noticed two other robed figures in the room. One was about my size, and the other one was larger and broader. Their heads were covered with hoods, and I couldn't see their faces. The one in front of me was clearly in charge. The other two walked over on the first man's signal and removed the hoods of Val, Richard and Rachael..

"Ignore them," he said as I watched the two return to their stations. "They are merely here to observe and learn how to operate the machine so that we can begin harvesting from the Mind Legion. Up until now we have had to resort to using this simple extraction machine to sap sufficient energy from mere mortals to keep us alive and at equal power with the Mind Legion. Your sister has helped us over the last few weeks to restart the activation sequence of our master machine. Unfortunately for you, we require more energy as a catalyst to fully charge the master."

"And then what?" I asked.

"Then we let your friends go, and we keep you as an apprentice."

"I'll never be an apprentice to a Mind Thief."

"I'm afraid you won't have much choice. The master machine allows us to alter your mind enough to create a new reality. Once you have been reprogrammed, your highest priority will be the acquisition of knowledge and power by any means. The Mind Thieves, as you call us, are not what you believe us to be. We do not seek the destruction of the Mind Legion for the sake of destruction. We destroy them because they slow progress. Kallikrates is the worst of the Mind Legion. He is a hypocrite. He spent generation after generation here on Earth learning and increasing in power so that he could take over the Great Council. And yet, he does not allow others of the Mind Legion to harvest Earth's power because he fears that they will become greater than he is."

"You are wrong," I retorted. "Kallikrates would never do anything selfish. He did it to protect the Mind Legion."

"No, Darius, this is where you are wrong. You think you know him better than I, but that is not true. I was also an apprentice of Kallikrates."

"Kallikrates didn't destroy the Mind Thieves here on Earth," I responded in realization of what the history meant. "You destroyed the Mind Thieves. Or at least someone just like you. Your own lust for power drained the Mind Legion of its power and in turn left you powerless. That's why your master machine doesn't work anymore. That's why you cannot defeat the Mind Legion."

My last words evoked a tasteless response from the man before me. He struck out at me with the back of his hand and blood trickled down the corner of my mouth. Stars filled my eyes, and I rocked to one side slightly before returning to an upright position.

"You know nothing about our history," was his response as he turned his back on us and walked toward the other two figures.

"I know enough to realize that none of us are leaving this room with our mind intact. I can see that you intend to wipe every last ounce of energy from us to start your precious machine. What then? There will be no more Mind Legion on Earth to keep it going and it will come to a halt."

"One will come to see what happened. When he does, I'll harvest enough energy to restore those to power that have earned it by right."

At a gesture from the man, the taller man opened the door to the small room with the lone chair.

I levitated the training stone from my pocket and flung it across the room in the direction of the dark-robed man. He ducked just in time as it glanced off the wall and rebounded into the middle of the room. He turned to take in the situation just as a second stone flew across the room in his direction. It was done with such surprise and fury that he was unable to stop it before it glanced off his forehead. The blood trickled down his face as he looked fiercely at Val. Death was in his eyes as he calmly walked over to the stone and levitated it in front of him to get a closer look.

"That is not the purpose for which this stone is designed," he said before calmly hurling it across the room directly at Val. At the last minute it ricocheted in the other direction, glancing off the wall and hitting the tall man in the arm. He grunted in pain and grabbed his arm.

"That wasn't very smart, Richard," said the dark-robed man. "I had something special in store for you. I was going to make you my number two in command."

The tall man looked over in surprise. Obviously he'd heard such promises as well.

"You had such potential," the dark-robed man continued. "I trained you to be the best, and you were almost the best. If you would have listened to me you could have been the best."

"What's he talking about, Richard?" asked Val. "Is this your master?"

"Yes, he was my master," Richard responded in shame. "I should have told you guys sooner."

"You should have told us what? Richard?" Val said sternly.

"He kind of promised that I'd be the Captain if I'd help him get his machine going."

Rachael wept in silence as Richard continued, "He told me that nobody would be hurt and that the rest of you could go on living normal lives."

I could sense Val's discontent as she whispered, "I can't believe you would do something like this."

"I'm sorry," was all that Richard could mutter.

"What a sad ending," Cerys, Richard's master said with a slight smile as if he was actually enjoying the emotional pain he was causing.

"Where is your wife?" asked Rachael quietly.

For the first time Cerys looked slightly startled and pained. "She was willing to go through the years of planning. When it came time to take the final step she faltered."

"So you killed her?" Rachael said softly.

"She would have told the Council of my plans," he said as the anger began to build up in him again. "She thought I was going too far. She sensed your pain and her motherly weakness was getting in the way. She didn't understand that this was better than the Code. We could have more knowledge and more power than the Code could ever make possible. She couldn't see that the purpose wasn't the Code. The purpose was what the Code provided: Power."

"So you destroyed the one thing that you truly cared about in this existence to increase your own power?" Rachael continued.

"You don't know what you are talking about little girl," he said. "I destroyed her to make things better. She was sacrificed to provide the power needed to make the impossible happen."

"This machine can't bring them back," Rachael said compassionately.

"You don't know that. You sound just like my wife."

"Your wife often mentioned your father and mother. They were truly spectacular, but the machine cannot bring them back."

"Shut up!" he screamed. "You don't know what you are talking about."

"I know that you sit on the Great Council. I know that your Father was Chief Captain before Kallikrates. I know that he tried to negotiate with the Mind Thieves and they deceived and killed him." And then in a more reverent tone Rachael continued, "I know that you lost your children in the Great War. This machine can't bring them back."

"You are wrong," he said with finality as he sat in the chair. "This is where I prove you wrong. Start the machine."

Rachael leaned over and whispered something to Richard too softly for me to make out the words. The tall man walked toward the wall holding his arm and hesitantly pulled the lever. A shock of energy bolted through each of us.

An apple extracted from the pack in the Rock Room levitated by my side. It had travelled down a small cavern that must have been used to enter the room by the Mind Thieves. It landed near us. Almost instantly it began converting from an apple to a seedling to a small tree. The ground shook. Small fruit began to form on the tree and matured to ripeness.

"Val! Richard!" I shouted. "Now!"

Richard began hurling the apples toward the two men outside the booth-like room. Val would explode them just before impact. The two robed figures fled in fear.

"Cowards!" yelled Cerys.

Richard redirected the projectiles and they exploded on the glass like window that separated us from Cerys. Cerys merely smiled. Val began freezing the apples and the smile disappeared as the glass began to crack and shatter. Finally an apple shot through the other side and exploded near him. The explosion was enough to distract him from his efforts.

The machine had now been turned on for a minute or so. We felt the power seeping from us. I summoned my training stone from across the room. It levitated slowly and shakily.

"Richard! The switch." I said as I attempted to make the stone fly.

An apple dropped as he focused his efforts on my stone. The first attempt careened off the wall sending some sparks.

"Val. Rachael. We need you," I pleaded.

The stone levitated again. This times there was no shaking.

"One, two, three," I yelled out.

The stone flew toward the switch mechanism and shattered it into a million pieces with a giant explosion. The energy flowed back down into us.

Cerys had now reached the boiling point. He walked right through the wall on his way toward us.

"Val," I urged. "I need spontaneous combustion on these bands."

"But I'll burn you."

"Just do it, Val."

"I'm sorry," she cried out as my skin burned around my wrists and ankles.

I tugged at the cords and jumped up.

Cerys was right on top of me. He grabbed me by the neck in deference but underestimated my strength. I ran my feet up his body and kicked him in the face before performing a back flip and landing on my feet. Blood trickled down his slightly blackened face. His eyes were blazing. I charged him and in a fury threw punches at his mid-section and face before backing off and catching my breath.

I looked around in time to see the others behind me. Richard was levitating several apples and stones around him. Val was alternately combusting and freezing the apples that Richard was levitating. Rachael's tree was digging deeper and the power draining mechanism was making popping and cracking noises under the strain.

"It's over, Cerys," I stated with finality.

"Do you really think that the four of you can stop me?"

"Yes," we said in unison.

The tree finished its work as the machine was crumbled to rubble. Flaming and frozen apples filled the air. Cerys was hit and knelt near us, dazed by the blows. I approached him with some of the remaining rope. As I neared he flung the remains of one of the apples in my direction. I stopped it mid-air and said, "Don't ever try that again. Obviously our power is greater than yours."

He collapsed in exhaustion before us.

"Darius?" said a familiar voice.

"Kallikrates? How did you get here?" I said turning to see my Master face to face.

"I came down a dark tunnel between this location and the Rock Room."

We all laughed at the practical answer. "No, how did you get to Earth?"

"We left as soon as we knew the Great Council was breached."

"I wish you would have made it sooner," I said sadly.

"It looks like you didn't need me," he responded.

We looked around at the room. There were shards of rock everywhere and where the machine had previously been located there now stood a mature apple tree. Smoke still filled the upper part of the cavern from the combusted apples.

Kallikrates walked over to Cerys and knelt beside him. He reached out and gently rested his hand on his head.

"My poor friend. How did this ever happen?"

A tear trickled down the cheek of the Chief Captain of the Mind Legion as he knelt beside the body of Cerys. His last efforts to destroy us had drained all of his power.

"What will you do with him?" Richard asked.

"He must be returned to be tried by the Great Council. We, together, will decide his fate. Until then he will be held in a safe place here on Earth."

Kallikrates stood and turned toward me, "Darius, before we go any further, I must know if you have made a decision."

"I have made my decision but it is on two conditions."

"And what are those conditions?" he asked, his eyebrows rising slightly at the request.

"First, you must never leave me alone again, and second, I want you to find new masters for Rachael and Richard."

Richard looked up in astonishment and gratitude, and Rachael threw her arms around me.

"I'm sorry, I can't meet your conditions," said Kallikrates flatly.

We all groaned in dismay. "What do you mean?" I asked. "After all that has happened, I don't think I can go on without you or each of them."

"I am sorry, Darius, but I won't always be able to be with you. It is impossible, and is not the way of the Mind Legion. It would cripple you and slow your ability to learn what you must learn. If you are willing to drop this first condition then you are the Captain of the Mind Legion."

I thought for a moment, and then looked around at my friends and my sister. If I said no, they would be forced to go back to their normal lives. And even worse, they would be powerless against the Mind Thieves on Earth. If I said yes, I would have to be solely responsible for their safety.

"You'll never be alone, Darius," said Val as she reached over and held my hand.

I looked over at Val and Rachael and Richard, and then I looked up at Kallikrates and said, "I think I can live with that."

Val hugged me and Rachael joined in, but not before grabbing Richard and bringing them into our embrace. For the first time, he wept.

CHAPTER 26

"Darius, you have company!" yelled my mother down the stairs.

Thinking it was Val and Richard; I casually rolled out of bed and splashed some water on my face before clambering up the stairs. I licked my hand and tried to get the rooster tail down on the back of my head without much success. As I entered the living room I saw Mrs. Williams sitting on the couch.

"Mrs. Williams? What are you doing here?" I said a little too curtly.

"Darius! Show some manners," my mother said nervously as she tried to smooth over the situation.

Mrs. Williams smiled and stood up from the couch as I entered. "It's okay. I'm sorry to disturb you this early in the morning. I just wanted to deliver something to you." She reached into her bag and pulled out a package wrapped in brown shipping paper. "This is something that I should have given you a few weeks ago. I'm sorry I can't stay much longer, but I have a pressing engagement this morning and didn't want to wait another day to deliver this."

She walked to the door and left somewhat unceremoniously. After her car pulled away down the street, I looked down at the package in my hand. My mother was staring at me.

"Why don't you open it, Darius?" she said as my father joined her in the room.

I opened the package to find a pile of small books entitled, *Words of Wisdom for High School and Beyond*. Beneath the title was the phrase: "Written by Darius Shannon." I opened the book and read a few paragraphs. I could not believe what I was reading. It was my essay from the spring detention sessions with Mrs. Williams.

"Well, what is it?" my mom asked.

"It looks like a book," my father responded, stating the obvious as usual.

"Of course it's a book," she said as she digged her elbow into his side.

I silently handed her one of the books from the package. As she stared at the title and then at me over and over again, I looked down at the package and noticed the corner of a white envelope sticking out of one of the books. I opened the envelope as my parents thumbed through the book. I read a letter that said I had qualified for royalties on the first lot of books to the sum of ten thousand dollars. Beneath the letter was a second sheet of paper containing the check made out to me for the total amount.

"Did you really write this?" asked my mother quietly.

I nodded in the affirmative and handed my father the letter and the check. He read and re-read the letter in disbelief. My mother hugged me. Even the Captain of the Mind Legion needed his mother sometimes. I hugged her back and my father joined in.

Later that day we all returned to the Rock Room dressed in our best clothes at the request of Kallikrates. We arrived in pairs through the hidden tunnel about twenty minutes apart. Rachael and I arrived first to what appeared to be an empty room. We looked around expectantly for Kallikrates but found nothing. We tried our stations, but the room seemed dormant. We then walked over to the tunnel that led to the machine of the Mind Thieves. I knocked on the panels, but they all sounded solid. We heard footsteps and turned to greet the twins. Richard looked sullen and ashamed. Val was holding onto his arm, almost as if she had assisted him along the way. She looked stunning in a summer dress that accentuated her finest features. I stared for a few moments before Rachael nudged me with her elbow and whispered, "Stop drooling."

Val looked at me with a smile and blushed. I smiled and greeted them, "Hey guys."

CRAIG WOLL

We stared on for a moment more in silence before Val said, "Any sign of Kallikrates?"

"No, not yet," Rachael responded.

"Maybe we should sit down and wait," Val was saying when the wall to the side of us opened into a new room.

We looked over at the new room in surprise but not astonishment. At that point we were becoming used to these kinds of events. I walked toward the opening. Val was to my right, and I felt her warm hand grasp mine from behind as we passed through the opening into the room. Rachael grabbed Richard by the arm and gently escorted him into the room. I glanced back in time to see her whisper something into Richard's ear and a spark of light flickered on his face as he entered the room.

Kallikrates stood at the opposite end of the room. His wife was by his side radiantly smiling in our direction. Her beauty was beyond any that I had seen before, except in the person alongside me. Her olive skin was a perfect contrast to the large green eyes. Her face was flawless despite her many years. She had flowing silver hair that accentuated the silver linings in the black robes that they both wore. The couple looked down on us as proud parents would on their children.

Kallikrates reached down on the altar-like table and retrieved an ornate box. He motioned me to come forward. I took one step before I realized I was still grasping Val's hand. I turned to her and gently released her hand before continuing forward to the base of the table. Kallikrates slowly opened the box and revealed two rings like those I had found. As I looked closer I realized that they were ornately decorated with wisps of silver design. It looked like ancient writing.

The rings were offered to me by Kallikrates. I reached to remove the rings on my hand, but they wouldn't budge. Kallikrates smiled and slightly shook his head while his eyes glanced down at my other hand. I slid the rings on the thumb and pinky on my left hand and felt a thrill of power surge through me as the memories of the previous year raced by in a single moment. The history of the Mind Legion on Earth also burned into my memory as if it were my own.

Kallikrates then led me to the side of the room where there was a hand indentation on the wall. He motioned for me to reach out my left hand. As I placed my hand in the indentation, we stepped into a small room. The door immediately closed before he began to speak.

"What I tell you now is in your trust and must not be shared until a future time. My wife will instruct the others in their duties while I speak to you about yours. You are now the Captain of the Mind Legion on this planet that you call Earth. This is a position of power and responsibility. You are young still and will make many mistakes as you learn to govern this place. As you make these mistakes, learn from them and become stronger, for someday you will need to attain great power if you are to defend your stewardship from our greatest enemies.

"The Council fears what may become of Earth, and I fear what may become of you as your Earth is restored to its prior glory. Many will be unable to control their ambition, as you saw with your young friend. He will learn from his mistake, but only if you lead him with love. Your sister will also need great support and confidence if she is to be successful in the Mind Legion. She is the youngest in years, but not in heart. She is wise, but still weak and must develop strength. Val will be one of the great leaders of Earth, and you would be wise to listen to her council in the coming months and years. She has a good master and learns quickly. Finally, you must now lead. The responsibility of the Mind Legion rests on your shoulders, and you must carry it forward."

Kallikrates stopped speaking for a moment, reached into a drawer, and retrieved a black bundle and handed it to me. I looked at him for approval to explore further and he nodded his affirmation. The cloth unfurled into what looked like a sheer black shirt. It felt like silk but was lighter than any material I'd encountered. I held it up to myself and peered down to see that it dropped down to about mid thigh on me.

"This material was designed here on Earth many generations ago and has been held here in secret since that time. Only a few of these remain known to us," he said as he pulled down at his collar to reveal what he was wearing beneath his outer garment. "You must keep this a secret, but wear it always. It will protect and strengthen you from the powers of the Mind Thieves that remain on Earth."

"What about the others?" I asked.

"They must wait some time before they will be ready for such things."

Kallikrates left after instructing me to put the shirt on under my clothes. I slowly stripped off my shirt and replaced it with the new one. It was soft and soothing.

My mind cleared and my senses felt enhanced. I could now hear Kallikrates providing instruction to the others as my hearing became more acute. He was telling them of my new responsibilities and how I was their leader, but I needed to support their development. After I finished dressing, I opened the outer room and approached the others.

Kallikrates finished what he was saying and waited for me to take my place.

"Each of you has new responsibilities. In the coming days you must choose your first apprentice. Yes, even you Richard," said Kallikrates as Richard looked up in surprise.

"Really, I'm not kicked out for what I did?" he said, nearly stumbling on his own words.

"No, you are not 'kicked out' for your actions. I believe that you have learned a valuable lesson about trust, friendship, and family. These three things are the pillars upon which a healthy leader of the Mind Legion can build."

"Kallikrates?" asked Rachael shyly as she looked over at Richard. "How will we be able to help others without our masters?"

"That is an excellent point. You will be appointed new masters. There is some work still to do on the Great Council, but your new masters will contact you shortly after I leave."

"Are you leaving so soon?" asked Val, looking expectantly at Kallikrates and his wife.

"Yes, if the danger had not been so great we would have stayed for some time to help train you, but our times of peace are over, and there is much work that must be done on other planets."

Kallikrates and his wife embraced each of us before departing. The Rock Room was silent for some time as we each sunk into our own thoughts. As usual, Richard broke the silence. "I don't know about you guys, but I'm starving. Let's get something to eat."

My heart swelled as I looked around the room at my sister, Richard, and Val. Their development and safety was a solemn responsibility. One from which I must never shrink. It is hard to believe that in one year I had found something that I never knew I was looking for – Love.

ABOUT THE AUTHOR

CRAIG WOLL graduated from Brigham Young University with a B.S. in Psychology. He graduated from Utah State University with an M.S. and a PhD in Instructional Technology. In describing *The Annals of the Mind Legion Volume 1: The Resurgence* he says, "I've always been drawn to stories that suspend reality, teach truth, and increase imagination. I believe that this is such a story."

Craig and his wife Emily live in New York. This is his first book. His website is www.craigwoll.org.

www.ingramcontent.com/pod-product-compliance
Lightning Source LLC
Chambersburg PA
CBHW062108170626
46813CB00002B/362